Praise for *Beach Rivals*:

'A delight. Ideally would have read it on a beach; still
bloody good served on the sofa'
Lauren Bravo, author of *Preloved*

'The perfect read for wet and rainy British spring!
I loved everything about this'
Five-star reader review

'Complete sunshine in book form . . . Fun and
swoonworthy, a delicious slow-burn love story as
well as a love letter to books, *Beach Rivals* is as
bright and engaging as its glorious cover'
Cressida McLaughlin, author of *The Staycation*

'Such a cute fast paced read. Great writing . . . Do yourself
a favour and pick up *Beach Rivals*!'
Five-star reader review

'*Beach Rivals* is the perfect slice of summer
escapism! Sizzling chemistry paired with swoony
romance, and two characters I completely fell
in love with. I read it in one sitting!'
Catherine Walsh, author of *Holiday Romance*

www.penguin.co.uk

BEACH RIVALS

Georgie Tilney

PENGUIN BOOKS

TRANSWORLD PUBLISHERS
Penguin Random House, One Embassy Gardens,
8 Viaduct Gardens, London SW11 7BW
www.penguin.co.uk

Transworld is part of the Penguin Random House group of companies
whose addresses can be found at global.penguinrandomhouse.com

Penguin
Random House
UK

First published in Great Britain in 2023 by Penguin Books
an imprint of Transworld Publishers

A CIP catalogue record for this book
is available from the British Library.

ISBN 9781804992234

Typeset in 10.75/14.4pt Sabon LT Std by Jouve (UK), Milton Keynes.
Printed and bound in Great Britain by Clays Ltd, Elcograf S.p.A.

The authorized representative in the EEA is Penguin Random House Ireland,
Morrison Chambers, 32 Nassau Street, Dublin D02 YH68.

Penguin Random House is committed to a sustainable
future for our business, our readers and our planet. This book
is made from Forest Stewardship Council® certified paper.

For Amy Jones

Chapter One

Clare was sure that when she'd left the house she'd looked like a normal human person. She hadn't bothered with make-up, but her skin had been clear, her hair and clothes neat. She flattered herself she'd been almost dewy.

She took out her phone and checked the selfie she'd posted earlier that morning as she was boarding the plane and, yes, no one could say she wasn't glowing. And she hadn't even used a filter – she was trying her hardest to stay away from filters and, honestly, in that light who even needed them? The light in question being the soft dawn glow she'd been awake for, thanks to her brutally early flight.

But now, in an airport bathroom on the other side of the world, it was an entirely different story. Her skin looked clammy, pale and, under her eyes, distinctly grey. Her hair was somehow both lank and dry, lying flat across the top of her head and crackling out to the sides with astonishing volume.

Amazing, really, what sixteen-odd hours in a plane could do to a person.

Clare passed a hand over her face and moaned. Not

putting make-up on for the flight had been the right call. Not putting any make-up in her carry-on bag had been the wrong one.

She splashed some water on her face, made one last attempt to ruffle her hair into something approaching beachy waves, and hauled her bag over her shoulder. Not the best first impression, but surely her new boss would understand. If you insist on meeting a new employee at the airport, you'd better be prepared to see them looking like a desiccated husk.

And if you insist on taking a job on the other side of the world, you'd better be prepared to turn up looking like absolute arse.

'Well, Clare,' she said, to her reflection, 'you're not getting any prettier.' And with that, she left the bathroom, ready to face her new life.

*

After an inordinate amount of time spent waiting at baggage claim and passport control, she stood motionless in front of the frosted-glass sliding doors that were now the only barrier between her and the new life she'd committed to on a whim just two weeks earlier.

It had seemed so simple when she'd seen the article – but everything seems simple when you're absently scrolling on your phone in bed at two a.m.

'*The Ultimate Dream Job: Reading on the Beach*', the headline had read. 'It seems too good to be true, but this bookshop wants to pay you to spend three months in Bali. The only catch? You have to sell a few books while you're there.'

Clare had sent it to her cousin Lina, saying, *OMG! Imagine if this was real*, then moved on. After all, no one actually applied for jobs like that, surely. They were a fantasy. The life you imagined yourself living whenever the real world got too grey. A customer complains for too long about his latte being cold and you close your eyes and pretend you're in your own little world, wandering in from the beach, pottering around your own little shop, barefoot, windswept, and alive.

Your biggest responsibility? To read as many books as you can so you can recommend them to people. You imagine yourself being unexpectedly good at it. You find a hitherto unsuspected talent for divining just what would suit each person. You build a reputation. 'Oh, I simply never buy a book without checking what Clare thought of it,' people start saying.

Eventually you're included in a list of must-sees for tourists visiting the area. 'No trip is complete without a visit to Clare's Books – just you try to leave without at least five crisp paperbacks.'

And one day the door opens, the bell set above it ringing softly to announce a customer. And you look up and see an intelligent-looking but strangely bashful man. You recognize him. An author you love. 'I hope you'll excuse me,' he says. 'This shop sells more of my books than any other. I had to come and thank whoever keeps recommending them.'

And you're simply happy for the rest of time.

It's perfect.

But it's not real. It's just something to distract you from the constant low-level dissatisfaction you feel all the time.

That dissatisfaction you feel so guilty about because isn't it your own fault that your life is the way it is?

Clare was very aware that she had squandered her potential somewhere along the way. She'd always been a good student, she'd gone to a good university, and then she'd fallen at the last hurdle. An understandable fall, given the circumstances, but she'd failed to get back up properly.

Clare had expected to wake up the next morning to a joke from Lina about packing it all in for Bali. They'd go back and forth all day on the lives they'd have out there. But Lina didn't joke. She'd sent a two-word reply: *Do it*.

Clare laughed to herself. *As if*, she thought. Lina had to know how unrealistic the idea was.

But, in the end, Clare had done it. Something within her had still wanted to believe in the glimmer of hope that she could take one big swing and set things, if not completely right, on a better course.

And after all, it wasn't like she had anything to lose.

And now she was here. It was all waiting for her on the other side of those doors. Which, somehow, she couldn't walk through. Because it wasn't simple any more, not now that it was real. Real things aren't simple. Real things have complications and compromises and failures.

'This is the dumbest thing I've ever done,' she muttered to herself. 'This is worse than dropping out of university with one year left to go. This is worse than meandering around the world for two years so you didn't have to face the fact that you dropped out of university. This is worse than running out of money and failing to find a job abroad and having to go home to your mum's. This is worse than getting fired *twice in a row* and winding up relying on temp work for months on end, knowing you'll never make something of your life now.'

She couldn't quite define how this was worse than all those things, but she felt deeply that it was. Maybe it was just that she'd let herself believe this could be the solution, when really she knew she was simply running away again, that this was just another temporary job, only in a nicer climate.

Let that be enough, she thought. *Just another temp job, but one that's letting you escape January in Surrey.*

She took a deep breath. Then another. And another.

Go through the doors, she thought. *You have to go through the doors. Even if it's just to leave Arrivals, go straight to Departures and get on a plane home, you have to go through the doors.*

That was the thought that did it.

So after what was surely a completely reasonable amount of dithering, she squared her shoulders and walked through the doors.

Chapter Two

There were people everywhere – other passengers barging past with their bags, taxi drivers clamouring for her attention. She'd never had to meet a stranger at an airport before, and suddenly it seemed complicated.

How was she supposed to find the right person? Would someone be holding one of those little signs with her name on it? What if someone else called Clare was being picked up? Why had she put herself in a position of such uncertainty if she was going to tumble into a panic at every new obstacle? Why had she worn her thickest blackest yoga pants on the plane when she was coming to a tropical paradise and was going to be boiled alive as soon as she got outside?

This honestly could have gone on for hours, but fortunately a saviour arrived, in the form of someone walking up and saying, 'Clare, I'm so glad you made it safely.'

The someone in question was a man vaguely in his sixties, whom Clare couldn't help thinking of as little. It wasn't that he was short – although he was only an inch or so taller than her. And it wasn't that he was slim – indeed he was a little round. That was it, she decided. He was a little short and a little round. He had a little twinkle in his eye. He gave a little smile. It all added up to a charming picture. He was exactly the sort of person Clare could imagine running a bookshop on the beach, or indeed in a fairy-tale.

He was dressed far more sensibly than Clare, in soft cream linen trousers and a rumpled pale blue shirt. He looked like someone about to become embroiled in a murder mystery on board a yacht.

It took her a moment, but she recognized him from her interview. 'Oh,' she said. 'Mr Hearn! I didn't expect you to meet me yourself.'

The little twinkle brightened. 'My dear, call me Adam. And who would I send? I'm sorry Lissie didn't come with me. She doesn't do airports.'

Clare had no idea who Lissie was, so she was completely truthful when she said, 'Oh, that's fine. I understand.'

Adam had taken the handle of her suitcase and was wheeling it alongside as he led her out of the terminal. 'Celestina,' he said, with the gravitas you might use to talk about Beyoncé. 'You'll meet her eventually. And Jack, of course.'

'Right,' said Clare, who couldn't remember either of these people being mentioned in her interview. There was a lot to take in, but she was sure it would all make sense eventually.

They stepped out into the car park and into the morning sun. The sky was a clear bright blue, and although the sun was still fairly low in the sky it had evidently been soaking into the tarmac for a while. Clare felt the heat swallow her for a moment before a slight breeze came through, and even then she felt sticky and sweaty immediately.

Adam didn't seem to notice the heat. He strolled calmly and crisply across the tarmac while Clare trudged breathlessly behind him, pushing her newly damp hair off her clammy face.

'Lovely morning,' he said, over his shoulder. 'You might find it a trifle warm later on, though.'

'It's going to get hotter?' Clare asked, dismayed.

'Oh, yes, dear. It's not even nine a.m. yet.'

Clare had a momentary vision of grabbing her suitcase from him and sprinting back to the terminal – whether to fly home or simply to cower in the air-conditioning she wasn't sure – but suddenly Adam was ushering her into a car.

'Too late,' she said, under her breath.

*

Clare gazed out of the window as the car slid smoothly along the road. Her earlier panic was starting to give way. This was right. This was perfect. The familiar sensation of visiting a new place came back to her and a simmering excitement took root.

Adam was driving along a coastal road, through a busy neighbourhood. Clare could see nightclubs and fast-food shops slipping past on the right, while the beach to her left was already crowded with surfers. She knew this kind of place. Every holiday destination had one: the loud, hectic, messy streets where chaos reigned, somehow both too shiny and too dirty, with a stag party on every corner.

But before long the nightclubs gave way to boutiques and spas. The beaches changed too, no longer packed with surfers seeking early morning waves but with brightly coloured umbrellas dotted around, waiting for people to relax beneath them.

Clare smiled in anticipation. She could almost feel it already, the sun soaking into her pale winter skin, the salt of the ocean refreshing her spirit, the sound of the waves sanding down the rough edges of her mind. *It's real*, she thought, *I'm here, I've actually made it.*

She felt guilty about how good it felt to be there, to be away from her home again. She knew it wasn't fair, but she couldn't help it: she'd made a break for freedom and it had worked. Like she'd crawled along a tunnel hidden behind a poster and made it to paradise.

She knew, really, that it wasn't her home she'd escaped. Not her mother or her jobs. It was something in herself. Some fear or hesitancy that had taken root when she'd moved back and trapped her in uncertainty.

'We'll give you a couple of days to get acclimatized before you get started in the shop, of course,' Adam was saying, as he drove, 'but you'll be living in the little flat behind it, so you'll get to see it now. I'm sure you'll need to rest after your journey, but if you want company I'll be in the shop all day.'

'I'm actually feeling all right,' Clare said. 'I might go out and explore a bit.'

'Well, of course, if that's what you'd like,' Adam replied, pulling into a parking space.

The journey to the bookshop had taken a little over half an hour and, before she'd had a chance to catch her breath, Clare was right smack in the middle of disillusioned reality.

In the fantasy bookshop, the one she'd imagined so clearly before she arrived, the door had opened with the chiming of a little bell. The fantasy shop was charmingly cluttered, without feeling crowded, airy and light, yet cosy in the kind of paradox that works in a daydream. There would have been tables covered with new releases and recommendations, shelves so crowded with books that more were laid across the tops. A broad wooden staircase would lead up to a second floor with armchairs and spindly little tables covered with books in a way that left plenty of room to sit and read.

The real bookshop was not like that.

Adam led her from the car to a simple shop front, with a dusty window, set partway off the beach, where the sand started to turn to scrubby grass but there was still enough of it to creep over the doorstep. It looked as if it had once been painted blue, but now it was weathered and faded, and the sign hanging over the door reading 'Seashore Books' seemed like it might only have a couple more months of legibility in it.

The door opened with a raspy groan. The shop was cluttered, yes, but not in a cosy way: it was cramped and awkward. Despite the brightness of the morning outside, the shop itself was dingy and dark. As well as being dusty, the window was blocked by a heavy black cloth. There were a couple of tables near the door with books piled on them, but the stacks seemed haphazard and disorganized. And while the bookshelves were crowded in some places, in others there were gaps, with books flopping onto their neighbours. There was a small mezzanine, with a wrought-iron staircase curving up towards it, but it was dark and appeared to be full of boxes. The stairs were roped off with a sign reading 'Staff Only'.

'What do you think?' Adam said, smiling at Clare's wide gaze.

Clare laughed. She'd known she shouldn't expect the bookshop that had sprung to life in her head, but she was surprised by how far from it the reality was. The shop looked as if no one had taken charge of it properly in months, maybe years. She found herself wondering just what was expected of her. The ad and the interview had made it sound like a low-pressure job that mainly involved sitting on the beach, but the shop clearly needed a complete overhaul.

Clare looked over at Adam, who was still waiting for an answer.

'Yeah,' she said, nodding. 'It looks great.'

'The previous pair have left you a bit of a clean-up, I'm afraid.'

'Oh, thank God,' Clare said. 'I was worried you were going to say, "I have a system," and I wouldn't be allowed to fix it.'

Adam laughed. 'It's a while since I've had any part in the system here,' he said. 'But, please, don't worry too much about the state of things. You're here to enjoy yourself. Come on, the flat's around the back.'

The flat was tiny, but Clare didn't mind. There was a small living room with a kitchenette in the corner. Three doors led directly off the living room, one to a bathroom and one to the bedroom. The third, Clare assumed, was a storage cupboard.

'I'm sorry about the single bed,' Adam said. 'It was either that or there'd be no room for a wardrobe.'

'Oh, it's fine,' said Clare. 'I didn't come here to spend all my time in bed.' Realizing what she'd said, she blushed right up to the roots of her dark red hair and coughed awkwardly.

Adam just twinkled at her. 'Well, if you want a lie-down

before you set off to explore you can test it out. But I'll be in the shop if you need me.'

Alone in the flat, Clare took a deep breath and shook herself out. She was fine. This was fine. This was good. The shop looked a mess, but it was right on the beach. Adam seemed nice, and he seemed to like her. Of course, her last boss had seemed nice, and as though she liked Clare, right up until the day she fired her.

But there was no reason to think Adam would do the same. Surely you'd have to be pretty terrible to be fired from a three-month working holiday. Clare wondered what would happen if she did get fired. Would she be sent home straight away? Probably. She'd have to make room for someone else.

She saw herself turning up at home two weeks in, having to tell her mother that she'd been fired for the third time in less than two years. Clare put her hands over her face and groaned.

Maybe a twenty-minute snooze was a good idea.

She dumped her bag on the floor, lay on the bed and closed her eyes.

Chapter Three

Clare had dropped out of university at twenty-one, after her father died. Her mother had been supportive. Encouraged her to take the time she needed, to go back with her mind refreshed. And when Clare had spent two years backpacking around the world, her mother hadn't minded. 'Lots of people take a gap year,' she'd said. 'It's good to experience different places, different cultures.'

When Clare had come home, her room had been waiting for her, everything set up to help her settle into a new job before she found her own place to live. And when she'd been fired the first time, her mother had been philosophical about it. 'It's a tough job market,' she'd said. 'You'll find something else.'

It wasn't until Clare was fired the second time that her mother suggested she finish her degree. Clare had said she'd think about it, and she meant to. And then September came and went without her making a move and that was when her mum had started to worry.

She'd wanted to know why Clare wouldn't go back to university, and Clare didn't have a good explanation. And then she'd wanted to know why Clare hadn't had any job interviews recently, why she didn't seem worried about finding another permanent job, why she'd stopped trying.

The evening after Clare had seen the ad for the bookshop on the beach, she was picking at her dinner and had looked up to find her mother watching her, a worried crease between her eyebrows.

'Anything promising in the job search recently?' she'd asked.

'I'm sorry, Mum,' Clare had said. 'Something will come up. People are still just getting back after New Year's.'

Her mum had regarded her sadly. 'I just . . . I worry about you, Clare. You're not happy. You're not even trying to be happy.'

'I'm not trying to be unhappy.'

'I know,' her mum said, and after a moment, 'I know you miss your dad. Even I miss him, and we'd been divorced for a decade when he died. But you still have your own life to live.'

'It's not about Dad,' said Clare. 'I don't know what it's about.'

'I just wish I knew what your plan was,' her mum said. 'It's not right to still be living at home at your age, working a new job every month.'

Clare knew her mother meant well. She also knew she had no satisfying answer to give her.

'I don't know what's wrong with me,' she said on the phone to Lina later that night. 'I know she's right. I should just find a permanent job, any job that will keep me, move out and be an adult.'

'Probably,' Lina said. 'Aunt Maggie is often right, in my experience. Or you could apply for the bookshop in Bali.'

'I know,' Clare said. 'I wish.'

Lina laughed. 'Come on,' she said. 'Why not? You could get it – you could escape the long grey that is Britain in January.'

'I bet thousands of people apply for those kinds of things. I wouldn't get it.'

'Someone has to.'

'Yeah, well, someone has to win the lottery too.'

'Look,' said Lina, sounding firmer now, 'you're obviously in a funk. You're not doing yourself any favours by mooning around about it all. Shake things up! And what will it cost you? It's just one more job application.'

Clare paused. 'Shouldn't I be trying to find something long term?' she said. 'Shouldn't I be trying to figure out a career plan?'

'Maybe,' said Lina. 'But figuring out your long-term career is a long-term goal. In the short term we just need to get you to liven up a bit. Then you'll have, I don't know, more decision-making energy. Or something. And you never know, you might get some ideas out there.'

'Do you think?'

Lina was a wedding photographer. She'd spent ten years establishing herself while working part time as a receptionist and had managed to go full time a couple of years earlier, although Clare knew it was still touch and go as to whether she'd be able to pay her bills.

'How did you know you wanted to be a photographer?' Clare asked.

'Well,' Lina said, 'I always liked playing around with

cameras, was always the one taking photos of my friends. Then one of them asked me to shoot her wedding, because she couldn't afford to pay anyone, and I just . . . I just loved it.'

'Do you still love it?' Clare asked. 'Now that . . .'

'Most of the time,' said Lina. 'I wish so much of it wasn't hustling for the next job, but I still love the actual taking-photos bit.'

Clare couldn't think of anything she loved, like Lina loved photography – enough to face ten years of grinding just to get to do it as a job.

'Look,' Lina said, 'I never really had a plan for this. I just did the job that was in front of me. And then the one after that. And I kept going because I loved doing it, and now it's a career. It's okay to be unsure, but don't let that stop you trying things. Taking risks.'

Clare brought up the ad again after she'd hung up. It still felt impossible, it still felt like a fantasy.

Do it. Lina's voice sounded in her head. *Do it*.

So she did it. She wrote an application. And one Zoom interview and one miracle later, she'd got the job.

*

After that it only took one brutally long flight, one seventy-minute train journey to get to the brutally long flight, and one car ride to the station.

Clare's mum had driven her. Clare had been worried she'd try to stop her going, that she'd be annoyed with her for running off – for running off *again* – but she'd actually seemed relieved. *It's probably not that she's glad to be rid of me*, Clare told herself. *It's probably some other, nicer reason.*

They turned into the station car park just as a train was pulling away.

'Was that your train?' Maggie asked.

'Naturally it was,' Clare said, checking the timetable on her phone. 'There's another in twenty minutes. I've given myself plenty of time to get to the airport. This isn't my first rodeo, Mags.'

To her surprise, her mum switched off the ignition and undid her seatbelt.

'It's okay,' Clare said. 'You don't have to come in and wait with me.'

Maggie stared at her. 'Don't be daft,' she said. 'It's the last time I'll see you for three months. Of course I'll come in and wait.'

Clare hefted her enormous suitcase out of the boot, slung her backpack onto her shoulder and they crossed into the station, settling down on the platform to wait. 'I'm sorry,' she said, as they sipped terrible railway-station coffee.

'For what?'

'I don't know, that I'm running away. Again.'

'Do you feel like you're running away?' her mum asked. Clare shrugged, cupping her hands around the hot paper cup.

Maggie sighed. 'I'm not upset with you for going. I'm glad you've made a decision about something.'

'A spontaneous, reckless decision,' said Clare, with a wry smile.

'Oh, Clare,' her mum said. 'I've been expecting spontaneous and reckless from you since you were two years old. I've missed spontaneous, reckless Clare.' She paused, biting her lip. She seemed to be searching for the right words. 'I'm happy you're doing something you seem excited about,' she said. 'That's what's been so difficult to watch this past year or so. You've just been drifting. Bored. You were never one to let yourself get bored when you were young. You'd always be off on some tear somewhere. Recently it's been like you've lost that. Like you can't make a decision for yourself. Like you don't know what you want.'

Clare was silent. She didn't want to tell her mum how right she was, and how scared that made her feel. Scared, not just that she couldn't decide what to do with herself but that there wasn't anything out there she did want.

Her mum sat beside her, gazing out onto the train tracks.

'Look,' she said, 'I'm happy that you're doing this – I think it'll be good for you. But it's only temporary. It's just three months. And then what? You just come back here and carry on as you are now?'

She turned to look at Clare, who was staring down at the cup between her hands.

'Clare, all I want is for you to use these three months to think about what's next for you. Do you want to go back to university? Do you want to start a career in something specific? Do you want to get a solid, reliable, boring office job that lets you commit to some wild hobby? Whatever it is, I'll support you, but it has to be a decision. If it's just to keep drifting from one thing to another, then ... I'm not sure I should let you continue living at home.'

Clare snapped her head round to look at her mother. 'Maggie!' she said. 'Are you kicking me out?'

Her mum gave a wry smile. 'Don't call me Maggie,' she said. Then she sighed. 'Clare, you're twenty-five. You should be fleeing the house. But, yes, I suppose I am.' She gave her shoulders a little shake. She looked quite proud of herself.

'Jesus, Mum, will there be a grace period at least?'

'I suppose so,' she said. 'You'll have jet lag, after all.'

Clare laughed in spite of herself. 'Okay, great. So, I'll get back, have a couple of days to recover and then it's all over.'

The train pulled into the station and Clare and her mum stood. Clare shouldered her bag and gave Maggie an unwieldy hug. 'Love you, Mum,' she said.

'Love you too. Have fun. But have a bit of a think, too. About what you want to do.'

'Sure,' said Clare. 'I'll have a bit of a think about what I want to do. With the rest of my entire life.'

She got onto the train, slung her backpack onto the floor, and slumped into the window seat. No pressure, then. She closed her eyes and let her head fall back, the rhythm of the train soothing her as it carried her away. It would be fine. She had three months. Three months of sun and sea and books.

Surely that was plenty of time to decide on a future.

Now, twenty odd hours and twelve thousand kilometres later, Clare fell asleep with her mum's demand ringing in her ears.

When she woke up a few hours later she knew there was someone else in the flat. At first she couldn't tell how, but after a moment she heard what was clearly a person moving. It sounded like bare feet on the wooden floors.

Adam didn't seem the sort of person who'd drop in whenever he felt like it, but who else could it be?

Clare sat up and listened intently. Something creaked.

Maybe the couch, maybe someone was sitting down. Who thought they had a right to come into her (temporary) home and sit on her (temporary) couch?

For a moment she wasn't sure what to do, and she was a little annoyed with herself. She'd spent two years travelling alone, and she had a very well-established system for keeping herself safe. But here she'd let her guard down simply because she had a job waiting for her.

But then the injustice of it stung her. This microscopic flat was her home for the next three months. How dare some random make her feel afraid?

She narrowed her eyes, stood up and stormed into the living room. 'Who the hell are you?' she said, furiously.

The figure on the couch turned to face her, one dark eyebrow raised.

'I'm Jack,' he said, and turned back to the laptop perched on his knees.

Clare blinked in the silence. 'Well,' she said, a bit more limply than she'd planned to, 'what are you doing here?'

Jack sighed and looked back around at her. 'I live here,' he said.

'No, you don't. I live here.'

'And whoever heard of two people sharing an apartment?'

'But there isn't another bed—' Clare stopped talking, noticing for the first time that the third door was open. Open on what was unmistakably another bedroom, with another single bed and an open suitcase lying on the floor beside it.

'Oh,' Clare said. Adam had mentioned a Jack, hadn't he, when he picked her up from the airport? And had he mentioned someone else during the interview? She couldn't quite remember. She'd assumed she'd be working with Adam. She hadn't questioned further. But this Jack must be here on the same deal as her.

'I didn't realize,' she said. 'So we're living together.'

'Apparently.'

Fantastic. Three months spent in a flat the size of her foot with a strange, snide man.

'Did you just arrive?' Clare asked.

'Yep,' he said, with a solid full stop palpable in his voice.

He seemed determined to avoid an actual conversation at all costs. Clare rolled her eyes and moved to the kitchen to look for coffee.

'There's nothing there yet,' Jack said, as she opened a cupboard. 'Adam said he had supplies coming for us soon, though.'

Clare cocked her head to the side, looking at him properly for the first time. His dark hair was cropped short, and the eyes that were fixed so steadily on his laptop screen were a deep brown. They were narrowed in focus, but they were large and intense. He'd spoken in an American accent, but with a softness to it, like he'd spent a lot of time outside of the States. He was dressed in dark trousers and a grey shirt, which stretched over his shoulders. A blazer was flung over the arm of the couch and – she looked at the shoes by the front door – yes, he'd been wearing oxfords. He was, she concluded, decidedly good-looking, if a little too neat.

And a little too abrupt. She didn't want to find this abrupt man attractive. She definitely did not want to find this abrupt man – this rude man – attractive if she was going to be stuck in this miniature apartment with him for three months.

'Do you always dress like that in the tropics?' she asked.

He glanced up at her. 'Do you?' he said.

Clare looked down at herself and flushed. She was still wearing her yoga pants and the loose flannel shirt that had made sense for a journey to the airport in the icy London dawn. She'd given her coat to her mother as she boarded the train, but she was still decidedly dressed for winter. Grimacing, she lowered her nose to her shoulder and took what she hoped was a subtle sniff.

'I think I'm going to shower, if you don't mind,' she said.

'I really don't,' he said, with – was that relief? 'I really, really don't.'

Chapter Four

The flat was empty when Clare got out of the shower. Which was a great relief since, in the heat, her moisturizer was refusing to absorb properly. She sat in her dressing-gown in front of the fan for a few minutes, waiting for the swampy feeling to leave her skin.

She was a little unsure about sharing such a tiny flat with a stranger, but she could make the best of it. It wasn't like she was intending to spend much time there. And she supposed that, with two people working in the shop, she'd have plenty of days off, plenty of time to enjoy the beaches and jungles of Bali.

From the look of the shop, she couldn't imagine it got enough business to justify three people being there all the time. Although, now that she thought about it, she wasn't sure if Adam would be there full time. After all, from the look of things he hadn't been there while the previous booksellers were around. If he had, it surely wouldn't be in the state it was.

Well. Even two people felt like a lot for that shop.

It's a shame, she thought. Seashore Books could be so

cool, right on the beach as it was. But it clearly hadn't been given any real care in a long time.

*

It was getting towards mid-afternoon by the time Clare made her way back to the shop, and she was starving, but dressed much more appropriately. Her hair wasn't quite dry but was doing a saucy tousled thing over her forehead that almost looked deliberate. She'd pulled on some denim shorts and a T-shirt and when she glanced into the mirror she was more or less satisfied.

Adam seemed to agree when she made her way into the shop. 'Yes,' he said, 'you'll be much more comfortable now.'

Clare laughed. 'You didn't like the thick flannel for me?' she asked.

'Oh, I did, of course,' he replied with a smile, 'but this is much more of the moment, you know. It's giving Betty Boop at the carwash.'

'Exactly what I was aiming for,' Clare said.

'Now,' Adam said, suddenly more businesslike, 'we have important issues to discuss – first, that you will be coming to us for dinner tonight. Lissie absolutely insists.'

'Oh! Well, of course, that sounds—'

'And second, that I'm not going to ask you to start work for the next few days, so you have a chance to acclimatize, recover a bit from your jet-lag, and get to know each other.'

Clare looked around, realising that she and Adam weren't alone. Jack was standing a way back into the shop with a book in his hands. Like her, he'd changed into clothes more appropriate for the weather, although he'd chosen a more professional, formal look. Where Clare was wearing sandals, he was in boat shoes; where she had her legs on full display, his crisp tan trousers went all the way down; and where her T-shirt was casually knotted at the waist, his smoky-blue shirt, though a rumpled linen, was primly tucked in. His one concession to being on a resort island appeared to be rolling up his sleeves. It was a good look on him.

He seemed to realize he was being watched and looked up from the book in his hands to Clare and Adam.

There was a moment, a millisecond, as Jack's gaze shifted from the book in his hands to Clare, when the air in the room changed. There was something sleepy about him, as if he was surprised to find himself awake. Something benignly startled, something endearing.

His eyes met Clare's and she swallowed and looked down, her eyes falling on the sinews in his forearms shifting as he turned the book over in his hands. Yes, rolled-up sleeves were undeniably a good look on him.

Good grief, Clare, she thought. *Stop this. He called you smelly earlier. He as good as called you smelly. Do not gaze at this man's nice arms.*

She forced herself to look up at his face again, to study him properly so she could find something wanting. Something to prevent any burgeoning feelings of attraction from taking root. He wasn't particularly tall – maybe five eight – but seemed so next to Clare's plump five foot two. He had dark brown eyes that were peering at her a bit too steadily, and a mouth that curved slightly up at one corner.

His shoulders under his rumpled shirt seemed well built – tight rather than bulky – and Clare found herself wondering

25

if she should suggest a trip to the beach. Just as an experiment, not for any other reason.

So far, so good, which was *not* what she'd been aiming for. But there was the hair. Yes. Jack's dark hair was so neat as to be almost prim. A careful, studious cut, gelled enough to keep it in place, but not so much as to be shiny and crunchy. A business haircut if she'd ever seen one. A haircut that said, 'I'm not here for fun and games, no matter how wry my mouth appears.'

That's more like it, she thought. *Focus on the prim haircut, not the well-defined shoulders or sinewy forearms.* Her eyes dropped to his hands again. *Damn it.*

Clare wrested her attention from Jack's general person to the wider room, turning back to Adam. 'Thank you,' she said. 'That's very thoughtful. A few days to get used to the place sounds perfect.'

'Thoughtful nothing,' Adam said. 'These are the fruits of experience. I've seen what disasters are wrought by installing someone fresh off a twelve-hour flight behind my till. Now, off with the two of you. No doubt you're hungry. Have some lunch, explore the place, get to know each other.'

Clare turned back to Jack, who'd lost the wry twist to his mouth. He looked singularly appalled at the prospect of getting to know her.

Wonderful, Clare thought. *This could end up being a long three months.*

*

'Well,' Clare said, as she and Jack walked away from the shop, 'shall we find somewhere to eat?'

26

The bookshop was part of a row of stores along a small stretch of sand. Clare could see a clothing boutique, a nail salon and a couple of small restaurants, all opening straight onto the beach. The sand was pristine, white and warm as it pressed up around her sandals, trickling between her toes. A little way down the beach she could see the umbrellas she'd glimpsed from the car, making bright dots of red and orange against the blue of the ocean. They curved up to a point at the top and had tassels hanging around the sides.

She closed her eyes and turned her face to the hot sun, feeling it seep into her. She breathed in the salt and smiled. This really was paradise.

When she opened her eyes, Jack was peering down at her. The quizzical twist to his mouth seemed even more pronounced than it had in the shop. Because of her, Clare decided. It must be because of her. She was annoyed. He'd barely talked to her – he'd made a point of barely talking to her – and now he was twisting his mouth at her? He was probably judging her, thinking she was strange.

Her feet planted a bit more firmly, she swallowed and, instead of glaring back at him, tossed her head as if she hadn't noticed him gazing at her like she was some kind of strange insect.

'We could get something from a food truck and eat on the beach?'

'Oh,' he said. 'Is that what you'd like to do?'

'Sure,' Clare said. 'That's what I like to do on the first day of every holiday. Find some grungy cheap local food and eat it outside. Did you want to go to a restaurant or something?'

'Right,' he said. 'On holiday.'

'Yeah,' Clare said slowly. 'A working holiday, obviously. But we don't have to do my thing. What did you want to do for food?'

'I hadn't really thought about it,' Jack said. 'I assumed I'd just pick up some groceries and eat at home.'

'On your first day here?'

'I don't see why it being the first day makes that much difference.'

Clare opened her mouth and closed it again. It took her a moment to figure out what to say. She started walking, pressing her lips together in thought, mildly surprised to see Jack turn and walk with her, although she couldn't have said why. Finally, she said, 'It's like the equivalent of meeting someone for the first time and deciding not to ask them about themselves until some unspecified later point. Not their name, not what they do, not what brought them to wherever it is you've met them. It's like just shaking their hand and walking away. And in this specific case, you're doing it with a place you're going to spend the next three months. You've just been introduced to your new home, and you want to ignore it in favour of sitting in a flat.'

'But in this case there's plenty of time to get to know it,' he said. 'If you meet someone you know you'll be spending a lot of time with, you don't have to worry about getting everything done immediately. You can ask those questions any time. And better questions, hopefully.'

'But at the first opportunity to get to know them a little you've chosen to let them remain a blank.'

'I wouldn't say that. There are things you can learn about someone without asking them anything.'

Clare stared at him. 'You think you can learn about people without talking to them?'

Jack shrugged. 'Not everything,' he said. 'But some things.'

Clare shook her head. 'But you'll learn more if you put a little effort in,' she said. 'If you engage properly.'

'And I'm going to learn something profound about Bali by buying some cheap food and eating it on a beach?'

'I didn't say it would be profound, but it'll be something. Something that lets you get up tomorrow in a place you're a little more comfortable with than you were before.'

Jack didn't reply immediately, and as they walked, Clare stole a glance at him. His brow was slightly furrowed.

'What is it about eating cheap food outside that makes it the best first thing to do?'

'Stop putting words in my mouth,' Clare said, surprised by how frustrated she felt. She'd just met Jack and he was already getting under her skin. And she had to live with him. And work with him. For three entire months. 'I didn't say *the best* like the definitive best possible way to start a holiday. I just said it's what *I* like to do.'

'Fine,' Jack said, a bit shortly. 'Why do you like to do it?'

Clare didn't answer immediately. She'd never really thought too deeply about why she'd developed this habit. It was one of those traditions that grew without you noticing. The first few times she'd probably just arrived somewhere hungry. And she'd always travelled on a shoestring, trying to make her money go as far as possible. But somewhere along the way it had taken on a greater meaning for her. A way of settling into a new environment that made her feel comfortable.

'I guess because it's one of those unguarded things you do when you're at home. It's not an event, you know, not something you plan for or dress for. You just think, *It's a nice day and I'm hungry*, then grab something to eat in a park or wherever.'

'And that makes it a better introduction than eating in Bali's finest Michelin-starred restaurant?'

'Oh, I never go to them at all,' said Clare, laughing. 'But if we're comparing it to the type of nice restaurants I can actually afford, then yes. It's a more casual introduction. No one's putting on airs.'

'Like meeting someone by strolling over when they're in the middle of doing the gardening instead of dressed up for a red-carpet gala.'

Clare laughed. 'Exactly. Yes.'

For a moment she thought she was getting somewhere, that they might be able to understand each other, but when she glanced at him there wasn't even a hint of a smile on Jack's face. He was staring straight ahead as he walked, his hands thrust into his pockets.

Clare deflated a little. She was too exhausted for this. 'Look,' she said, pointing a little way ahead. 'Food stalls. Let's get something to eat.'

There was a row of small trucks with rice and noodles heaped in large pans. The spices and smells hit Clare's nostrils and she was suddenly starving. She picked a stall and stood in line.

'You've gone for the one with the longest queue,' Jack said. 'Maybe we should go somewhere else.'

'You can if you want,' said Clare, 'but if you have nothing

else to go on, always choose the place with the queue. It's probably there for a reason.'

Twenty minutes later she was holding a cardboard container of *nasi goreng*, sitting on pristine white sand and looking out over a perfect blue ocean, with a black hole of charisma sitting beside her. A good-looking hole, but a hole nonetheless, who seemed determined to contribute the bare minimum to the conversation.

'See?' Clare said, a few mouthfuls in. 'This is delicious.'

'It is,' Jack said. 'Point Clara.'

'Clare.'

'Right. Sorry. Clare.'

They ate in silence for another few minutes. Clare had taken off her sandals and dug her feet into the warm sand. There were people lying on deckchairs and large beanbags, some walking in the shallows. Clare could picture herself spending a whole day out here, reading in the sun.

She turned back to Jack. 'So,' she said, trying to keep her voice breezy, despite the feeling that she was doing the conversational equivalent of dragging a sack of wet sand up a steep hill, 'what made you apply for the bookshop?'

'I thought it would be good work experience.'

'Experience for what?'

'I've just finished my master's. I have a job starting in a few months. I thought I'd use the time in between to see how a small business runs from the inside.'

'Right. Sure.'

Jack merely grunted in reply.

Clare tried one more time. 'Why this particular small business?' she said.

'I hadn't been to Bali since I was a teenager,' he said. 'I've missed it.'

Clare stared at him. 'You let me go on and on about meeting Bali for the first time and you'd already been here?'

'Practically grew up here,' Jack said. He smirked, his eyes suddenly sparkling. He reached out for her empty container, his hand brushing hers as she passed it to him. Clare felt a jolt in the pit of her stomach.

'I think I need a nap,' Jack said. 'I'll see you later.'

He wandered back towards the shop, dropping the containers into a rubbish bin as he went. Clare stared after him, her head spinning.

Who was this guy?

Chapter Five

Clare spent the rest of the afternoon in gentle exploration. She was sure that if she sat down for too long she'd fall asleep again, and then she'd be awake all night. One of her travel rules was never to buy anything other than food on the first day, but she wandered past stalls and shops, making mental notes of the places to come back to.

Just before five, she headed to the bookshop. Adam had suggested having dinner early to allow for Clare's and Jack's jet lag. He and Jack were standing outside the shop, chatting. At least, Adam was chatting and Jack was answering occasionally.

'Ah, here's our other new bookselling starlet,' Adam said, as she walked up to them. 'Splendid. Are we all awake, all surviving?'

Clare smiled. 'So far, I think. But I'll apologize in advance in case I fall face-first into a bowl of soup later.'

'Don't worry, my dear,' said Adam. 'If that happens, Lissie will make you so comfortable in your bowl you'll feel like you're sleeping in your own bed.'

The sun was already getting low in the sky as Adam drove

them smoothly back past the airport and out onto the peninsula to the south. The evening light hit the green of the forest, making it feel unearthly. Magical. They passed some slick-looking resorts and hotels, but as they drove on, up through the streets, they thinned out, leaving a calm, quiet, breathtakingly green road ahead of them. Adam kept up a steady stream of chatter as he drove, letting Clare and Jack sit mostly in silence, taking in the views.

Before long, they pulled up at an elegant bungalow and Adam ushered them inside, calling out as they opened the door: 'My love, we are arrived.'

A vision walked into the entranceway.

'Lissie, my love, this is Clare and this is Jack, our new shopkeepers. This is Celestina Lai, my wife.' His voice grew warmer as he introduced her, and Clare wondered if they were only recently married. Celestina was tall, and unspeakably elegant. She was dressed in a flowing gold kaftan that set a glow in her warm brown skin. Her hair was silver and flowed down her back in gentle waves.

'Welcome, welcome, angels,' she said, her voice low and honeyed. 'You must be simply aching with exhaustion.'

She walked up to Clare and grabbed her chin, pulling it up and gazing down into her eyes. 'Yes,' she said. 'You. You're a right one. A kindred, I think.'

Clare swallowed, feeling strangely vulnerable. From anyone else this would have seemed pretentious, artificial, but there was something grounding about Celestina, in all her lavishness.

She moved from Clare to Jack, placing a hand on either side of his face.

'You don't want me to see it,' she said, 'but it's there. Yes. There's something there.'

Clare glanced at Jack, trying to see how he was taking all this. His brow was furrowed. He seemed a bit confused.

'Well, my love,' Celestina said to Adam, letting go of Jack's face, 'you've done better this time. This time might be special.'

'Well, well,' said Adam. 'I'm sure they'll do all right.'

'You have a lovely home,' said Clare.

'Yes, don't we?' said Celestina, a dreamy smile on her face as she gazed around the room. 'We bought it for absolutely nothing last century and it's been a dream ever since.'

So, they weren't newlyweds, Clare thought. But there was an air of freshness about them all the same.

Adam broke in: 'I wouldn't say that. It was falling to pieces. It took years to make it properly liveable.'

Celestina waved a hand. 'Yes, but I didn't have to worry about any of that. You did it all.'

Clare couldn't help but grin. She'd never met anyone so charming. She was pretty sure Celestina could say anything she wanted and still be nothing but delightful.

'Now come through to the dining room and we'll get you comfortable.'

Even Jack gasped as they walked into the next room. It was elegantly furnished and painted a deep, luscious blue, with art on every spare inch of wall. But the real star of the show was the southern wall.

As they'd entered the house, it had seemed like a normal bungalow, in a quiet, leafy residential street on a hill, surrounded on either side by lush greenery. But now Clare saw they were on top of a cliff, looking out over the Indian Ocean.

The entire wall was a vast folding glass door that had been pulled to the side, letting the spectacular view into the whole room. The sun was lowering to the west, staining the sky pink and orange as it sank into the inky sea. In the east stars were appearing, sparkling in the sky in much greater numbers than Clare was used to. Birdsong came in from all sides, and Clare breathed it all in. She'd seen a lot of beautiful places that day, felt the sun-soaked holiday energy catching at her, but this – this was magical.

Adam looked at Clare's and Jack's awestruck faces and chuckled. 'Yes,' he said, 'rather good, isn't it?'

Celestina gently clapped her hands together. 'Now, cocktails?'

'Of course, of course,' said Adam, moving to a bar set up on the far wall.

*

Two Old Fashioneds and one exquisite sunset later, Clare was feeling very at peace with the world.

Celestina rose from her chair with the air of someone about to announce Best Picture at the Oscars. 'I believe it's time to eat. *Mon cher*, if you would select a wine. White, I think.'

Clare stood up, with significantly less elegance. 'Can I help you bring things through?'

'My dear, I will simply never refuse help in the kitchen.'

Clare followed Celestina through the house. 'It smells amazing,' she said, as they walked into the kitchen, where a vast array of boxes was spread out across the countertops.

'Now I must let you in on my darkest secret,' Celestina said.

'You're not great in the kitchen?' said Clare.

'How dare you? I am marvellous in the kitchen. I am extremely good at plating. I merely have no interest in learning to actually cook.'

'I'm not sure I'll be much help with plating,' said Clare.

'Then you shall bring me plates as I direct you and watch me create art.'

It was immediately clear that Celestina hadn't been bluffing. She unpacked box after box of food – refusing to tell Clare where it had come from – and installed it carefully on plates and platters, through some art or magic that Clare couldn't follow, making it look even better than it smelt.

'You and Adam seem to have such a lovely life here,' Clare said, as they worked. 'Did he move here for you?'

'It was more the other way around,' said Celestina. 'I was born on Bali, but I didn't grow up here. My parents moved to California – to Malibu, darling – when I was a baby. We visited a lot, of course, but I never lived here. Adam and I came here together shortly after we met and he fell in love with it.'

As Celestina placed some carefully selected garnishes on the dishes, Clare looked around the kitchen. It was spacious, much more minimalist than the dining room, with just one framed picture on the wall – a photo. A younger Adam by some twenty or thirty years sitting on a balcony with a tall Indonesian man. It appeared to be somewhere in the Mediterranean. They were sitting at a small café table, both leaning in towards each other, half-drunk glasses of wine between them.

Celestina noticed Clare looking at it and came over to stand beside her. 'I do adore this photo,' she said. 'My favourite picture of us BCE.'

Clare looked up at her, confused.

'Before Celestina Era, my dear.'

'Is it strange for you?' Clare said. 'Having photos of yourself from before, I mean.'

'There are some old photos I prefer not to look at,' Celestina said. 'But I'm still me. She's in there, she just doesn't know it yet, although she definitely suspects.'

Celestina stroked her old face in the photo with affection. 'We are each of us made up of all the times in our lives,' she said, 'and there are plenty of times when we aren't fully ourselves. But that doesn't mean those times aren't important or beautiful.'

'That's a lovely way of putting it,' said Clare.

'Yes, aren't I wonderful?' said Celestina. 'Really, I love this picture for Adam. Look at him. See how much he loves me.'

She was right. Adam was gazing at her as if he couldn't bear to look away. But also as if he knew he would never have to.

'I have wondered sometimes,' Celestina said, 'why I was never afraid to tell him who I really was. I should have been. It's a lot to ask of a person, and plenty of relationships don't survive it. But . . .' She fell silent for a moment, gazing at the photo. 'Even then he was seeing me, you understand. Really seeing me. He didn't know he was seeing a woman, but he knew who I was. In my bones.'

Clare was speechless. She suddenly felt small and alone. She didn't think anyone had ever seen her that deeply. It seemed impossible that anyone ever could.

Chapter Six

The next few days passed peacefully enough. Clare decided that, while she was ready to get to know Jack and would chat whenever chatting was called for, she wasn't going to strain a muscle trying to be companionable just to see him smirk at whatever she had to say.

Adam categorically refused to let them start working in the bookshop before they'd had a few days to recover, so Clare spent her days exploring the beaches and markets in the neighbourhood.

She gave herself the promised full day on the beach near the shop. She rented herself a bright beanbag and an umbrella, and lay there reading, getting up only for food and drink.

She wandered through the colourful market, haggling over sarongs and necklaces, picking out souvenirs for her mum and Lina. She found a quieter beach a bit further west, with fewer restaurants and bars lining the sand, and went swimming in the pristine blue sea. She explored further east, visiting the surf beach she'd seen from the window of Adam's car on her first day. She watched the surfers for a while, and resolved to try it herself before she left, although she did not expect to find herself naturally gifted at it.

She was still longing for bed by around eight thirty or nine each night so she decided to wait for a while before trying some of the clubs she walked past. They'd be there for her when she was more awake.

She wasn't sure how Jack had been spending his time, although she had her suspicions. She'd come back to the flat for a change of clothes after a particularly messy lunch on the second or third day to find him sitting on the couch with his laptop.

She couldn't help laughing. 'You know it's a paradise out there, right?' she said.

Jack looked a bit embarrassed. 'Oh,' he said, and – wait, was that a blush? 'Yeah. I just wanted to catch up on some stuff.'

Clare raised an eyebrow and left him to it. She wasn't sure what he could have to catch up on if he'd finished his master's and not started his job yet, but she decided that was none of her business. The next day as she came in from a swim, she spotted him sitting on the sand under a beach umbrella, laptop open in front of him.

'That's better,' she called to him as she passed. 'Only a tiny bit better, but still.'

He nodded in reply, keeping his eyes on his screen.

Aside from that, Clare's interactions with Jack were limited to 'Good morning,' and 'Do you mind if I have a shower now?'

That and mumbling 'Excuse me,' as she squeezed past him

in the kitchenette, trying to get to the milk for her morning coffee. Which was how she discovered that he smelt nice – knowledge she did not at all want to have.

And she might have caught herself staring at Jack's fore-arms while he chopped vegetables in the tiny kitchen once or twice, but surely that was normal. Surely staring just a couple of times was normal, and it wasn't like he'd caught her at it.

After four or five days, Clare was beginning to get antsy, so she was relieved when Adam finally allowed her and Jack to start their new working lives.

*

Adam took the pair of them quickly through the operational elements of the shop.

'Really all that matters are the practical things,' he said. 'How to sell books, how to order books, where the petty cash is. I always hope that people will feel able to put their own stamp on things. I think a lot of the time they don't want to tread on my toes, so they keep things much as they are, but there's really no need to worry about that. For as long as you're here, you can consider the shop your own.'

'Will you not be working with us?' Clare asked.

'Oh, no,' said Adam. 'I'm all but retired so I'll leave it to you. But you can call me, of course, if you need help with anything.'

'Do you need to take us through the accounting?' asked Jack, just as Clare was saying, 'Does the shop have an Insta-gram account?'

'Oh, you don't need to worry about the accounts,' said

41

Adam, lightly, to Jack. 'I've never done them myself, always farm out the boring stuff. And I think a couple of years ago someone did set up an Instagram account – the login details are probably in the notebook under the till.' He pulled it out and passed it to Clare. It must have been several years old and contained notes ranging from 'Bob to collect broken chair Thurs' to 'Had small fire in kitchen. Out now.'

Clare flipped through it until she found the Instagram login, pulled up the account and looked through it. The profile picture was a blurry shot of the shop's logo, and the feed was nothing but selfies – on beaches, by waterfalls, at nightclubs. None at the bookshop. If the bio hadn't mentioned books, no one would have known what the account was for, and even then it simply said, 'Bali, books and babes'.

Jack looked at Clare's phone over her shoulder. 'I think that seems more like your area than mine,' he said.

Clare's head jerked up. Did he think she was going to do the same kind of posts as this? He had already moved away from her, now looking at the petty-cash receipts. Well. Whatever. This *was* her area.

'Is it okay if I do a rebrand?' she asked Adam. 'And maybe delete some of these old posts?'

'Oh, whatever you think,' said Adam. 'I never look at it.'

It felt to Clare that Adam had only given them a cursory demonstration of how the shop was run, but he seemed satisfied with what he'd told them, and wandered off after a couple of hours.

'Does he seem a bit too, I don't know . . .'

'Unconcerned?' said Jack. 'He really doesn't seem to care at all.'

'I don't get it. If he doesn't care about the shop, why does he go to all this trouble? Hiring new staff every three months when he could just take on a manager and leave them to it. Or he could sell the place.'

'I guess it takes the pressure off. Clearly, he doesn't mind if his staff spend all their time on the beach taking selfies.'

There was something in the way he said it that put Clare's back up. He sounded like he was giving her good news. Like he expected her to be happy about it.

'Do you think that's all *I'm* going to do?' Clare said.

'I have no idea what you're going to do,' he said. 'I barely know you.' He went back to the petty-cash logbook, leaving Clare standing there blinking. 'I wonder if I can find the number for Adam's accountant,' he said.

*

Clare left Jack to his detailed records of times when people had dug into the petty cash for a box of teabags and wandered around the shop, taking stock of where things were. The shelves were a mess, with books seemingly put wherever they would fit. It appeared no effort had been made to highlight specific books, no covers facing out, no staff recommendations, no bestsellers or new releases.

Clare had never thought about how bookshops should be run before, but she'd spent a lot of time in them. She and her dad had had a tradition – he'd take her to one on the first day of the school holidays and give her thirty pounds to spend on whatever books she wanted. He'd always told her to take as long as she liked to decide. Which was how she'd ended up reading *The Shining* at the age of eleven, but also how she'd discovered most of her favourite authors. Amy Tan, autumn half-term when she was thirteen. Terry Pratchett, Christmas, aged eight – she'd bought *Hogfather* and her dad had started reading it to her on Christmas Eve. By New Year they'd got through *Mort* and *Small Gods* as well. Jane Austen, summer, aged sixteen. Browsing bookshops had always made her feel safe. Grounded. Small, but in a good way, like there was a universe surrounding her to be discovered slowly, calmly, knowing that she'd never run out of things to learn and see.

This bookshop did not make her feel like that.

The window, which was dirty, had three faded paperbacks sitting on a dusty black cloth, like a display that someone had started setting up ten years previously and forgotten to finish. The tables at the front were overwhelming, crowded with a random hotchpotch of paperbacks.

After half an hour, Clare found herself desperate to change something, and she knew where she wanted to start. She was nervous, though, hesitant. It felt a bit like staking a claim on something that wasn't really hers, even though Adam had said it was. And she'd never done anything like this before. She knew what she wanted to do, she could see it in her mind's eye, but she couldn't help feeling the reality would be a disaster.

She closed her eyes to give herself a talking-to. *Do it, Clare,* she said to herself. *You can't very well make the shop look worse.*

She swallowed, opened her eyes and set to work, ignoring the flutter of fear in her belly.

She ransacked the shop and the tiny storeroom for crates,

stepladders – anything that would make a small platform. She found a couple of dusty old lamps stashed away. She burrowed into cupboards and on shelves to find cleaning supplies and collected everything in the corner by the shop's window. She stepped outside and looked at the display, picturing what she could do to change it, before heading over to Jack.

'I'm popping out for some things,' she said. 'Can I have some petty cash?'

Jack looked up at her from the maths he was apparently doing. 'Why? What for?'

'We need to freshen up the window display.'

'The window?'

'Yes. So the shop looks nice. And people want to come into it.'

'I'll just have to work out what we can afford to spend.'

'Never mind,' said Clare. 'I'll just pay for it myself.'

Jack started to say something, but Clare was already out of the shop. She was suddenly full of drive and energy, and she didn't need financial caution holding her back.

The market was crowded and loud, humming with life. Sweat prickled on her skin as she walked through, resisting the calls of the vendors showing off beautifully crafted leather bags and colourful jewellery.

The ocean breeze didn't penetrate the crush of bodies, and by the time Clare had found everything she needed, she was sweltering and starving. She made her way back through the crowds and stepped into the air again with relief. Stopping by a food truck, she grabbed some lunch for her and Jack and headed back. 'I bought you food,' she said, as she walked in. 'Sorry, I know I was gone for an age.'

Jack handed some change to the customer he'd just served and went back to his calculations. 'That's fine. Like I said, I don't think Adam cares.'

'Well, if you want to take a break to eat, I'll look after things here.'

'Maybe in a while,' Jack said, not looking up.

Clare rolled her eyes and left him to it. She downed her lunch in five minutes and got to work. She bustled back and forth for three hours, almost forgetting Jack was there. Occasionally customers came in, but he didn't seem to need her help with them, so she left him to it. Every time someone appeared at the till, he seemed slightly baffled, but managed to put the sales through just fine, although he didn't chat much to the customers.

Finally, Clare was done. Sweaty, covered with grime, and satisfied to the point of smugness, she stood outside inspecting her handiwork, a tired smile on her face.

'Do you want to have a look?' she called in to Jack.

He took a moment to pinpoint where she was calling from. He looked exhausted, too. He passed a hand across his face and stood up, stretching out his back before walking outside.

The window was gleaming and lit warmly with the two battered old lamps Clare had put on either side. Footstools, boxes and tables were carefully arranged, each with a stack of three or four books, the top one propped open, its cover facing out. A stack of classics, with Jane Austen's *Emma* on top, some fun recent releases, capped by an Emily Henry. And *The Seven Moons of Maali Almeida* topping a stack of literary-prize winners. A sheet of sheer, gauzy off-white cotton hung behind everything, separating the display from the shop behind it, while still letting in the light, and with window chalk, Clare had drawn a large circle, with strands of blue and green, surrounding the shop's name in gold: Seashore Books.

'I need to do some research into what's selling well now,' she said, 'particularly in airports or other holiday destinations. We should make sure the books in here are things people will have heard of to bring them in. And once I've sorted things inside, we might bring the gauze down to let people see the shop properly. Although I kind of like the effect. It shows just enough to be tantalizing. Or it will be tantalizing when it's rearranged.'

'I think you're right. I like the gauze,' said Jack.

Clare looked at him in surprise. She hadn't expected a compliment. 'You like it?'

'It's definitely much better than before,' he said, which kind of took the weight out of his praise. Clare could have emptied the window, and cleaned it, and it would have been better than before. 'Ah, I've cleared an impressive bar there. I'll be competing in the window-display Olympics in no time.'

'Do you have your receipts?' Jack said.

'Why?'

'Just give them to me.'

Clare fished them out of her pocket and handed them over. Jack went back inside and opened the petty-cash tin.

'Oh,' Clare said. 'Don't worry about it. I said I'd pay for it.'

'Just take it,' said Jack. 'But I have to do a budget for this stuff.'

'Yeah, yeah. Thanks.'

Clare went back outside and carefully took a photo of the window, with the shop's name bright in the centre. She opened Instagram and swapped out the blurry old profile picture. Then she called to Jack again. 'Come outside for just one minute.'

He walked over to her slowly. Before he could resist, she spun him around and pulled him to her side, standing up on her toes to make it easier to frame. Swooping her hand high and making sure the shop's name was clearly visible behind their heads, she took a few quick photos.

'It won't all be selfies,' she said. 'I promise.'

Jack gave a small laugh.

'That's okay,' he said. 'I mean, good. But one or two is fine, I guess.'

Clare looked at him. He looked a bit uncomfortable. They were still standing close enough together for her to feel the heat coming off his skin. She cleared her throat and stepped back.

'Right,' she said. 'Just enough to give it that personal touch.'

'Yeah,' he said. 'Yeah, I get it.' He nodded at her awkwardly and stepped back inside.

Clare tweaked the photo before uploading it. She looked tired in it, but happy. There was a light in her eyes that she realized she hadn't had in a while. She smiled to herself and tapped out a quick caption:

Hi there, readers of Bali. We're Jack and Clare, and if we look exhausted that's because we are. We'll be your booksellers here at Seashore Books for the next three months and we've spent all day working ourselves ragged, getting acquainted with this special shop. We're so excited to get to know you all, so please stop by and tell us what you love to read. Keep an eye out for recommendations, events and more as we dip our toes into life on this beautiful island. *Suksma*!'

Chapter Seven

The next morning, Jack took up his position at the till again, bending over papers and notebooks, poking at an actual calculator instead of just using the one on his phone. Clare left him to it and began a careful survey of the shelves. There were faded signs at the top of some, indicating that, theoretically, they held science fiction or cookery or authors between F and K. And it was true that they all included at least some books that fitted their category. But on each there was an encroaching tide of unrelated titles. Nigella's *At My Table* sat alongside Kazuo Ishiguro's *The Buried Giant*, both shelved among the graphic novels. There were copies of Anne Brontë's *The Tenant of Wildfell Hall* and Evelyn Waugh's *Decline and Fall* under New Releases, while *The Girl with the Dragon Tattoo*, by Stieg Larsson, was in young adult fiction.

There was, in short, an overwhelming amount of reorganizing to be done. Clare found herself grinning at the prospect, although she knew from bitter experience that her excitement wouldn't last.

She was stricken every year or two with the need to reorganize her bookshelves at home, and it always went the same way. She would start in a glow of energy and optimism, revelling in the chance to rediscover books she'd owned for years and not seen in months. She'd ponder possible organizational strategies, trying to hit on the perfect system. She'd done colour-coded, authors' nationalities, height, width and – her personal favourite – 'if you liked . . .' where she'd arranged them by similarity of mood or feeling. Somehow she didn't think that system would work for an actual bookshop.

She let out a sigh. 'If only,' she muttered

'What was that?' Jack said from behind her.

She spun on her heel. She hadn't heard him approach.

'Oh,' she said. 'Nothing. I was being silly.'

Jack peered at her.

'Do you think Adam would mind if I rearranged things a bit? Or a lot?'

'What do you want to rearrange?'

'Everything. All of the books.'

'They definitely need tidying up a bit. Is that *The Princess Diaries* under classics?'

'Well, it is a classic. So, it's clearly one of the few that's shelved correctly. But I'm not talking about putting everything back in the right place. I want to redo the whole system from scratch.'

'I don't think Adam would mind,' said Jack. 'I might, though.'

'Really?' Clare said. 'But you're so busy doing all the maths.'

'You say that like the maths isn't important.'

'Oh, I know it's important,' Clare said, 'but so are shelving systems. You're doing that, so I can do this.'

Jack shifted from foot to foot. 'I just mean don't make any big decisions without me. I'm responsible for the place.'

Clare bristled. 'We're both responsible for it,' she said.

'Yeah,' he said. 'Sure. But, you know . . .' He trailed off.

'I know what?' Clare said.

'I thought you'd want it this way,' Jack said. 'You get to have a holiday in paradise and all you have to do is put in a few shifts at the bookshop.'

'While you run it?' said Clare.

'Look, I'm not trying to be a dick, but I know what I'm doing here. You don't have to worry about things.'

'I see. I just have to work on my tan and post selfies in front of waterfalls on the shop's Instagram account.'

Clare felt as if she was trapped in a flashback of a poorly dressed and completely unsympathetic HR rep giving her the thanks-for-your-time-but-we-have-to-let-you-go talk. The you-don't-quite-match-the-serious-important-vibe-of-the-company talk. The you-smile-too-much-and-talk-too-much-you're-too-flighty-and-too-loud talk.

'Isn't that what you want to do?' Jack said.

'Wow,' Clare said. 'Cool. Thanks for that. You've really got me pegged.'

Jack flushed a little and the corner of his mouth twisted up. 'Isn't it, though? You said it yourself. You spent two years travelling, but you couldn't afford to keep going, so you applied for this job so you could do it for free.'

'When did I tell you that?' Clare said.

'The other night at dinner. You said it to all of us. How

glad you were to come here when usually you couldn't afford to.'

Clare could feel a lump rising in her throat. It was like a skipping record. *You're not good enough, Clare. You're not a serious person. You're not a real adult.*

She swallowed the lump. 'And that means that *all* I want to do while I'm here is lounge around in the sun?' she said. 'That I don't have any interest in the shop at all?'

'There's nothing wrong with that,' said Jack. 'It's obviously what Adam expects.'

Clare could feel her eyes getting hot and prickly. At any moment she'd start crying, and Jack would think she was upset, when actually she was furious.

'Fine,' she said. She could hear her voice starting to wobble. 'I'll leave you to your serious bookshop work and swan around somewhere.'

She grabbed her bag and stormed out of the shop. She managed to get around the corner before she burst into tears.

*

Clare was as good as her word: she went to the beach. She walked across the sand and out into the ocean, past the food stalls, past the sunbathers, past the beginners' surf class taking place in the shallows. She swam out until she found a quiet spot in the sea, with nothing in front of her but blue. The salt water lapping around her was refreshing, and the vastness was calming somehow. It made her feel small but important, as if she was a tiny part of a greater organism. She breathed in, tasting the salt, slowly coming back to herself.

Why had she got so upset? It shouldn't matter what Jack thought of her – she barely knew him and what she did know of him she didn't like. He was smug and uptight and boring. He might have good arms and a nice smile, but not nice enough to make up for the perfect-business-boy attitude. He might smell good sometimes – and don't think she hadn't noticed how good he looked fresh out of the shower with nothing but a towel around his waist – but that didn't mean he had a free pass to look down his nose at her.

If she was willing to be a little more honest with herself, she would have admitted that Jack's assumptions about her stung because they were pretty close to the truth. She *had* applied for the job as a way of visiting Bali without having to pay to visit Bali. She hadn't thought much further than that, not about the reality of things. She'd imagined her fantasy-bookseller existence – in which the shop in question didn't need anything from her. In which it was already everything it could and should be.

It wasn't until she'd arrived, until she'd seen what a state it was in, that it had started to feel like something more. Something about the shop made her feel needed. She could help things, she knew it. She could make things better.

She thought back to what her mum had said to her before she left. Her request that she use this time to decide what was next. Clare didn't feel any closer to knowing what she wanted to do, but somehow she was starting to feel that there was something she *could* do. Had that been her problem all this time? She was so uncertain of herself, of her abilities, that she hadn't been able even to start thinking about what kind of job she could do. About where she could be useful.

Sure, so far she'd only tidied up a shop window, but other ideas for improving the shop were beginning to crowd each other out in her mind, and she was genuinely excited about doing all that work. She could feel the energy of it snaking through her veins. She was excited to spend some time relaxing on the beach, yes, but for the first time in ages she felt like she had something to contribute.

Jack clearly didn't take her seriously. She couldn't let that stop her. She was here to figure out what she wanted, what she was capable of doing. If she let him get to her she'd lose all this motivation.

The first thing would be organization, of course. A review of how things were arranged, what was stocked, what was missing. Then a change of decor, maybe. A fresh paint job, maybe a new logo, if that wasn't going too far. She'd have to find out if the shop ever did events – launches, signings, panels. As things were, she didn't see how events would be possible – there was barely any room for people.

The shop should be partnering with local bars for book-related cocktail nights on the beach. There were so many options, and she couldn't wait to get started.

Her mum had been right, she realized. She had been bored. She'd been bored for so long. She'd been bored even before she'd come home. She'd loved her two years off, two years spent travelling the world, working in whatever bar would hire her, but during the last few months she'd felt she was just frittering her life away.

It was ironic, really. She'd travelled because she'd been afraid of wasting her time. When her dad had died she'd found herself panicking about how short life was, how suddenly it could all be over. But then travelling for so long without a plan or focus also felt like it had been . . . not a waste entirely but not as good as it might have been.

She liked a project. She'd been craving it.

Well. She couldn't let Jack get in the way of that. She would show him and his perfect-little-business-boy butt.

She stayed in the ocean for a while, letting the water soak into her, turning her rage into righteous indignation, then into firm resolve. There was a steely glint in her eyes as she swam back to shore, and as she lay on the sand feeling her skin prickle in the sun, her mind whirled with ideas.

Satisfied with her plan, Clare stood up, wrapped a sarong around her waist, and slipped on her flip-flops. She grabbed a quick bite to eat, then took to the markets once more. A busy and energizing afternoon of browsing and haggling later, she had everything she needed to get started.

*

She didn't mention anything to Jack when she saw him that night at the flat, and she made sure her purchases were well out of sight in her room.

The next morning, she let herself wake up slowly, stretching and turning over when she heard Jack go into the shower. She was eating a bowl of cereal and doing a crossword when he emerged from his room, dressed for work.

'Have a nice day,' she said, as he opened the front door. He looked at her but didn't say anything, just gave a small smile and left.

Once he left, Clare got to work. There was a lot to do, and she wanted to have it cleared up before Jack returned to the flat. As it was, she had to hope he'd be sticking to his previous routine of staring at the till all day with his calculator and his piles of accounts. If he came back here for lunch, it would be much more awkward.

She pushed the little coffee table to the side and tipped out her shopping bags in the middle of the floor. There was a pile of moss-green felt, a bunch of slender driftwood sticks, some charcoal cotton and a packet of needles. Clare propped her laptop on the couch, stuck on an old season of *Bake Off*, and sat against the wall, legs stretched out in front of her, happily stitching away, half an ear listening for approaching footsteps. By mid-afternoon she was staring at the results of her labour with a satisfied smirk. She cleared up all the scraps and spread her work in front of her.

They would do, she thought. They would do quite nicely.

*

The next part of Clare's plan involved some light deception. Some low-grade manipulation. She almost felt guilty about it – or at least she would have if Jack hadn't happened to say, 'Enjoying your vacation?' as she walked through the lounge on her way to bed that night.

She stopped dead in her tracks but with some effort kept her voice breezy. 'I am,' she said. 'Thanks.' She waited a second. 'You look tired. Stressful day?'

Jack sighed. 'I just—' He cut himself off. 'It's fine,' he said. 'I'm fine. There's just a lot to go through.'

'Yeah, you've been working really hard the last few days,' said Clare. She smiled benignly. 'Look, you don't want to wear yourself entirely out in the first week. Let me cover for you tomorrow. I'll mind the shop and you can get some rest.'

'It's okay,' he said, passing a hand over his face. 'I can manage. I'm not here for a holiday.'

Clare bit back a retort and tried to inject some warmth into her voice. 'A day off isn't a holiday. You won't be able to do your best work if you don't get some decent rest. Even just going to bed tonight knowing you don't have to be up in time to open the shop tomorrow.'

Jack didn't reply immediately but Clare was sure she was getting through to him. He really did look exhausted.

'I know you think I'm a frivolous ne'er-do-well or what-ever but I can actually manage for one day. I won't ruin everything, I promise.'

'Don't be silly,' Jack said. 'Of course I don't . . .' He trailed off and yawned.

Clare smiled to herself. 'That's it,' she said. 'Look at you. I'm banning you from the shop for twenty-four hours.'

Jack sighed. 'I'm honestly too tired to argue,' he said.

'Good!' Clare said. 'And while, unlike me, you're not here for a holiday, you should still do some fun things while you're here. You can't spend three months in Bali and not go home with at least a little bit of a tan.'

Jack just grunted.

*

Clare had hoped he'd still be in bed when she left the next morning, but he was up. He wasn't dressed, though. She showered, threw on some clothes and came out of her room to find him eating cereal in boxers and a T-shirt. That could be a problem. Not because the sight of him in his boxers did things to Clare's insides – well, not just because of that – but because she needed to sneak all her supplies past him.

'Morning,' she said brightly. 'Sleep well?'

'Yeah, actually,' said Jack. 'I feel a lot better. I probably will come in after all.'

'No!' Clare yelled, a little too loudly. 'Twenty-four hours. We agreed. You need a proper break. Go and relax on the beach. Learn to surf or something.'

'I'm actually pretty good at surfing,' said Jack.

'Huh,' said Clare.

Jack gave a crooked smile. 'Surprised?'

'No,' said Clare. 'Not at all. The moment I set eyes on you I knew you for a surfer. One look at your pristine short back and sides and your crisply pressed trousers, and I thought, *Toe to tip, that's a surfer*.'

'Jeez, it's not that bad,' Jack said, running a hand over his head. 'You make me sound so boring.'

'You've been doing maths for four days.'

'That's a low blow.'

Clare grinned at him.

'Well, if you're sure you're okay in the shop –'

'I'm sure.'

'– then I guess it's not a terrible idea to have a day of recreation.'

'A day of recreation. That's the phrase you're going with.'

Jack didn't answer for a moment, then, 'Yes,' he said. 'Apparently it is.'

'Okay,' said Clare. 'Good.' She headed towards the door

and gave what she hoped was a natural, and in no way over-dramatic start. 'Oh,' she said, 'my phone.'

She went back into her room and casually batted the door until it was ajar. She didn't want Jack to be able to see her, but it would seem strange if she closed it entirely. She grabbed her bag of felt and lowered it out of the window into a bush. Then she fished her phone out of her pocket and left the room, waving it aloft and saying, 'Found it,' as she walked towards the door. As she retrieved the bag and made her way to the shop, she worried that Jack would take a while to go out, then wander past the window later today and see what she was up to. But there was a lot to get done and if she didn't start early, it wouldn't be finished by the time he came back.

But she was reckoning without his business boy's sense of efficiency. Twenty minutes after she'd left him in his pants eating cereal he walked past the window, in shorts and a T-shirt no less, waving at her as he passed. She waved back lazily, phone still in her hand, like the wannabe influencer he believed her to be, then dashed to the window and craned her head out, peering after him as he walked down the street and turned the corner.

Right. Now was the time.

Clare took a deep breath and turned to the shop. She couldn't do it all in one day, but that was fine. She just needed proof of concept. Her focus was the set of shelves just to the right of the door, the first you saw when you walked in. There were a couple of tables in front of them, but she wanted to do a better audit and probably order some new things before she dealt with them. Today was about working with what she had.

She spent the morning walking back and forth through the shop, pulling out the books that would suit her needs and stacking them at the front. Next, she cleared the shelves she wanted. She figured that there was no sense in trying to do that in an organized way, given how chaotic the rest of the shop was, so shoved most of them into the gaps she'd just created.

She was getting grimy and sweaty, and when a customer walked in around lunchtime, she was suddenly aware that she might look a little unprofessional. She tried to make up for it with a bright, welcoming smile.

'Hi!' she said, a little too cheerily. 'How can I help?'

'Oh,' said the customer, a tall man of around fifty. 'I'm sorry, are you closed? I can come back.'

'No, no, come in,' said Clare. 'We're not closed, but we are in disarray, if you can deal with that. Things are a bit disorganized and I'm trying to set them to rights. Were you after something specific, or did you just want to browse?'

'It looks like finding something specific might be tricky,' the man said, with a smile.

'It's definitely a good time to take a punt on something random you've pulled from a shelf with your eyes closed, but if we have what you want, I'll hunt it down – or we can order it in, of course.'

'What are the odds of my sticking my hand into a random pile and pulling out something by, say, Ayn Rand.'

'Not zero,' said Clare, apologetically, 'but all adventures come with some risk.'

'It's tempting,' said the customer, 'but maybe another time. I'm just here to pick up a book Adam ordered in for me. It'll be under Bethany.'

'Sure,' said Clare. 'Of course.' She looked in the box of special orders under the till. There was only one book in it – a Jon Klassen picture book with a Post-it on the cover that said 'Bethany'.

'Oh!' Clare said, surprised. She didn't know what she'd expected, but it wasn't that. 'Is this the one?'

The man smiled. 'Yes, excellent. She loved the hat ones, you know.'

Clare didn't know, but she nodded anyway.

She sold him the book and he left her to it. She wasn't interrupted again, which, though convenient, made her worry a little. Well, she couldn't solve every problem in one day. For now, all she could do was shelve a few books.

*

Clare was sitting outside the door of the bookshop with an ice cream when Jack came back from his day off. She noted his pleasantly tousled hair and said, 'Looks like you made it into the ocean.'

He smiled. 'I may have surfed. And you were right, I did need it.'

'Good,' she said, then grinned a little nervously. 'Now, don't be mad . . .'

Jack's shoulders went from relaxed to rigid immediately. 'What have you done?' he said.

'You're going to love it. It's good. It's great, actually.'

He sighed and let his head fall back. Clare got the distinct impression that he was counting to ten while he stared at the sky. He looked back at her, and she beamed at him.

'Okay,' he said. 'Show me.'

'You could say it a little more cheerfully,' said Clare, 'if you wanted.'

'Noted,' said Jack, as he followed her into the shop.

He didn't say anything for a couple of moments, but Clare smiled happily as she surveyed her handiwork. The shelves by the entrance were transformed. They were neatly organized and adorned with Clare's new pennants. The largest one spread across the whole width of the shelves and read 'On holiday?' The shelves immediately below each had their own pennant, with labels that included 'Romance (Modern)', 'Romance (Historical)', 'Mysteries (Thrilling)', and 'Mysteries (Cosy)'. The shelf to the side was marked 'Indonesian & Balinese Authors'.

Clare looked up at Jack. 'Well?' she said.

'I think most people would say "thrillers" rather than "thrilling",' he said.

Clare grimaced. 'I know, but the others were all adjectives, I didn't want a rogue noun messing up the flow.'

'Are these the only kinds of books people read on holiday?'

'They're the only kinds of books I read on holiday.'

'What about non-fiction? Airport books, like political memoirs and pop econo—'

'You want a Freakonomics shelf?' said Clare.

'Some people might want a Freakonomics shelf,' Jack said. He sighed again. 'How much did you spend?'

'Not a lot. Obviously, it would be better to get proper signs made but I knew you'd say we have to budget for that—'

'No, Clare, I have to budget for everything. Every cent.'

'Adam didn't say we had to—'

'Adam didn't say anything about money at all, did he? Why do you think I've had to go over the books like I've been doing? Because he hasn't told us there *is* no money.'

Clare stared at him but didn't say anything.

'How many sales did you make today? Any?'

'Yes, but—'

Jack walked over to the till and hit a button. 'One,' he said. 'One sale. Which is one more than I made yesterday.'

'Obviously the shop's not in a great state,' said Clare. 'That's why I'm doing this. To help it get better.'

'You're not listening,' said Jack. 'The shop's not in a bad state. It's dead. It hasn't made enough in the last year to cover our flights here. We are already more than this place can afford without frittering money away on signs.'

Clare was silent. She could feel that lump in her throat again. She'd been so sure that she was helping things. That she was contributing. What a joke. She should have known.

'But why?' she said eventually. 'Why would Adam bring us here if things were going so badly?'

'I don't know,' said Jack. 'But he must be paying for us out of his own pocket.'

'Maybe we should talk to him about it,' said Clare. 'The three of us could work out a plan.'

'I've tried. I've been trying. I've tried talking to Adam, I've tried talking to the accountant – whose number, by the way, it took me two days to find because Adam wouldn't give it to me. He said I was being officious.'

Clare gave him a sidelong glance, and she could almost have sworn he blushed. 'Look, the signs and stuff, I don't need the shop to pay for—'

'The shop will pay you back. Just give me the receipt. But the petty cash, that's got to be coming from Adam's pocket as well.'

'But this . . . this is to help,' Clare said. 'If we make the shop better, things will improve. But we have to invest in it, right? We can't turn things around without some kind of spending.'

'Come on, Clare,' said Jack. 'You think we're going to bring this place back from the brink with a few handmade signs and a positive attitude?'

Clare was stung. 'I don't think we'll do it without those things,' she said.

'Look, I'm trying to take care of things,' said Jack. 'Just leave it to me.'

Clare turned to face him, her eyes narrowed, her arms crossed. She had made her mother the wrong promise, she realized. It wasn't about deciding what she wanted to do. It was about proving that she could do something. Anything. She was going to leave Bali in three months knowing she had something to contribute to the world, and she wasn't going to let Jack get in her way. 'No,' she said. 'I'm going to help, whether you like it or not.'

'Clare—'

'Don't you want to do more than *take care of things*? Don't you want to turn this around? This shop could be special. We can make it special.'

Jack passed a hand over his face. 'It's not enough just to be special. It has to be profitable.'

Clare scoffed and Jack rolled his eyes.

'I'm not saying it has to bring in millions in profit, but it has to make enough money to cover its expenses.'

'Okay,' said Clare. 'It has to turn a profit and there's no guarantee you and I can make that happen, not in three months. But we could try, couldn't we?'

Jack laughed, then sighed. Clare knew she was being a bit overdramatic, but she kept going. She couldn't give up, and that meant she couldn't let Jack give up either.

'We could make this place special for its own sake. And then if it helps the bottom line that's great. And if it doesn't at least we'll know we did our best.'

'We did our best and failed,' said Jack. Clare frowned. He seemed so defeated. Why would it mean so much to him if they failed?

'We can't fail,' she said. 'If the shop's already dead and we don't bring it back to life that's no surprise. But if we do, it's a miracle. We would have performed a miracle.'

'You're just saying that because you think we'll succeed.'

'Well, Jeez, one of us has to,' Clare said. 'Come on. Let's just try. Let me help you – let me contribute.'

She held Jack's eyes. She just needed him to have one tiny speck of hope. They could do this. She was sure they could. 'Jack,' she said.

He bit his lip. 'I'm going to regret this,' he said.

'Is that a yes?'

'God help me.'

Clare beamed. 'Okay. It's decided. You and I are going to save this shop. We're going to do our best to save it, and if it still dies, at least it'll die pretty.'

Jack laughed reluctantly. 'Okay,' he said. 'Okay.'

Clare clapped her hands together. 'The first thing we're going to do is reorganize the rest of these shelves.'

'I don't—'

'I think we should close tomorrow and get it all done with no distractions.'

He looked bemused and still a little unsure but she didn't let up.

'We can't operate a bookshop without the books being in the right place on the shelves,' she said. 'I promise I won't buy anything else.' Jack shook his head but his eyes were softer. Warmer.

'Fine,' he said. 'Fine.'

Chapter Eight

They ended up closing the shop for two days. By the end of it, they had a clean and organized shop floor, a crate of books to return, a bargain bin out at the front, and two tables by the door stacked with new releases. Well, the newest releases they could find.

'Next, we need to tackle the mezzanine,' Clare said, as they sat outside the shop drinking a beer at the end of the second day. The lowering sun was warm on her face as she dug her toes into the sand. 'But I don't think we need to be closed for that since it's not being used as part of the shop.'

'Let me guess, you have a big plan for it,' said Jack, with a grimace.

'Well,' said Clare, straightening in her deckchair.

Jack muttered something under his breath.

'What was that?'

He shifted awkwardly. 'Nothing?' he said.

'What did you say?' He didn't reply. 'Come on,' she said. 'I won't get mad.'

Jack sighed. 'Fine. I said, "Terrifying".'

'Terrifying?'

'Yes.'

'Me?'

'Look,' said Jack, defensively, 'we don't know each other very well. I was just talking to myself. It's not important.'

Clare crossed her arms and raised an eyebrow.

'See? This is what I'm talking about,' Jack said. 'Sometimes, when you have a sudden idea, or when you think you have to defend yourself, it's like your whole demeanour changes. You get this evil gleam in your eyes and your centre of gravity shifts. It's like watching a demon take over your body.'

'And it's terrifying?'

'It's terrifying.'

'I'm terrifying.'

'Much more so than I was expecting when I met you.'

'Hmm,' said Clare.

'Look, I'm sorry. I shouldn't have said it. Obviously,' said Jack.

'I really don't think there's anything to be scared of,' Clare said. She wasn't sure whether she was offended or flattered. She'd never thought of herself as intimidating – she was short, a little plump, and she crocheted. How could someone like that be intimidating? It made her feel almost powerful. She kind of liked it.

'It's not just the transformation,' said Jack. 'It's that it feels like you might have some scheme up your sleeve that I won't be able to stop or control because you're so sure you're right.'

'But there's no need for you to stop or control me,' said Clare, 'because I am right.'

'You see? This is what I'm talking about!'

'Oh, come on, Jack. My ideas are good.'

'Are they?'

Clare didn't know how annoyed she was for a moment. Did he really think she was doing all this work on some ill-considered whim? Just throwing her weight around because she liked being in charge? 'Hold on. You said the window was good.'

He gave a nod in acknowledgement. 'The window is good.'

'And you said the signs were good.'

'The signs are good,' he said.

'And having the books shelved in a way that makes sense is good.'

'It is.'

'Which means that, so far, all my ideas have been good. What reason do you have to be afraid of the next one?' she demanded.

Jack's mouth had started pulling up at the corner in the way it did sometimes, in the way that was starting to make Clare furious every time she saw it.

'It's not a particularly robust data set,' he said.

'I swear to God—'

Jack put up his hands in a conciliatory way. 'Look, it's not that the plans aren't good. It's that you come up with them out of nowhere and you barge ahead without asking any-one, without checking what the costs will be, or knowing if there might be consequences.'

Clare didn't know what to say, which annoyed her even more. It was true that she hadn't spent a whole lot of time weighing up the possible pros and cons, but there hadn't seemed to be that many to weigh up. Everything had worked the way she'd thought it would.

'Just because you can't see what's going on inside my head,' she said, 'doesn't mean there's nothing there.'

'That's what scares me,' said Jack. Clare took a breath, but he raised a hand to stop her. 'Look, I'm sorry,' he said. 'Your ideas so far have been good, and you're right, I have no reason to think the next one won't be too. But I also don't know enough to be sure it *will* be. All I have to go on is a window and a sign. And your insistence.'

Clare wanted to say something, but the words didn't come. Was he expecting her to trust his judgement when he had no faith in hers?

'I'm just a cautious person,' he went on. 'I take time to make decisions, I like to be sure I have all the information before I commit, and I studied for years to understand how best to interpret that information. You don't seem to do that. You trust your instincts, I guess. I just don't know your instincts that well yet.'

Clare didn't reply. She didn't know how to. He'd taken the wind out of her sails. She didn't know if he was criticizing her for being too impulsive or praising her for having good instincts. Either way, he was definitely holding his superior education over her head.

Jack took a sip of his beer. 'Will you please tell me your plan for the mezzanine?'

Clare took a breath and cleared her throat. She tried to keep her posture relaxed, her voice gentle. 'I was thinking we should consider repurposing it as an event space. If we clear it out, we can put café tables up there, maybe, and we could host book signings and things. We could keep space around the sides for more bookshelves, and maybe a gift section, but then have this more relaxed seating space in the centre.'

'God,' said Jack. 'Somehow that was even more horrifying.'

Clare was so outraged she almost stood up and walked out. 'I can't—' she started, but Jack broke in.

'I was joking, I was joking,' he said. 'I think it's a good idea. We need to go through all those boxes anyway. There are probably more books up there, and maybe some shop records. But I don't know who we'd invite or if they'd come. We can't afford to bring people here, so we'd have to find authors who were already on the island or coming soon. We'd have to get in copies of their book to sell. So maybe this one is something we can work at in the background while we try to get the everyday business to pick up.'

For a while they sat in a silence that was almost companionable.

'Can I mention something obvious?' Clare said.

'I'd really rather you didn't,' said Jack.

'We need to order more books.'

Jack didn't say anything. He'd seemed fairly cheerful while they sorted the books, but now his shoulders were slumped, and he looked deflated.

He seemed so uptight all the time, but Clare was starting to wonder if that was circumstance more than personality. He was taking this all very personally. It was strange – she had been the one to convince him they should try to save the shop, but now he'd agreed, he was taking it even more seriously than she was. It seemed important to him, and Clare wondered why.

But then why was he so stubborn about letting her help?

Clare took stock of the shop. It felt brighter, less cramped. It was still small, but now it felt like it could fit a few people in without everyone tripping over each other.

'We should start a book club,' she said. 'Weekly, maybe on a Wednesday evening.'

Jack was looking at her, his eyes a bit brighter, his mouth curving up at the corner. 'What would we read? Something new?'

'We don't have anything new,' Clare said. 'What do we have a lot of copies of?'

'Check the returns box – there are a few things we had too many of. Maybe we can sell them instead.'

Clare went over to the box, which was sitting against the far wall, and began sorting through it. 'We've got a lot of Arnold Schwarzenegger's autobiography – maybe not the vibe – and, ooh, a few copies of *House of the Spirits*?'

'I've never read it,' said Jack.

'Oh, it's great. I read it when I was at school.'

'Well, if you think it's a good fit . . .'

Clare grinned and pulled all the copies she could find out of the box. She stacked them neatly by the till and grabbed some cardboard for a sign.

'I'll put a call out on Instagram, but maybe we should do some fliers too.' She bent over the desk, carefully writing, 'This month's book club'.

'And,' she said, as she added some flourishes, 'we should look at stocking things made by local artisans. Bookmarks and key rings, things like that. Postcards by Balinese artists. There are some amazing leatherwork stalls in the markets – and before you say anything, we could sell on behalf of the artists, rather than buying things off them to sell.'

'Okay, okay, you have a lot of ideas, I get it. Can we talk about it later?'

Clare smiled, satisfied. 'Absolutely,' she said.

*

They were barely open the next day when Celestina walked in, wearing a flowing burgundy robe, with gold make-up flecking her face in a way that, on anyone else, would have looked ridiculous outside of an Oscars after-party, but which on her looked perfectly normal for five past nine on a Friday morning.

'How does that eyeshadow look like it bloomed on you naturally?' said Clare.

'Because it did, darling one,' Celestina said, taking the compliment as if it was no more than her due. 'Well, well, my angels, look at what you've done with this old place. It almost looks alive again.'

'The signs are all Clare's work,' said Jack. 'I just moved things around.'

Clare looked at him suspiciously. Was he trying to make sure she got the credit? Or the blame? 'I know they're obviously handmade,' she said defensively. 'It would be better if we could get some professionally done, but for now I hope they'll do.'

'Everything has to be made by someone's hands,' said

Celestina, waving away Clare's comment elegantly. 'Why are your hands less worthy than those of others?'

'Oh, I'd say a basic lack of skill,' said Clare.

Jack frowned. 'I think they're very impressive,' he said. 'I couldn't do that.'

Clare turned to look at him, eyes wide. Why couldn't he have been paying her compliments like this the whole time? They'd have been getting on much better if he had. 'Well, I'm glad that my girlhood obsession with crafts has finally paid off,' she said.

'Clare has big plans for the mezzanine as well,' Jack said to Celestina. 'She wants to turn it into an event space, for signings and . . .'

Celestina appeared to have stopped listening to them. She was walking around the shop, taking in the environment, almost sniffing the air. After a moment she stopped and nodded to herself. 'Yes,' she said quietly, 'I think I will.'

'You will what?' said Clare.

'Oh, don't you worry,' said Celestina. 'I'll take care of everything.'

'You'll take care of what?' Jack said.

'Well, dears, it's been a while. The shop's been in such a state, as no doubt you noticed, and I've been telling Adam for years, but he just didn't seem to take it seriously. But now that you've both done such a marvellous job, making everything look much more as it should, I think it's time I made a reappearance. My fans must be simply longing to see me. I think it's been at least nine or ten years.'

'An appearance?' said Clare. 'Here?'

'You're right about the mezzanine,' she said. 'We used to have events up there all the time – mixers, book launches, things of that nature. But they sort of fell off. People started getting harder to book. Everyone wants their events to be in big cities, where you can draw a crowd, sell a lot of books. Eventually staff started leaving things on the mezzanine and it devolved, you understand, into a clutter that no one ever wanted to deal with. And now, well . . .' She wafted a hand sadly at the pile of boxes upstairs.

'So, if we clear it out you'll . . .' Clare trailed off, not really knowing what kind of appearance Celestina was planning.

'Yes, beloved, it is decided. I am going to do a reading.'

Clare and Jack glanced at each other. Jack looked as astonished as Clare felt.

'A reading?' he said. 'From what?'

'Hmm, yes, that is the question,' said Celestina. 'What would best suit my first appearance after a long hiatus? Perhaps something from *His Eyes Were As Daggers*. Or maybe *The Scarlet Abbess*. No, not them. I think, after all, it should be a return to my true heyday. I think *The River Over Them* is the one.'

Clare blinked a few times in rapid succession. 'Celestina,' she said, 'you didn't tell us you were an author.'

'Yes, darling. That is how Celestina came to be, in fact. It was my *nom de plume* for years before it became my real name. Adam and I met when I did a signing at a bookshop he managed in Brooklyn.'

'Can you show us your books? Are they in the shop?' said Clare, eagerly. 'I'm sure I would have noticed when we were reshelving everything—'

'Oh, no, dear, they're all long out of print, of course. But true fans don't come to these things to buy books. They come to see me.'

Clare suspected that Jack had different ideas about the purpose of events, but she found herself more and more delighted by Celestina with every passing second. She should be asking her to mentor her in everything from philosophy to how to dress.

'Please come here more often,' she said.

Celestina smiled graciously but didn't reply. Instead, she gently clapped her hands together and said, 'Well, loves, I must leave you,' and walked towards the door. She turned back just before she left and said, 'Oh, and we're taking you out tomorrow night, Adam and me. Somewhere nice, so dress pretty.'

And with that she was gone, leaving a cloud of delicate perfume in her wake. Clare immediately pulled out her phone.

'What are you doing?' asked Jack.

'I'm trying to find out if there are digital versions of Celestina's books, obviously.'

Chapter Nine

Celestina's demand that she 'dress pretty' would have sent Clare into a panic if she were at home. She would have spent hours in front of her wardrobe, trying on and discarding every possible iteration of every nice outfit she owned, worrying about which shade of lipstick looked best with which dress, wondering if maybe those shoes were a little too chunky for something with a long skirt.

But she had always been a light packer and that was the saving of her. She'd brought several options for work, naturally, and a few different pairs of swimming togs for days at the beach. She had good walking shoes for exploring caves and trekking to see waterfalls, and her most comfortable, well-worn tracksuit bottoms in case of illness or epic hangover.

She had all those things and exactly two nice going-out dresses. And one of those was decidedly on the short side, more suited to a sweaty night in a club than a nice dinner out. That left only one option: a dusky blue, bias-cut wrap dress that set off the dark red of her hair, and made her boobs look amazing.

She paired it with strappy silver sandals, which she mirrored with metallic eyeshadow and big silver hoop earrings. After a few days of hauling around books in a T-shirt and shorts, she felt spectacular.

She came out of her room just as Jack was coming out of his, and she stopped still. 'Woah,' she whispered to herself.

He was wearing a rust-coloured shirt that hugged his shoulders, with the cuffs rolled up showing off those forearms. His hair was tousled and soft-looking, rather than neatly slicked down like it usually was. For a moment she noticed his gaze flickering over her too, and she smirked a little in satisfaction.

'What?' he said, when he caught Clare looking at him. 'Celestina said to dress pretty.'

'That she did,' said Clare.

Jack waved her through the front door ahead of him and she muttered to herself, 'God bless Celestina.'

*

'God damn Celestina,' Clare said half an hour later, as she dangled precariously over a ravine in the middle of a jungle, grasping the sides of a rope bridge as she tried to extricate her heel from a knothole in one of the planks of wood while Jack watched, pale, but bemused.

'Do you need a hand?' he said, just as Clare wrenched her shoe free, panting.

She glared at him as she bent over her foot trying to unbuckle it one-handed while grasping the rope for dear life, the bridge swinging from side to side underneath her. 'She said to dress pretty,' she said mulishly.

The rope bridge was the final step in the saga to get to the 'nice' place Adam and Celestina had picked for dinner.

It had started when their taxi had pulled up in what looked like the middle of nowhere. To the right were tiered rice fields, gentle and golden in the early-evening light. To the left was a forest. For a moment Clare thought maybe the car had broken down, but the driver was staring at them, clearly expecting payment. 'Sorry,' she said, 'is this the right place?'

'Raja's, yes,' said the driver, waving his hand to the left.

'O-*kay*,' Clare said, glancing at Jack, who also looked confused, but was pulling his wallet out of his pocket. Clare grabbed some cash for her share of the fare and the two got out of the car. Once outside, Clare looked around for a couple of minutes before she saw it – low to the ground, a small wooden sign reading 'Raja's' with an arrow pointing down a small path through the trees.

'Well,' said Jack, who had noticed it too, 'this is interesting.'

'This is exciting,' said Clare.

'There's barely a path.'

'That's what makes it exciting.'

She looked up at Jack and was surprised to see he seemed hesitant. 'Maybe we shouldn't have sent the cab away,' he said.

'Come on,' said Clare. 'Are you seriously saying you don't want to go?'

'Am I saying I don't want to walk blindly into the jungle with nothing but a handmade wooden sign to guide the way?'

'What's the point in leaving the house if you're not willing to have an adventure?' Clare laughed.

'Apart from personal safety?' He was joking but Clare could tell he was genuinely nervous. 'Are you always so gung-ho?' he asked.

'Learned it from my dad,' Clare said. 'Kind of. Don't live your life never doing the thing.'

'What thing?'

They definitely didn't have time for *that* conversation. Clare shrugged. 'Any of them. Now, come on, kid,' she said, stepping towards the path. 'We'll be fine.'

'We're putting a lot of trust in Adam and Celestina,' said Jack. 'But okay.'

The path was nothing more than well-packed earth for the first few minutes, but eventually gave way to large slabs of stone. It really did start to feel like an adventure. Celestina and Adam had clearly picked somewhere exciting for dinner, and Clare felt energized and thrilled by it.

The stone path curved through the trees and, for a moment, Clare thought they were coming to a clearing, that the restaurant was about to materialize in front of them.

She was wrong.

What did materialize was a stone staircase, climbing up through the trees. Initially Clare was even more excited. *They must be going somewhere really special*, she thought, *to be worth this kind of journey*. But after several long minutes of climbing the uneven stone stairs, her energy and enthusiasm started to flag.

'There had better be some incredible food at the end of this,' she panted. 'Like I'm talking one of those burgers with real gold on them.'

'I can't imagine that makes them taste better,' said Jack.

'That's not the point,' said Clare. 'I just want my efforts here to be rewarded in some grand and ostentatious way.'

'By food that includes indigestible metals?'

'Or some equivalent.'

'A trophy, perhaps?' said Jack.

'Anyone can get a trophy,' said Clare.

'Depends on the trophy.'

It was at this moment that the rope bridge appeared.

'Oh, no,' Jack said quietly.

'Are you okay?' Clare asked.

'Yeah,' he said. 'I'm fine. I'll be fine.'

'Are you . . .'

'I don't love heights,' he said, 'but it's fine.'

'Well, I can go first,' said Clare. 'That way if we fall, I'll be the first to die.'

'Did you think that would be funny?' said Jack, staring at her with wild eyes. 'Did you think it would be helpful?'

'Okay, okay, I'm sorry,' said Clare. 'There's just always something about finding out that a stoic, serious person has a phobia. It's unexpected, makes them interesting.'

'You don't think I'm interesting?'

Clare kept her face deadly still. 'Of course I think you're interesting. You're a fascinating person.'

'Shut up,' said Jack. He closed his eyes and shook himself out. 'Okay,' he said. 'Let's go, but can we go quickly, please?'

'Of course,' said Clare, stepping onto the first plank of wood and grabbing the rope railing.

They were just past the halfway point when her foot got stuck.

'It's okay,' she said, 'you go on, get off the bridge.'

'Oh, that's fine,' said Jack. 'I'll wait with you.' Was it just Clare or did he look nervous? Would he really rather stay on the bridge with her than get off it as fast as possible?

He gripped the sides with white knuckles while she fought to free herself, trying as hard as she could not to shake the bridge. Once she was free, she took off her silly, strappy heels and continued in bare feet.

'Want to lay a bet on me getting a splinter?' she asked, as they finally continued on their way.

'Don't even joke,' said Jack.

But the wood was soft, worn smooth by countless feet before Clare's, and they made it to the other side without any more incidents.

Jack heaved a sigh of relief when they stepped onto solid ground.

'You really didn't have to wait for me,' said Clare. 'You could have got off the bridge way sooner.'

'The lesser of two evils,' said Jack. 'It's always worse when I'm by myself. It's like losing your grip on reality, if that makes sense. The world spins away from you. Having another person nearby is, I don't know . . . grounding.'

'Huh,' said Clare. She knew phobias didn't discriminate, but the idea of someone so quiet and serious being scared of heights had never occurred to her, and something about it charmed her. Jack looked younger in his mortification. He clearly hadn't planned to reveal that side of himself.

'That makes sense I guess,' Clare said casually, trying to let him know subtly that she didn't think it was a big deal. She started putting her shoes back on – there was nowhere to sit, so it involved doing a small, shuffling dance on one foot while she fiddled with the tiny buckle.

'Wait,' said Jack. 'Let me help.'

Clare's mind went blank. 'Oh,' she said. 'Okay.'

Jack knelt in front of her as she slid her foot into the first shoe. As his fingers moved over her ankle, she lost her balance and put a hand onto his shoulder to steady herself. He finished with the buckle and moved to pick up the other shoe. Clare gulped as he held her foot and slid the shoe into place.

Was it just her, or did he linger a little over the second buckle? He set her foot on the ground and stood, facing her, colouring slightly. Nope. Not just her.

'Thank you,' she said. They were standing very close. The energy that seemed to exist around them seemed to pull them together, like a lasso slowly tightening. Something about it scared Clare a little. She'd be lying if she said she hadn't come to Bali hoping for a little fun and flirtation, looking forward to a casual fling in paradise. But this didn't feel fun or casual. This was static charge before a thunderstorm.

Clare looked up at Jack, leaning forward a little. She felt his fingers close around hers, his thumb brushing over her knuckle.

'Jack,' she said, 'I think—'

A voice from behind cut her off. 'Ah,' it said. 'You managed to find it.'

Clare turned to see Adam and Celestina stepping off the rope bridge looking for all the world as if they'd arrived by gliding through the air rather than hiking up three hundred stone steps. 'Did we?' she said. 'I wasn't sure we had.'

They moved towards Clare and Jack, looking like Oberon and Titania – if Oberon were shorter and twinklier than he's usually portrayed and wearing more linen. Adam was the epitome of rumpled class, in a moss green linen suit, with a loosely knotted cotton cravat. Celestina was spectacular, as usual, in a stormy grey silk dress that matched the silver of her hair, which was piled on top of her head.

'My, my,' she said, looking from Clare to Jack, 'don't we all look marvellous? Shall we go in?'

And she stepped behind a tree and disappeared.

*

Clare stared after Celestina for a moment wondering if the rope bridge had deposited her at the top of the Faraway Tree. She looked back at Adam, who smiled and twinkled, and said, 'After you.'

Clare took a step forward and, instead of more trees, she saw a small path leading to a door in a wall. Celestina was standing in the middle of a pool of light, looking back at Clare, who walked up to meet her and followed her through the door.

She found herself in a narrow corridor, with simple, brown-papered walls. She could hear voices coming from the other end as she walked down the hallway, Jack and Adam following her. Eventually the corridor gave way to a wide, wooden balcony. Clare stepped out onto it and gasped.

'Yes, it's good, isn't it?' said Adam, from behind her.

Across from the doorway they'd just walked through, the balcony gave way to a large waterfall, cascading over a series of rocks and surrounded by greenery. There were tables and chairs around, but just a few – for a balcony it was large, but for a restaurant it was fairly small. The furniture was simple, solid and well worn. There was little decoration except for a few woollen banners hanging from the ceiling to help dampen the noise.

A tall, broad man came towards them, arms open. 'Lissie,' he said, 'it's been too long, far, far too long.'

'Don't be absurd, Vik,' she said, leaning to kiss his cheek. 'I was here last month, surely.'

'No, no, it's been at least a year, longer even.'

'Now you mustn't say things like that,' said Celestina. 'You'll make me feel like I'm ageing.'

The man, Vik, laughed. 'Never,' he said, 'never. Come, your table is ready.'

He led them to a table so close to the edge that Clare worried they'd be splashed. She glanced at Jack, wondering if this would set off his fear of heights again.

'It's okay,' he said, when she caught his eye. 'As long as the ground under my feet is solid, I'm all right.'

Clare nodded, although as far as she was concerned the ground under her feet was far less solid than it should have been.

'Now, Lissie,' Vik was saying, 'have you told your friends the rules?'

'I will, Vik. I will.'

'Rules?' said Jack.

'This place is a well-kept secret,' said Adam. 'Vik works hard to keep it from being overrun by tourists. That means no photos, no social media, no revealing the entrance.'

'No Instagram?' said Clare, before she could stop herself.

Jack rolled his eyes and Clare glared at him. 'I mean this is such an extraordinary place it seems a shame not to share it,' she said.

'Not all extraordinary things are meant to be widely shared,' said Celestina. 'This place has a magic to it that would be stretched thin if too many people knew it was here.'

'It's only locals who know about it,' said Adam.

'Does that make us locals?' asked Jack.

'It was Lissie's idea to bring you here,' Adam said, smiling. 'So I suppose, to her, you are.'

'I told him about the marvellous work you've been doing in the shop,' said Celestina. 'When you came to us for dinner, I thought you'd be a good pair and you're proving me right. I love being right. It seemed only fair to let you in on one of our favourite parts of Bali.'

'I hope we haven't changed too much,' said Clare. 'I know it's your shop, Adam. I don't want to go too far with it.'

'Oh, it's no matter,' said Adam, waving a hand in the air. 'But don't work yourselves too hard – you're supposed to be experiencing this beautiful place, not slaving away all day every day.'

Clare glanced at Jack. 'But we want to do the best we can for you,' she said. 'We're so grateful to be here, the least we can do is make an effort in the shop.'

'I wouldn't worry too much about it,' he said.

Jack furrowed his brow and said, 'You know, I think I can help turn things around—'

But Adam interrupted: 'There isn't a set menu here but they do a fresh catch every day, so I recommend some kind of seafood.'

'But—' said Jack, and it was Celestina who cut him off this time.

'Darlings, this isn't a work dinner, this is your leisure time. Now, I want to hear more about your previous travels, Clare. What a joy to get to see so much of the world when you're so young.'

The rest of the dinner passed pleasantly – Adam and Celestina had a lot of outrageous stories and a gift for pulling people out of themselves. But Clare couldn't quite enjoy herself completely. It seemed like Adam had just given up on the shop. He didn't appear to care what happened there at all. But if that was the case then why bring them here at all? Why keep the shop open?

Chapter Ten

Jack was quiet in the taxi back from the restaurant. Which wasn't unusual, but some instinct pushed Clare to ask him if he wanted to stop somewhere for a drink before they went home.

'Oh,' he said. 'Sure, if you like.'

They walked to one of the beachside bars and took a table outside, at a distance from the music. The moon shone down on the ocean, and the sound of the waves rushing into the shore was soothing.

Clare watched the crowds for a while, waiting for Jack to feel like talking. A group of guys was daring each other to do cartwheels in the sand, cheering each other on. One seemed to be giving the others tips, but she hadn't seen him try it himself yet, so she was sceptical of his authority. She turned to point them out to Jack, but he was grimacing at his beer bottle, picking at the sticker with his thumb. 'You okay?' she asked.

'Oh,' he said, 'yeah. Just a bit tired. It's been a week.'

'Lemon, it's Tuesday,' she quipped.

'What? It's Fri— Oh, right. I get it. *The Office*?'

'God, you are tired,' said Clare. 'It was *30 Rock*.'

'Right,' he said. 'Right.'

Clare said nothing for a while. She was starting to worry about this uptight dickhead who always wanted to pour cold water on her parade.

'Maybe this is a waste of time,' said Jack, under his breath. Clare didn't know if he was talking to her or to himself. 'Maybe I shouldn't have come here. I should have . . .' He trailed off.

'Why did you come?' Clare said, after a minute or two. 'You said you used to come to Bali a lot. Did you already know the shop?'

Jack didn't answer immediately. He turned his beer bottle around in his hands a couple of times. 'My grandmother was from here,' he said, after a while, 'so my dad used to bring us out a couple of times a year to visit her.'

'This is where you learned to surf?' Clare asked.

Jack nodded. 'We did mostly the outdoorsy stuff. My dad and my brother are both big on that kind of thing – hiking, cave-diving, paragliding. I didn't join in on the paragliding,' he said, with a rueful smile. 'It's not like we came to Seashore Books a lot. Just once or twice one of us had a reading list for school, or something, and we'd come in to get the books. I guess it was Adam mostly running it back then, and he was always interested and helpful. I didn't think much about it. It was just like any other shop, but it was nice.'

'Does Adam know?' Clare asked.

'Yeah, I mentioned it in my interview. It didn't seem to make much of an impression, and then I thought, you know, loads of people must come to the shop, so I guess it's not that big a deal.'

He'd peeled the entire label off the bottle. He looked down at it and dropped it into an ashtray.

'Anyway,' he said, 'my *nini* – my grandmother – died when I was sixteen and we stopped coming. I missed it. So when I saw the job listing, and saw where it was, I thought, *Why not?* Find out what it's like to live here properly for a bit. I guess I thought it would all be the same.'

Clare felt a wave of compassion for him. She wanted to reach out and put a hand on his arm, to comfort him, draw him close, but something held her back.

Jack rubbed the back of his head. 'Or maybe I didn't. Obviously, things change – things have to change. It's just . . .' He trailed off for a moment, staring out into the blackness of the ocean. 'When I was a kid it seemed like there were a lot of people who really cared about this shop. I thought there still would be. I thought Adam would be one of them.' His face hardened. 'Well, it'll still be good experience for when I get back.'

'Right,' said Clare. 'You said. I still don't understand what for, though.' She was so confused by him. She knew he'd agreed to try to turn the shop around, but he'd made it seem like he was doing it as a favour to her. But he took it so personally when it seemed that they might fail.

'I wanted to get a fuller picture of things,' he said, 'I have a job starting in April with a consultancy that specializes in mergers, acquisitions, receivership, that kind of thing. I've already interned with them twice, and I've interned with a conglomerate that franchises small businesses. I know that side of things, the big business part of acquisitions, but I don't know much about what happens on the other side, what happens to make a small mom-and-pop store join a franchise or sell out to a corporation.'

Clare's mouth had dropped open while he was talking. She wanted to interrupt but the words wouldn't come. She'd been thinking of Jack as 'business boy' but she hadn't really thought about him in the context of an actual business. A corporation. Especially not one that specialized in taking over small businesses. Businesses exactly like the one they were trying to save.

'I always thought,' Jack continued, 'that it must be out of desperation, that people must have fought tooth and nail to keep their business, that they'd started them because they loved them. But I guess sometimes they just don't care. They're doing it out of habit. Maybe it's a relief to be bought out.'

He fell silent.

'What are you saying?' Clare said.

He sighed. 'I don't know. I thought we could do something to turn the shop around *for* Adam, you know? But . . . do you think sometimes a little business like this becomes a millstone around your neck? Something that weighs you down but you feel like you can't cut it free? Because, I don't know, it would look like failure or something?'

Clare stood up. She didn't want to hear this. They had decided to save the shop. Jack had agreed to save the shop. Now he was talking like he wanted to let it close, like everyone would be better off. Everyone except Clare. If they let the shop close, she'd have to go home knowing she'd failed again. She had to follow through. She was vaguely aware that this was an unreasonable goal to pin her self-worth on, but she was also certain that it was too late. 'Jack,' she said, 'are you giving up? Are you telling me you want to give up?'

Jack looked at her. It took him a moment to focus on her face. 'What?' he said. 'I—'

'You can't give up. We can't give up. Just because Adam doesn't seem to mind what we do, that's no reason to sit back and let it all fall apart.'

'I didn't say that,' said Jack. 'I didn't say I wanted to give up.'

Clare was breathing hard. She knew she was in the middle of overreacting, but she didn't know how to wind herself back down. 'Good,' she said, and walked away.

*

Clare took off her shoes and went down to the shoreline. She stood at the very edge, letting the waves rush in to meet her toes before receding again. She wanted to swim right out into the night, to be lost in the darkness of the ocean until she felt calmer.

She was already starting to feel embarrassed. She hadn't even let Jack finish explaining. And he was right about Adam – he definitely didn't seem to care too much about the shop or what happened to it. Why had she flown off the handle like that? Just when they were starting to get to know each other. Just when it was beginning to feel like they could be friends. Just when she was starting to wonder if maybe there was more here than mere friendship. That moment by the swing bridge might have been a precipice in more ways than one – who knows what would have happened if Celestina and Adam hadn't interrupted? But now she'd ruined it by throwing a tantrum, like a child.

You're not a serious person.

And she had to go home soon to the tiny flat they shared. She had to go crawling back, would have to admit she'd been an idiot.

A wave came in that didn't quite meet her feet and Clare stepped forward to catch it.

'Ah, you don't want to do that,' said a voice. 'Dress is too nice for a midnight dip.'

Clare turned and saw a tall, very well-built, golden-skinned man wearing nothing but board shorts. She recognized him as one of the cartwheelers and now that he was up close she was taken aback, by him, the muscles, the hair, the Australian accent, like some kind of Hemsworth. 'It's not midnight,' she said, rather limply.

'Yeah, but "ten past eleven dip" doesn't sound as good,' he said. 'What are you doing down here alone? You have a fight with your boyfriend?' He nodded back towards the bar where she'd been sitting with Jack.

Clare's lip curled. 'He's not my boyfriend,' she said.

The Hemsworth nodded sagely. 'Cheater?' he asked.

Clare shook her head. 'No, no, we're not together. We've never been together. I just work with him. I just have to work with him. At a bookshop.'

'Right,' said the man, but he sounded confused. Which was fair, Clare decided. It was hard to imagine what kind of workplace drama could lead to someone storming off like she had.

'Well, you look like you could use some company,' he said, 'and maybe a drink.'

'Aren't you with your friends?' Clare asked.

'Nah, they've all packed it in. Want to get up early tomorrow for a surf.'

'And you're not going with them?'

'Nah, I still will.' He grinned. 'I'll sleep when I'm dead. I'm Toby, by the way. Tobes.'

'Clare,' said Clare.

*

Tobes, it turned out, came to Bali every year with the boys for a full month. It was a tradition that had started when they were all eighteen, celebrating the end of high school. The group had drifted and changed with time – not all the original boys still came, some were new recruits – but the tradition itself held.

'It's like a paradise,' he said, 'and it's so easy to get to. Well, easy to get to from Perth.'

'But isn't Australia already a paradise?' Clare asked.

'Yeah,' he acknowledged. 'But this is different. Nice to have a change. You go surfing in Perth, and it's great and everything, but you know that over among all the buildings and stuff is your work. You come here and everything around you is nothing to do with you. You surf, you drink, you eat, and you don't think about anything but surfing, and eating and drinking.'

He was a very restful person, and Clare found herself relaxing into his company as if it was a hot bath. He listened to her talk about the shop, about her mum, about her terrible jobs at home, but he didn't put forth any opinions, and he was just as attentive when she talked him through her ranking system for *The Great British Bake Off*.

This wasn't a precipice. This wasn't a thunderstorm. This was a tonic. She felt her brain wrinkles smoothing out under the influence of Toby's consequence-free chatter. Or maybe it was the cocktails.

Either way, she felt the way you should feel on a trip to Bali – at peace with the world, forgetful of its troubles. How could there be troubles when the beach in the moonlight was this peaceful, when the man at her side was this beautiful?

They chatted their way through a couple of drinks, and then he walked her home. She pointed out the bookshop as they passed it.

'Ah, so this is your window,' he said.

'It is. Do you like it?'

'Yeah, nah, it looks great to me,' he said. 'I like what you did with the cloth there.'

'It's better when the lights are on.'

'I don't know, I think it's pretty good already.'

'Well, thank you,' Clare said. 'I like it.'

They stood together in silence for a moment.

'I think you look pretty good too,' he said. Suddenly Clare came over all giggly, and embarrassed.

'Well,' she said, 'I am all dolled up.'

Toby shook his head slightly, putting out a hand and tugging on her fingertips. 'The dress is good,' he said. 'The dress is *very* good. But it's been given a solid head start.'

This, Clare thought. *This is the fling in paradise you want.*

'I can't ask you in,' she said. 'The flat's the size of a cupboard and two of us live there.'

Toby let his head fall back, his hand coming to his heart

in mock woe. 'A devastating turn of events,' he said. 'We'll have to plan better next time.' He lowered his eyes to hers and said, 'If you would like?'

'Um, yeah?' she said, peering up at him with a smile. 'Yes. I would like.'

'Good,' said Toby.

He bent his head and tucked a finger under her chin. Clare rose up on her toes to meet him, her hands on his broad, solid chest, and as his lips met hers, she thought, *Yes. This is what I need. A gentle, undemanding kiss from a gentle, undemanding man.*

*

Jack's door was closed when Clare got in, and she was relieved. She knew she needed to apologize but she wasn't ready to face the embarrassment. She went to sleep telling herself it would be easier in the morning.

It wasn't. She came out of the shower to find Jack dressed and eating breakfast.

'Jack,' she said, 'hi.'

He nodded a greeting. She stepped forward. 'Look,' she said. 'I'm sorry about last night. I was tired, I guess. Got worked up about nothing. I just . . . I really want to make this work. The shop. You know?'

Jack gazed at her. She was very aware that she was wearing nothing but a towel.

'It's okay,' he said.

He took another bite of his toast, looked back down at his phone. Clare stood there awkwardly for a bit. She felt like she owed him more of an explanation for storming off so late at night, but he didn't seem to expect one. She wondered if he'd worried about her. He certainly didn't seem concerned now. Well, she was an adult, after all, responsible for herself. He was just her colleague and flatmate. Where she went wasn't his business.

And she didn't want it to be his business, did she?

Clare left him to his toast and went into her bedroom to get dressed before heading to the shop.

There were still some shelves in need of signs, so she had brought in the rest of her felt and sat working on them. She posted a shot of her progress to Instagram, encouraging people to come in and see the shop's new look.

A customer came and browsed for a while, and Clare left Jack to deal with her since his lap wasn't covered with needles and thread.

He said a quiet hello to her, and then left her to browse. She went straight to the cosy mysteries shelf and started shuffling through them. After a few minutes she went to the till and asked if they had any other Dorothy L. Sayers in stock.

'We don't, I'm afraid,' said Jack, 'but if you want to order something in, we can take care of it.'

'No, that's okay,' said the customer. 'I'll be gone by the time it comes. It's just that I've already read the ones you've got.'

Jack nodded. 'Sorry,' he said, and let the customer wander back over to the shelves. Clare rolled her eyes and carefully laid aside the sign she was working on so she could stand up and walk over to the customer. 'Have you read Ngaio Marsh?' she said. 'You might like her as well.'

'No, I've never heard of her. Is she good?' the customer said.

'I think you should give her a try. Also, whodunits have been making a comeback – if you want a more recent one, Richard Osman's really popular.' She pulled out a copy of *The Thursday Murder Club*.

'Oh!' said the customer. 'Yes, I've heard of this, I think. And it's good?'

'I haven't read it yet myself, but everyone I know who has raves about it.'

Clare sent the woman back to the till with three books and went back to her sign-making station. Just as she went to sit down the door opened again and another customer walked in – one Clare recognized.

'Hi!' she said. 'Did you have another order to pick up for Bethany?'

'Hello. Yes,' he said. 'That is, no, I haven't ordered anything, but I did want to buy another book for her. I don't have a particularly comprehensive selection, you see.'

'Right, of course. You want a range to suit every mood.'

He chuckled. 'Yes, something like that.'

Clare showed him to the newly reorganized kids' section. 'I was looking through these the other day,' she said, 'and this one was my favourite.' She pulled out an Oliver Jeffers book. 'But we also have a lot of the classics that I loved when I was a kid, things like *Peepo!* and *Where the Wild Things Are* and *Hairy Maclary from Donaldson's Dairy*.'

'Oh, wonderful,' the man said. 'They all look marvellous.'

'Perfect,' said Clare, beaming as she led him to the till and handed the books to Jack to ring up.

The customer noticed the stack of Isabel Allende paperbacks and picked one up. 'You're starting the book club again?' he said. 'That's splendid.'

Clare jumped at the chance. 'We are,' she said. 'Would you like to come? It's a fantastic book.'

'I'm not sure,' he said. 'It's not always possible for me to get time away.'

Clare was already riddled with curiosity about the distinguished older man and his growing picture-book collection, but she didn't feel she could ask. Perhaps if she could just get him to the book club, she could find out more about him. And he could tell her what the shop used to be like.

'Oh, it's very casual,' she said. 'Did you used to come? I'd love to know what the old book club was like.'

'On occasion,' the man said. 'It was always a little unpredictable, not to a set schedule you know, but somehow they always drew a crowd. Perhaps because there was always marvellous food.'

Clare laughed. 'I don't know if we'll manage a good spread this time,' she said. 'It'll be something to work on, though.'

'Ah, well, it was more than just that, of course. I never came regularly but it was always so welcoming. A real community, this shop was. Or it seemed like it to me.'

Clare smiled. That was it. That was what she wanted to bring back. 'If you can't make it on the day there's no harm done,' she said. 'But why don't you take the book and that way if you do end up being free you'll be able to slot right in? I'm Clare, by the way, and this is Jack.'

'Do you know, I think I will. It's been an overwhelming time . . . Perhaps I could do with a night out just for myself.'

'I'd recommend it,' Clare said, with the air of someone who knew exactly what kind of overwhelming time he'd been having.

'Yes. Thank you, Clare,' he said. 'Oh, and I'm Joyo.'

As Joyo left the shop, Clare turned to find Jack looking at her. 'You're pretty good at that,' he said.

Clare frowned. 'What?' she said. 'Talking about books?'

'Yeah. But it's more than that. You know what people will like.'

Clare thought about it. She'd never really considered talking about books, recommending them, to be a skill. 'I think it comes from my parents,' she said. 'They were always talking about books when I was growing up. They were always around. They actually named me after my mum's favourite Maeve Binchy, and even after they split up, they always talked to each other about what they were reading. And then I went to uni to study comparative literature. Talking about books is just normal. For me.'

Jack was looking at her, a curious smile playing across his lips, pulling them up in one corner.

Clare found herself grinning in response. 'Sometimes,' she said, 'I like to give people a book, but my own copy, instead of a new one. I like to give them a copy I've read, and sometimes I'll write notes for them in the margins about bits that make me think of them, or that they'll find funny or whatever.'

'Don't you ever worry about people just reading the notes and not the book?'

Clare stared at him. 'Who would do that?' she said.

'Are you so sure you wouldn't? Flick through ahead to see what they'd written?'

'Huh,' said Clare. 'I hope not. I don't know, no one's ever annotated anything for me.'

Jack smiled. 'Yeah, I've never heard of anyone doing that before.'

Clare shrugged. 'I like to share books. Not just give them to someone but share the experience of reading them.'

'Did you never want to go into publishing?' he said. 'You could look into it when you get back.'

Clare frowned a little. 'Maybe,' she said. 'But I don't know that I'd be good at it. Giving notes, helping shape things. And it must be emotional. You must have to hurt people's feelings sometimes. I like the finished product. I'm not sure I'm the person to help make it.'

'That makes sense,' said Jack. 'But you could be a book publicist. You'd be great at it. No one walks away from you without buying a book.'

Clare frowned. 'It's possible. Or maybe I should just work in a bookshop back home. I think I'm pretty good at that.'

Jack grinned at her. 'You're definitely very good at that,' he said.

*

The rest of the morning passed pretty quietly, and Clare was just about to offer to go and pick up lunch when the door opened and her broad-shouldered midnight kiss came in.

'Hi, mate,' he said to Jack. 'Clare around?'

Jack looked from Toby to Clare as she stood up from her perch on the stairs. 'Hi,' she said. 'I didn't know you were coming in.'

'Thought I'd get a look at the place in daylight,' he said.

Clare appreciated the logic of this now that she was getting to see *him* in daylight. He was even more impressive, the sun glinting off his hair and biceps. He was wearing a T-shirt and shorts but his hair was wet and tangled – he'd clearly just come in from surfing.

'A friend of yours?' Jack asked Clare.

Toby held out a hand. 'Tobes,' he said genially. 'You must be Jack. I might take Clare off for lunch if you can spare her for an hour.'

'Of course,' said Jack. His mouth was curving up at the side and there was a hard, glittery look in his eyes. 'Take your time.'

'Thanks,' said Clare. 'I can bring you something back.'

'Don't worry about it,' said Jack. He'd already returned to the work spread out before him.

'I don't suppose you and the boys want to join a book club,' Clare said, as she and Toby headed outside.

'Not really our thing,' he said. 'But I'll tell them to come here if they ever want a day off surfing.' He let out a barking laugh at his own comment, and Clare decided not to hold out hope.

Lunch was just as relaxing as drinks had been the night before and Clare was relieved that it hadn't just been the alcohol. It would be nice to have a friend here – for a while at least. Someone to talk to who didn't think she was terrifying.

He told her about his friends, and how their tradition had developed over time. 'The first few trips we just hung around Kuta,' he said. 'Surfing in the morning, partying all night. We were young, you know,' he said, with a chuckle, 'idiots. Wasn't till our fourth trip that we realized how much more there was to do here.' He glanced down at her, a twinkle in his eyes. 'You been to any of the hidden waterfalls yet?' he said.

'There are hidden waterfalls?' She'd been taking it easy on the exploration, knowing she had three months to get to know the island. Now she felt like she'd already wasted time.

'I'll take you,' said Toby. 'Don't worry, I know all the best ones.'

It felt like it was all falling into place. She could save the bookshop with Jack, explore paradise with Toby, and go home a completely new woman.

*

Jack proved exactly why she needed Toby the moment she walked back into the shop after lunch. 'Oh,' he said, looking mildly surprised. 'You're back.'

'Of course I am. I took an hour for lunch. Now it's your turn.'

'It's okay,' he said. 'I thought you'd take the rest of the afternoon. With your friend.' He put a weird stress on *friend*. 'When did you meet that guy anyway?'

Clare bit her lip, not meeting Jack's eyes. 'Last night,' she said. She felt a bit guilty. She and Jack had had that moment outside the restaurant and then she'd stormed off on him and run straight into the arms of another man.

Don't be ridiculous, she said to herself. *You don't owe him anything.*

'Well,' said Jack, 'he should make your time here more enjoyable.' There was a snide twist to his face.

'Are you doing this on purpose?' Clare said, crossing her

arms. 'Acting like I'm a flaky chit who's going to run off and leave all the work to you? Are you just trying to get under my skin?'

'No!' said Jack. 'But you heard Adam last night. He doesn't care about the shop. He wants you to experience Bali.'

'He wants both of us to experience Bali,' said Clare, 'not for me to swan about the island while you huddle inside with your maths.'

'I'm not huddling,' said Jack. 'I went out the other day.'

'You went out one day. You don't take lunch breaks even.' She took a breath trying to steady herself. She wasn't going to work herself up over this, not again. 'You need to have time away and it seems like you're not going to unless I actually push you out of the door.'

'Don't be ridiculous.'

Clare sighed. 'Well, at least you're not giving up,' she said.

Jack looked at her, startled. 'No,' he said. 'I'm not.'

'Good,' Clare said. 'I'm not either. I'm here to do this job well. I want to make this shop better, but don't make me feel bad because I'm not *only* here for that.'

Jack was silent.

'Look,' said Clare, 'this shop needs our help, but it doesn't need both of us to be here around the clock. I think we need to agree that both of us – *both* of us – take a day or two off from time to time. You said yourself you wanted to experience what it was like to properly live here. You can't do that by working twenty-four seven. Three months will go by quickly, and if you're not careful you might as well have spent the time working at a shop in wherever it is you live.'

'Chicago.'

'Right. You might as well have been working at a shop in Chicago.'

Jack was silent.

'Come on, Jack,' Clare said. 'I know you've spent a lot of time here, but you can't have learned everything about the island. There must be things you've always wanted to try, but never have.'

Jack passed a hand through his hair. 'Sure,' he said, 'of course, but nothing important.'

'That's my point. Do something that's not important. Something you're bad at. Try something new, have an adventure.'

She waited for a bit, peering up at him. He was biting his lip, unsure. 'Come on, Jack,' she said again. 'Do we have a deal?'

Jack sighed. 'Fine,' he said. 'Yes.'

Chapter Eleven

Clare had hoped that her relationship with Jack would stay comfortable. Maybe with fewer breathless moments on clifftops, fewer gazes held a little too long. It had taken them a while to understand each other, but it had finally seemed like they were becoming friends. And she wanted to be friends.

But now things were as awkward and tense as they had been at the beginning. Jack was brusque with her, and she snapped at him, and under it all it felt as if there was something neither of them was saying. And Clare didn't know what it was.

The two of them settled into a rhythm you couldn't quite call comfortable but that at least didn't include all-out fights. Clare put in occasional requests for money to spend on small improvements and Jack turned her down. They picked through the boxes on the mezzanine, sorting books to sell from books to return, sifting through piles of junk, occasionally finding things to repurpose, more often finding things to throw away.

Clare was spending most of her days off with Toby, who was of a more adventurous spirit than she was. He took her diving, and she marvelled at the beauty of the tropical fish. She came home exhilarated and blissful and in love with the entire island, to find Jack sitting on the couch with his laptop. He said, 'Hi,' shortly, without taking his eyes off the screen, and she felt deflated.

She and Toby went hiking through a lush jungle that led to an exquisite waterfall. Toby pointed out a bungee-jumping platform and, in what felt like an out-of-body moment, Clare nodded. She threw herself into the air and came home feeling like a goddess. And when she entered the flat Jack was already in bed, and there was a note on the bench saying, 'We're out of coffee.' Clare went to bed grumpy.

But two could play at this game: Clare refused to show any interest in what Jack was doing with *his* days off either. Even if she did wonder about it more often than she liked to admit.

The shop was starting to draw more customers and Clare was enjoying herself there. Jack had been right, she was good at finding people books they'd like. When she wasn't sorting through boxes, she was flicking through books she didn't know – carefully, trying not to bend the spine – so she would have a wider range of knowledge about them. She had always loved reading and talking about books, but she'd never had to look outside her own tastes before. She enjoyed the challenge of searching for what someone else would like instead of just what she personally believed everyone should read. She even found herself having to make an effort not to barge in on Jack when he was the one dealing with a customer. He tended to merely point them in the direction of the sections they'd asked for and offer to order books the shop didn't have in stock.

He didn't even seem to read – at least, Clare had never caught him at it. She figured that this job had simply come along at the right time, that he would just as happily have worked at an ice-cream shop or a place that sold craft beer.

She didn't want to criticize his work, but she started trying to intercept customers before they got too far into the shop to save them from him.

They didn't talk to each other much. Clare assumed Jack was happy to sit thinking his business thoughts instead of talking to her. He didn't seem very interested in what she was doing or how she was finding Bali. So she was surprised and stung one morning when, out of nowhere, he commented on her enjoying her time here with her 'beefcake'.

'What?' she said.

They'd been in the kitchenette at the same time for the first time in a while, both having breakfast. The silence between them had got to Clare enough that she'd started talking – not about anything in particular, just wittering on about her surfing misadventures and the restaurant she and Toby had gone to the previous night. She hadn't been paying much attention to what she was saying, or to Jack, but the word *beefcake* snapped the room into focus. Why would Jack say something so rude?

'I mean, you seem to be having a good time.'

She stared at him. 'I am,' she said.

'Yeah,' he said. 'That's what I said. With him.'

'Why did you call him a beefcake?'

'I don't know,' he said. 'I didn't know what else to call him.'

'You could have gone for his name.'

'Right. Tobes.'

Clare blinked a few times. What was wrong with him? Was he jealous? 'Is there a problem?' she said.

'No,' said Jack. 'I'm glad you're having fun. You should be.'

Clare shook her head as if she was trying to clear water from her ears. She had no idea where this conversation had come from. 'Are you mad at me?' she said. 'Are you mad at Toby? What did he ever do to you?'

'No, nothing,' he said. 'I'm sorry. I'm tired. Sometimes I get snide when I'm tired.' Clare stared at him but didn't say anything. 'Anyway,' he went on, 'do you have plans with him today? It's your day off.'

'No,' she said slowly. 'He's going skydiving with his friends. I think I'll visit one of the temples. He never wants to do that stuff.'

'No, I wouldn't think that was his vibe.'

'What's the *matter* with you?'

'Nothing, nothing. Ignore me.'

'Gladly.'

*

Clare had been walking for twenty minutes when she realized she'd left her phone in the flat. She stopped short, her head falling back in a groan. Jack would be the worst when she turned up for it. She'd be proving herself to be both flaky and addicted to her phone in one fell swoop.

Slowly, reluctantly, resentfully, she turned and trudged back the way she'd come. When she got to the shop she slunk past on the other side of the street, hoping Jack wouldn't choose that moment to look out of the door. Then she doubled back and crept down the path to the flat.

It wasn't until she got to the front door that Clare found she'd forgotten her keys as well. She sank against the locked door, picturing her phone and keys sitting comfortably on the bench inside. There was no getting away from it. She'd have to confess her idiocy.

She trudged back down the path to the front of the shop and walked through the open door. Jack wasn't at the till and, for a moment, she thought the shop was empty, but then she heard a woman's voice coming from somewhere further in.

'. . . but all he ever wants to read about is spaceships and planets. I mean, I'm not complaining – he's sixteen and I'm delighted he's reading – but I thought it would be nice for us to read something together that we can talk about. He might think it's beneath him, of course, to talk about a book with his mum, but I thought if I could find something in his wheelhouse, I could talk him into it.'

'But you're looking for something that's not sci-fi?'

'I don't know anything about those books. I tend to read more contemporary fiction. People like Sally Rooney, Hanya Yanagihara. I like books about people more than things. Relationships.'

Clare could almost hear the corner of Jack's mouth twisting up.

'Do you think you could cope with some spaceships if there are also intricate relationship dramas?'

The woman laughed. 'If he's okay with it, I am.'

'In that case you have loads of options. There's N. K. Jemisin's *Broken Earth* trilogy, Iain Banks's *Culture* series, Margaret Atwood's *The Blind Assassin*, Ursula Le Guin's *The Left—*'

'Wait, wait, let me write these down.'

'I can give you a list. But I'm going to try to sell you on my favourite.'

'Your favourite science-fiction book?'

'My favourite book of all.'

Clare heard Jack pull a book off the shelf.

'It looks extremely spaceships,' said the customer.

'Yeah, the cover's about marketing,' Jack said. 'It doesn't give you the whole picture. I read it when I was seventeen or eighteen and I reread it every couple of years or so. It is science fiction but there's a lot more going on.'

Jack's voice was getting a little quiet and Clare found herself holding her breath to listen.

'It's a multigenerational family saga,' he continued. 'It follows two timelines – one about a young couple living on a wasted earth, trying to gain passage on a colonial space vessel, the other following their great-grandchildren as the vessel nears a viable planet.'

He was excited, Clare realized. He was holding himself back, even, from showing just how excited he was.

'There's a spaceship and some action and even a laser or two, but it's also about legacy and connection. The tension of trying to colonize other planets when it was colonization that ruined this one. But the real reason I love it so much . . .'

Clare leaned forward a little, inexorably drawn towards his voice.

'. . . is because of the parallel love stories in the two timelines. One between two teenagers, discovering romance for the first time. The other between pensioners, finding one last spark as they close out their lives.'

The customer started to respond, but Clare was no longer listening. She had never heard Jack talk like that about anything. She'd thought he viewed the books they sold as products to sell. It had never occurred to her to even ask him what he liked to read. She'd assumed that, if he read at all, he read business books – how to be a millionaire before your twenty-seventh birthday, where to invest to look smart for your peers. That and the *Financial Times*.

She ducked behind a shelf instinctively as Jack brought the customer to the till and made the sale. As the woman left the shop, two identical books in hand, she caught a glimpse of the cover. *A Wind over Dofida* by Simone Adair.

Clare stood stock still behind the shelf, not sure why she was still hiding. Just as she was about to step forward, she heard Jack swear under his breath. He got up, put the 'Back in five' sign on the desk, and walked out. Figuring he must have left something in the flat too, Clare darted further into the shop, straight to the Sci-Fi/Fantasy section. She looked up at the top shelf, and there it was: Adair. There were a few other books by the same author, but only one more copy of *A Wind over Dofida*. She grabbed it, making a mental note to pay for it tomorrow, and dashed out of the shop.

She didn't even risk looking over her shoulder as she ran down the street. She'd get her phone and keys later. The temple could wait. A day reading on the beach sounded perfect.

Chapter Twelve

Clare read all morning. She kept the book in her hand while she queued at a food truck for lunch. She was still reading that evening when she chose a quiet outdoor table for dinner and a glass of wine.

The book was incredible, and she couldn't imagine how she hadn't heard of it before. It was epic, sweeping, yet there was an intimacy to it. A warmth and affection for its characters that held even when the scope of the story was vast. Even in its moments of tragedy a core of hope ran through it.

Clare was so transfixed, she almost forgot where she was.

She felt a wave of resentment when someone sat down across from her at the table and said hello. It took her a moment to look up and see Celestina.

'Ah,' Celestina said, when Clare raised her head, 'Simone.'

'I'd never heard of her,' said Clare. 'She's amazing.'

'Yes, well, it's been years since she published anything, and longer still since she stirred out to promote her books.'

'Oh, that's so sad.'

'Yes, isn't it?' said Celestina, wafting her hand vaguely in the air, and bringing a waiter scurrying over with a glass of wine. 'She made a bit of a splash back in the nineties, and then she just disappeared. And naturally the world moved on and everyone forgot about her.'

'Not everyone,' said Clare, quietly.

'You know,' Celestina leaned forward conspiratorially, 'she lives here. Or at least she used to.'

'In Bali?'

'Yes. You know the title of that book is referring to an Indonesian star? So this place must have had some meaning for her. I don't think she's Balinese herself, but there is clearly some connection. For a while in the early 2000s there were a couple of people claiming they'd seen her here. Of course there were also people claiming to have seen her in Vienna or in Burbank or wherever. But after he heard she might be here, Adam tracked her down. He wanted her to do an event at the shop. This was back when the shop was all he cared about, you understand. He was always coming up with plans for it.'

A reminiscent gleam lit Celestina's eyes. 'It used to be quite something. There were readings all the time – he persuaded David Mitchell to do a book launch there once. There was a monthly reading night on the beach. Not a book club, just a time to come and read by a bonfire with a drink.'

She smiled sadly.

'Anyway, when Adam heard the rumours that Simone Adair actually lived here, he was so excited. There are plenty of wonderful authors in Indonesia, of course, but Simone's renown at the time was on another level. Someone with that kind of international clout as a local author ... Well, it's good for any bookshop. And it took him a while but eventually he found her.'

'Did she do the event?' asked Clare.

'No. And she told him never to call her again. Her husband had died the year before, I think, and she just wanted to be left alone.'

'I can understand that,' said Clare.

She and Celestina sat in silence for a while. Clare hesitated, but eventually asked, 'When did the shop stop being what Adam cared about?'

'Oh, it must be at least a decade,' Celestina said.

'Did something happen?' Clare asked.

'I don't know that something happened,' said Celestina, 'or not in the way you mean. It was a slow disenchantment, I suppose.' She looked out at the horizon. 'He always saw the shop as being the centre of a community. He thought he would help children who were learning to read to pick their first books, then see them coming in year after year, growing into adults in front of his eyes.'

'And that didn't happen?'

'Things like that are never quite the way you imagine them. There were people, of course, who loved the shop and came again and again. But naturally it was only ever a tiny sliver of their lives. Not the centre, as it was for him.

'And I think that every time someone didn't seem so firmly attached to the shop as he wanted them to be it cost him something. And as the costs added up, he retreated. A little at a time. And the more he retreated, the more the shop suffered, and the more people ceased to find it an indispensable part of their lives.'

'So it goes,' said Clare.

'Ha! Yes, Vonnegut's great rule of writing – when you find a perfect phrase, use it over and over again the whole book long.'

'That must have been so painful to watch.'

'Yes,' said Celestina. 'Well, yes, I imagine it was, or would have been, but . . .' She leaned forward and lowered her eyes. 'I am not always able to give people my undivided attention. I suppose I could be called self-involved. On occasion.'

She leaned back again and took a sip of wine. 'I didn't notice as early as I might have. And so, you see, I was not able to help. I have tried, of course, over the last few years, but he just smiles at me and goes on with his day. I don't think he likes being in there.'

'Is that why he does the bookshop holidays? So that he doesn't have to work there?'

'Oh, no, if it were that bad he'd be much better just hiring someone full time. That way he'd never have to think about it at all. I believe he still has hope. Hope that someday someone else will love it the way he used to.'

*

Clare kept reading *A Wind over Dofida* all the next day in the bookshop. It was Jack's day off so she had to interrupt herself every time a customer came in – they still weren't exactly getting a hum of traffic into the shop, but it was a little steadier than it had been a couple of weeks earlier.

But although she was engrossed in the book, she welcomed each interruption. She was determined to turn the shop back into something Adam could love, and she was fast developing the next stage of her plan. She'd looked up Simone Adair online and there was still a large contingent of what Clare would have described as rabid fans.

The rumours of her living in Bali were still rampant – in fact, they had grown over the years. There was an unofficial convention that happened every year. The most diehard of Simone's fans, or at least those most able to afford nice trips, met on one of the black sand beaches to toast her work and listen to readings.

It seemed that it had started small, with just a group of friends making the trip in the hope of finding her, but it had grown every year since, and sometimes even included famous actors doing readings.

'And this year is the thirtieth anniversary of the book,' said Clare, when she outlined her plan to Jack that night.

It was late. The one time she was eager for him to come home and he'd stayed out until after ten. She'd accosted him as soon as he walked through the door, started talking immediately and had still not stopped.

'So, if we could find her, if we could persuade her to do an event here, it would be incredible. There would be so many people and they'd be so excited to see her.'

Jack didn't reply.

'Don't you think it would be wonderful?' she said. 'And we'd have to order books, but we'd definitely sell them. Everyone would want autographs.'

Jack continued to say nothing. He was staring at her as if he'd never seen a person before.

'Jack?' Clare said. 'What do you think?'

He started to talk and then stopped. And then started

again. 'You read *A Wind over Dofida*?' he said. 'Because you heard me talking about it?'

'Jack, that was the first thing I said. Tell me you heard the rest. All of it was much more important.'

Jack passed a hand over his face. 'I—' He stopped talking again. 'What?'

'Are you serious?'

'No, yes, I mean I heard you. I'm just trying to take it in.' He was silent for a few moments. Then: 'And she lives here?'

'Apparently. Or she did at some point. And Adam found her. He talked to her. He might still have her number, or maybe it's in the shop somewhere.'

Jack nodded a few times but didn't say anything for another few minutes. Clare wondered if he was dozing off. 'But if she didn't want to do an event back then, why do you think we could persuade her now?'

'She was grieving then,' said Clare.

'She might still be grieving.'

'Maybe. But what if she's just living a comfortable life with no idea how important her books are to so many people. Maybe she thinks everyone's forgotten about her. Maybe she'd be happy to know that she's still so loved.'

'And if she's not?' said Jack.

'I mean, for God's sake, Jack, if she doesn't want to do the event we won't make her, but why are we debating that part of it when instead we could just find her, ask her, and go from there? Anyway, even if she's not keen, there will be dozens of her fans here, and we could offer them a reading at least.'

'Okay,' said Jack. 'I . . . Okay. I need to sleep. I need to think about this. I'm going . . . I have to go to bed. But thank you. For talking all this at me.' He wandered into his room.

'You're welcome,' Clare said, to his closed door.

*

When Clare got up the next morning, Jack was leaning on the kitchen bench, his hands around a cup of coffee. When he saw Clare, he poured her a cup and pushed it towards her. They stood in silence for a few minutes, drinking their coffee.

After a while, Jack spoke. 'Was I dreaming?' he said.

'No.'

'You read *A Wind over Dofida*.'

'Yes, but—'

'And you found out Simone Adair lived, maybe still lives, here.'

'Yes, and—'

'And there's a bunch of her biggest fans coming here in—'

'In six weeks, and—'

'And you want to throw an event. With Simone Adair, if we can find her.'

'Yes,' Clare said. 'Yes, that's it. That's about it.'

Jack took a deep breath, in and out. He stared at his coffee, then drained the last of it. 'You have to understand,' he said, 'she's my favourite author. Ever. I can't convince myself that this is real.'

'Had you never heard the rumours that she lived here?' she asked.

'No,' he said. 'I never really thought about where she might live. I mean, I assumed she'd been to Indonesia because *Dofida*, but . . .' He fell silent for a moment. 'And when I first discovered her, it had been a few years since I'd been here, so it wasn't in my . . .' There was a stunned, starry look in his eyes.

Clare started to smile slightly. She'd never thought he'd get emotional about this; she'd never thought of him as an emotional person at all. She'd been surprised by how passionately he'd talked about the book but she hadn't realized his love of it ran so deep. She hadn't expected her idea to affect him so much.

She sipped her coffee, her eyes on his face, watching him continue to try and process the situation.

'Look,' he said after a while, 'I have to stop myself getting my hopes up. It's not unlikely that Adam has lost her details after all this time, and if he hasn't she might very well have moved – moved house, moved countries, anything – and if she hasn't it's entirely possible that she still has no interest in public appearances at all.'

Clare felt her smile growing. 'So that's a yes?'

Jack gazed at her, his eyes wide, his head shaking slightly in bemusement. He looked so young. 'We have to at least try,' he said. 'We have to.'

And Clare beamed.

Chapter Thirteen

Adam was a little less enthusiastic when they called to tell him about their plan and ask if he still knew how to get in touch with Simone Adair.

'If you want to throw an event, I don't see any harm in it,' he said, his voice booming out from Clare's phone, which was sitting beside the till. 'Although there's every chance she might resent this all happening in her name behind her back.'

Clare felt a little chastened. She'd already posted a tease about the event to Instagram. She'd shared a photo of the shop's selection with the caption 'Did you know that every year legendary author Simone Adair's biggest fans gather right here in Bali to celebrate her work? She's one of Seashore's all-time favourite authors and we're hatching plans to be involved this year. Not read her books? We recommend starting with *A Wind over Dofida* or *The Walk of the Hundred*.'

'But we don't want it to be behind her back,' said Clare. 'We really want to try to get in touch with her to see if she wants to be involved.'

'Well, that might be asking a little too much. I tried. I tried for a while, twenty years ago it must have been. Took me three months to track down her contact details and then she wouldn't have anything to do with us.'

'We know she wasn't interested in the past,' said Jack, 'but it's been a long time and we're hoping she'll feel differently now. Especially since she may not know how many fans she still has out there.'

'Perhaps,' said Adam. 'Perhaps.'

Clare and Jack looked at each other across the phone.

'Do you still have her number?' Clare asked. 'Or the number she had twenty years ago?'

'It's possible,' said Adam. 'But I don't know where it would be. Probably at the shop somewhere. There used to be a book somewhere around, I think, that had people's details in it. Haven't seen it for years.'

'Do you remember what it looked like?' asked Jack, an edge of desperation creeping into his voice.

'Brown, maybe?' said Adam. 'Really, I'm not at all sure.'

Clare and Jack leaned by the till, their heads in their hands, after the phone call had ended.

'I assume you haven't come across an address book in all your document reviewing?' said Clare.

'No,' said Jack. 'I assume you haven't, in all your rearranging things?'

'I have not.'

Jack sighed. 'On the bright side,' he said, 'there's still an enormous pile of crap we haven't gone through yet.'

'On the mezzanine?' said Clare.

'Yes,' said Jack, 'but also in here.' He pulled open a cupboard in the corner, which was stacked with boxes and papers. The top two shelves were neatly organized. Everything below them was chaos.

'That your work up the top?' Clare asked.

'I'm touched that you noticed,' said Jack, his lips twitching at the sides.

'Okay,' said Clare. 'It's fine. All we have to do is clear the mezzanine and make it ready for people to use, sort through an obscene amount of crap to find the one tiny piece of information we need, use it to contact someone who may not want to be contacted and persuade her to do an event she may hate the very idea of. Oh, and market the event so that people actually come to it, which we have to do in a way that doesn't promise a person we may not be able to deliver.'

Jack nodded silently, then brightened. 'Or we can contact her publisher – they may be able to help,' he said.

'That,' said Clare, 'is a very good point. Although it isn't going to save us from going through the rest of the crap up there, if we're going to have an event with more than, like, six people in this shop.'

*

Simone's publisher was discouraging, however. They hadn't had any contact with her since she'd delivered her last book for them in 1998, aside from sending her royalty statements every six months.

'They couldn't tell me where they send them, of course,' said Jack, when he relayed all this to Clare, 'but they did say it was a PO box somewhere in the United States.'

'Do you think that means she's left Bali?'

'Not necessarily. She may have an assistant who forwards

things to her or something. Maybe she never told her publisher her address here at all.'

Simone's agents were similarly unhelpful. The agent who had represented her had long since left, and since she hadn't written anything new for decades, their only involvement with her was funnelling her royalty payments through to her.

'What if,' said Clare, over noodles and beer on the beach one night, 'we told her agents we're producers who want to adapt one of her books. Then they'd have to put us in touch with her.'

'We might need some kind of legitimate credentials for that,' said Jack. 'There's a non-zero chance that it's a known way for stalkers to try to find contact details.'

'Maybe we should really become producers. Someone should adapt her books.'

'There was a film of one in the nineties,' said Jack. '*Persephone's Arrow*, I think. It was terrible, really cartoonish. And no one's tried since.'

'It's such a shame,' said Clare. 'More people should know about her. She's so great, it's not right.'

'You didn't know about her a week ago,' said Jack.

'Well, I mean, exactly! It's a damned shame!'

Jack laughed at her and took a sip of his beer.

'You know,' Clare said, 'we should start the rest of the planning. The bits we can do without her.'

'What do you mean?' said Jack.

Clare took a deep breath. She'd been thinking about this for days. 'I found this carpenter,' she said. 'Buana. He has a shop not far from here, and his stuff is really great. I talked to him about what we're trying to do, and he seemed interested – I think he knows Celestina. He said he has plenty of chairs all the time, but if we wanted tables he might have to make them.' She was talking a bit too fast, and not looking at Jack. She knew he was going to say no, but she wanted to get her point across. 'I think he'd give us a discount,' she said, 'if he could put a marker on them so people know who made them and where to find him. A little plaque or something.'

She fell silent and waited for the inevitable protests. They didn't come. She looked at Jack nervously. His brow was furrowed: he seemed to be thinking about something else.

'Jack?' Clare said. He looked at her.

'Sorry,' he said, 'I was just . . .' he reddened '. . . doing some math. I think we can do that. Buying local is a great idea, and getting a discount would help a lot. It'll be a chunk of money, but I think you're right. It's an important investment. But let me work out the details – I spent half my childhood here so I know how to haggle properly.'

Clare smiled blandly. 'You're supposed to haggle?' she said. Jack stared at her, and Clare laughed. He let out a breath and rolled his eyes.

'Thank God,' he said.

'That was extremely easy,' said Clare. 'I want you to go home and think about how to do better next time.'

Jack chuckled. 'I'll practise every day,' he said, then under his breath, like an incantation, 'Clare is joking. She's joking.'

Clare smiled. 'Really, though,' she said, 'thank you. I was sure you were going to say no.'

He looked startled at this. 'We agreed we were going to use the mezzanine as an event space. I've been working on a budget for it, so I know what we can afford. Well, afford is a bit of a stretch, but I know what we can manage.'

'Oh.' Clare was surprised. She'd been sure he saw her ideas as an unnecessary waste of money, that he'd just been humouring her. 'Well, good.'

Jack smiled and took her empty noodle carton from her, carrying it away to a bin.

Maybe it would work, Clare thought. Maybe the two of them could really make this work.

*

Clare was just finishing with a customer the next day when she heard a strangled cry from the mezzanine. They looked up towards the sound, then back at each other.

'I'm sure everything's fine,' said Clare, with an awkward smile. 'Have a great day!'

She crossed to the stairs and called up, 'Jack? Are you dying?'

His head popped out from behind a box. He'd been up there for a couple of hours and there was a smear of grime across his cheek. A clump of dust had attached itself to his hair.

'Jeez,' said Clare. 'Don't come down here till we've closed. You'll put off the customers.'

'Clare,' he said, ignoring her comment, 'you have to come up here immediately.'

Clare stared at him.

'Clare!' he said, sounding anguished. 'Immediately!'

'Okay, okay,' she said, starting up the stairs. 'What is it? A family of civets?'

But nothing could have prepared her for what was waiting for her upstairs.

Jack was sitting beside an open box, staring at Clare as if desperate for her to experience what he was experiencing. There were a few books piled beside him, as well as a loose stack of papers and a bag of rubbish.

Jack pointed mutely at the open box; Clare bent over it and gasped. 'Oh, my God,' she said. 'Oh, my God!' She knelt down beside him, staring from him to the box and back again. 'It's real.'

It looked like Jack had been halfway through sorting the box, which had mainly books in it, along with a few bits and pieces of bookshop-related ephemera. Lying on top was a paperback book with a dramatic illustrated cover of a woman, draped over the arm of an enormous man, her red hair streaming to the ground. They were both wearing clothes that were artfully torn, revealing rippling muscles on his part, and lavishly proportioned breasts on hers.

Scrawled across the stormy skies above them were the words *The Deadly Delicious* followed by, in a slightly smaller typeface, *Celestina Lai.*

Slowly, reverentially, Clare reached out and picked up the book. She went to open it, but the cover came away in her hand. The glue running along the spine was brittle and crumbling. 'Oh, no!' she cried in dismay. 'Do you think we can still read it?'

Jack took the book from her cautiously to examine it and a couple of pages slipped loose and fell to the floor. Clare screamed.

'Oh, God,' said Jack, tightening his grip on the book. 'Can you go and get some bulldog clips or something?'

Clare dashed to the till and rummaged in the stationery drawer to find something suitable, then darted back upstairs. Jack had laid the book carefully on the floor and was slowly leafing through it to find the right places to fit the loose pages back in.

'We can't read it like this,' said Clare.

'No,' said Jack, 'and I'm desperate to. I saw a line about someone flinging themselves upon an errant lance, and I have to know more.'

'Is that a euphemism?'

'That's the problem, Clare,' Jack said, in anguished tones. 'I don't know!'

He replaced the pages and closed the book, fastening it tight with the clips Clare had brought up. They both spent a moment gazing at it.

'Do you think we could get it rebound?' said Clare. 'Or would that be outrageously expensive?'

'I don't know,' said Jack, turning to her, his eyes lighting up. 'Maybe I'll look into that, see if it's possible.'

'I wonder if there are more,' said Clare. She and Jack looked at each other, then both grabbed the box, pulling it closer. There was an old compact dictionary, and a calculator, and Clare could see what looked like a box of pens. She began pulling stuff out of the box and throwing it aside.

'Careful,' said Jack. 'If there are more, they might be in the same condition as this one. And there may be other loose pages that have already fallen out.'

Clare nodded and they turned back to the box, removing the dross slowly and methodically. She felt like an archaeologist, brushing away mud and sand from a broken bowl that had been buried for centuries. It wasn't until they got to the bottom of the box that their search bore fruit, another book by Celestina. This one was titled *His Eyes Were As Daggers*.

'This is the best and worst day of my life,' said Clare. 'I can't believe we found them. And I can't believe we can't read them.'

'This box was stacked with those two over there,' said Jack. 'There might be more.'

The door downstairs opened, and Clare let out a low 'Nooo.'

There was no way Jack could help them in his current state. 'I promise.' He spoke as if making a sacred vow. 'I will alert you the moment I find anything.'

'You'd better,' said Clare, standing up and brushing the dust from her knees before heading downstairs.

*

By the end of the day, Jack had uncovered three more books. *The Scarlet Abbess*, *The Countess and the Hounds*, and *An Abundance of Thunder*.

They all had elegantly lurid covers and were all coming apart at the seams. Clare and Jack stood looking down on them after they'd closed the shop. Jack had bound them all together using clips and rubber bands to prevent losing any pages.

'This is agony,' he said.

'I would give my left boob to read these,' said Clare. 'And it is my bigger boob.'

'Wow,' said Jack. 'Noted, I guess.'

He studied the remaining piles of junk. 'It's more exciting now, though, isn't it?' he said.

Clare looked up at him and grinned. 'I'm almost sad to go home and leave all this here when we could be opening more boxes.'

Jack elbowed her in the ribs. It was friendly. For a moment Clare felt bereft at how friendly it was. *It's not enough.* Instantly she quashed the thought.

'That's just because you were downstairs all day,' Jack was saying. 'You're so clean.'

Clare sighed. 'Well,' she said, 'my turn tomorrow.'

*

But it turned out Celestina's books were the only treasures hidden in the junk pile. The next day, and the next, Clare and Jack sorted through the mess, finding nothing helpful, nothing interesting, only a seemingly endless pile of rubbish.

'And the worst thing is,' she complained to Toby, as they hiked through a lush green jungle, past a vast array of exquisite tropical plants, 'we can't just call it and throw everything into the bin. Because there *might* be something else good or important.'

'Yeah,' he said, over his shoulder as the foliage beside them opened out, showing a glorious view of vibrant green giving way to the rich blue of the ocean. 'Sure.'

'Simone's number could be up there. Great books could be up there. An uncashed cheque for enough money to save the shop could be up there.'

'Well, not the last one,' said Toby. 'Cheques expire.'

'Cheques expire?' said Clare. 'That's like money expiring.'

'Yeah, but imagine you wrote someone a cheque for a life-saving amount of money, and they didn't cash it for ten years. Maybe by that point you couldn't afford it. Now your life's over instead of theirs.'

'Okay. Well, it would have to be a suitcase of cash up there.'

'You think there's a suitcase of cash in the shop?' said Toby.

'No, but what if there was and we threw it out because we thought it was all only junk?'

They paused in front of a magnificent waterfall to take photos and Clare posted a selfie to her Instagram captioned, 'Can you believe this view? Love it here.'

'So, every day is just boxes and boxes of nonsense,' she continued, 'and it's so dirty. Can you see how swollen my eyes are from all the dust?'

Toby turned to peer at her. 'They look fine,' he said. 'Watch out, that monkey's after your phone.'

Clare shoved it safely into her pocket. 'Well, maybe they've gone down, but they were super-puffy when I woke up this morning.'

'That sounds painful. Maybe you should leave off clearing the mezzanine for a few days.'

Clare stared at him. 'But I can't,' she said. 'I have to know. I have to know if anything else is up there. I can't stop thinking about it.'

'I know, babe,' said Toby. 'I know.'

Chapter Fourteen

Clare woke slowly the next morning, quietly dreading another day spent among grimy boxes of mostly rubbish in the hope of finding Simone's details. She'd been so excited about the event when she came up with the idea, but it was starting to dawn on her that it might all be more difficult than she'd thought.

She turned onto her back and picked up her phone. She lay there for a while, scrolling idly through Instagram, liking her cousin Lina's latest wedding shoot, a friend's misadventures with sourdough, commenting 'OMG congratulations!!!' on the pregnancy announcement of someone she'd had a class with at uni.

Then she flipped over to the shop's account, screamed and dropped her phone on her face.

'Ow, shit!' she said to herself, rubbing her now very sore nose. Then she threw herself out of bed, shouting, 'Jack! Jack!'

But he wasn't there, because obviously he wasn't there, because it was ten forty-five and the shop opened at ten and he'd clearly woken up at a responsible time and gone to work, like she was supposed to do too.

Clare darted around the flat in a stew. She decided to get dressed and then changed her mind. In the end she threw her trench coat over her pyjamas, pulled on her shoes and dashed out the door.

'Jack!' she shouted, as she ran into the bookshop.

He gave her a pointed look, clearly telling her to shut up while he finished dealing with the customer in front of him. He handed the woman a paper bag with her books in it, told her to have a good day, and waited until the door closed behind her before he turned back to Clare and said mildly, 'Yes?'

'Jack,' she said, 'we've got ninety thousand followers.'

'What?' he said.

'On Instagram.'

He was silent and clearly baffled.

'Do you know how many we had yesterday?' she asked.

'I have genuinely no idea,' he said.

'Like, eleven thousand. Eleven to ninety overnight.'

'Huh,' said Jack. 'Congratulations.'

Clare stood stock still in her pyjamas. 'Do you not understand?' she said. 'We must have gone viral somewhere. The shop.'

She sat down by the till and started scrolling. She'd deleted all the old beach selfies and the feed was now full of pictures of the shop with the ocean in the background, sand spilling in over the door frame, piles of books arranged on the tables, books on the beach, books at pool bars, books being protected by an umbrella in a rainstorm.

They'd each got a little cluster of likes and comments

when she'd posted them, but they had all gone up by several orders of magnitude. People were tagging each other in the comments saying things like, 'We have to go here on our next trip.' People were sharing the photos to their stories with '#dreamlife'.

'And,' Clare said, as she showed it all to Jack, 'I've had like five DMs asking me to hold Simone Adair books for them.'

'That's nice, Clare,' said Jack. 'Why don't you go and put on some clothes?'

Clare looked down at herself. She was dressed for the weather in that her pyjamas did not have a lot to them. She grabbed the lapels of her trench coat and wrapped it around herself, before looking back up at Jack. There was a spark of amusement in his eyes.

'Whatever,' said Clare, 'it's not like you haven't seen me in less.'

The spark changed from amusement to ... something else. Something electric.

Clare gulped. 'I mean like bikinis,' she said.

'No,' he said. 'Yeah, I've seen you in ...' He cleared his throat.

'Right,' said Clare. 'I'll go and change.'

'Yes, please,' said Jack.

Clare poked her tongue out at him, but went back to the flat. And then back to the shop again to borrow his keys, since in her hurry she'd left hers locked inside.

*

She spent the rest of the day trying to figure out where it had all come from. It was mid-afternoon when she found it.

She was sitting cross-legged on the mezzanine next to a half-empty box she'd been slowly looking through in the moments she could tear herself away from her phone.

'Reddit!' she cried, triumphantly. She heard a sigh, footsteps, and then Jack's face appeared over the top of the stairs.

'Reddit?' he said.

'The Simone Adair message board shared my Instagram post to Reddit last night.'

'And they liked it?'

Clare scrolled through the discussion under the post. 'Well, some of them did.' A few people seemed excited about the post, speculating about what kind of event Seashore Books was going to host, but just as many seemed sceptical.

'I've never heard of Seashore Books,' one comment read, 'and I've been to Bali seven times.'

'Maybe it's a new shop?' someone had replied, but below it someone else commented, 'Nah, I've been there before. Place is a mess. Don't know what kind of event they think they can throw.'

Clare grimaced, then brightened. 'Look at this one,' she said, showing her phone to Jack.

'No other bookshop has got behind the fans this whole time,' someone had said. 'Maybe they won't be up to much, but it's nice they're trying. I'm definitely keen to see what they do.'

'And look how many upvotes it has!' Clare said excitedly.

'Do you think the upvotes will translate to sales?' Jack said, the corner of his mouth at high quirk.

Clare folded her arms and glared at him. 'Yes,' she said. 'I think they will translate to at least some sales.'

Jack chuckled. 'Well, I hope you're right. I'm happy for you and your ninety thousand Simone Adair fans,' he said, turning to go back downstairs.

Clare got up and followed him. 'They're not all Simone Adair fans,' she said. 'That's just where it started. It's mostly people who think the shop is cute. And it's a hundred thousand now.'

'That's wonderful,' said Jack.

'It *is* wonderful,' Clare said. 'It's great market—'

She was interrupted by two girls coming in giggling. 'See, I told you I knew where it was,' one said. 'I've walked past it loads.' She turned to Clare. 'Do you mind if we take a selfie?'

'Go ahead,' said Clare, smiling smugly at Jack. 'Make sure you tag us.'

The girls took a few shots, spent a few minutes tweaking them, then waved at Clare and Jack as they left the shop.

'See?' said Clare, as she posted their shot to the shop's Instagram stories. 'This stuff makes a difference.'

'They didn't buy anything,' said Jack.

Clare rolled her eyes. 'Okay, those people didn't buy anything, but some will, and the more people share the shop, the more will know it exists.'

Jack held up his hands in surrender, 'Okay, okay,' he said. 'I obviously have to bow to this unassailable logic.'

'Look, business boy, are you telling me that at your business-boy school they never explained marketing to you? Any marketing at all – billboards, celebrity endorsements, fliers slipped through letterboxes, all of it – probably only gets a handful of actual sales. Probably less than ten per cent. But the wider you spread the marketing, the bigger that ten per cent share is.'

'What did you call me?' said Jack.

'What?' said Clare.

'Did you call me "business boy"?'

Clare blushed suddenly. She'd got so into the habit of saying it in her head that it had slipped out of her mouth without her noticing.

'Anyway,' said Jack, 'how do you know all that stuff?'

'I don't know it, really,' said Clare. 'It just makes sense. How many ads do you see and how many of them make you go, "Oh, yeah, I'll buy that product"? Because I'm betting it's not most of them.'

Jack was looking at her, an odd expression in his eyes.

'What?' said Clare. 'I'm right.'

'Again,' said Jack, smiling, 'unassailable logic. I promise not to be dismissive about Instagram or Reddit or any of it.'

Clare gave a regal nod. 'Thank you,' she said. 'I'd appreciate it if you didn't.'

*

It was tough for Clare to keep the smug smile off her face over the next few days. The Instagram followers kept ticking up, more selfie seekers came into the shop, and a well-known columnist tweeted, saying, 'Sorry I didn't meet my deadline this week. I was dreaming about packing it all in to run a bookshop in Bali.'

And among all of that, there was a sharp increase in the number of people coming in to buy books. That Friday, they sold more in one day than they had in the entire previous week. They'd placed a bunch of orders for new books, including several copies of each of Simone Adair's books, all of which had sold out.

As Clare closed the door and flipped the sign to 'Closed', she sighed in happy exhaustion. 'We should go out,' she said. 'We should have dinner out. To celebrate.'

'I don't know that we can celebrate yet,' said Jack. 'And, besides, don't you want to go out with Toby?'

'He'll be fine without me for a night,' said Clare. 'And we should mark this. The first week where it felt possible, where it felt like we might really fix this place. This is the turn, I can feel it.'

Jack smiled, a little sadly, and nodded. 'Okay,' he said. 'I guess that's worth a meal.'

The sun was setting as they walked away from the shop, chatting comfortably. Clare found herself wondering again what Jack's deal was. She couldn't reconcile this Jack, the one who was reduced to silence by the prospect of an event with his favourite author, the one who had worked so hard to try to get the shop doing better, with the Jack who had studied and worked to become a specialist in corporate buy-outs. She couldn't make them go together and she didn't know which to believe in.

They were standing outside a row of restaurants, debating which one to pick, when a book fell out of Jack's jacket pocket.

'God,' Clare said, rolling her eyes. 'It's like pulling teeth for me to find clothes with pockets at all, while yours are big enough to fit whole books in the— Wait, what book is that?'

Jack reddened. He'd been trying to cram it back into his pocket – something made more difficult by the fact that he was carrying his jacket over his arm instead of wearing it – but he bashfully pulled it out to show the cover to Clare.

It was the fifth book in *The Princess Diaries* series.

Clare gaped. 'You do know you're not the target audience for that?'

'Is it my fault marketers don't know how to sell books like this to men in their twenties?' Jack said.

'Why are you reading *The Princess Diaries*?'

'You said you liked it.'

'I did like it,' said Clare, 'when I was twelve.'

'You should reread them,' said Jack. 'They're a lot of fun.'

'Wait, when did we even talk about those books?' Clare had no memory of any discussion of Meg Cabot at all.

'It's not like we had an involved conversation about them,' said Jack, 'but you mentioned it. Ages ago, when we were first here. You said it was a classic.'

Clare stared at him as if she'd never seen a human person before. 'I told you *The Princess Diaries* was a classic when we'd *just met* so you decided to read the *entire series*?'

'Well, no,' Jack said. 'I decided to read the first one. And I enjoyed it, so I read the second. And so on.'

Clare felt emotionally winded. She'd thought Jack wasn't interested in anything she said or did. He never asked how she was spending her time, never seemed interested in anything other than the shop, but he'd been reading books she'd mentioned this whole time?

'She reminds me a bit of you, actually,' Jack said. 'Mia. Always a bee in her bonnet about something.' He put the book back into his pocket, apparently without noticing that Clare had been rendered into stone.

'Anyway,' he said, 'how do you feel about this place? I think I'm in the mood for a burger.'

*

'You know,' said Clare, after their food had arrived and she'd recovered a bit of her equanimity, 'until I overheard you recommending Simone Adair, I wasn't even sure that you read.'

'Why would I want to work in a bookshop if I didn't like reading?'

'Yeah, I was very puzzled about that,' said Clare. 'I just never saw you at it.'

'There's been a lot of work to do,' said Jack. He paused. 'And I might have been a little embarrassed.'

'To be reading a book aimed at twelve-year-old girls?'

'No,' he said. 'I just didn't want you telling me you were right about something again.'

'I wouldn't have to tell you so often if you'd believe me when I said it.'

He laughed. 'Noted. But it's harder to tell someone they're right when they don't like you.'

Clare frowned. 'I like you fine,' she said.

'Oh, you like me fine.' He laughed again. 'The dream. But you didn't.'

'You didn't like me!' Clare said. 'You thought I was a frivolous travel bunny who was only here to take selfies on the beach!'

Jack's brow furrowed. 'Maybe I did,' he said. 'A little. I'm sorry.'

'Thank you,' said Clare. 'And I'm sorry I thought you were a miserly corporate robot.'

Jack's face fell. He looked hurt. 'Is that really what you thought of me?'

Clare's insides twisted. She didn't want to admit she had thought exactly that, that part of her was still afraid she'd been right. She didn't want to bring up what he'd said that night after their second dinner with Adam and Celestina. She liked this Jack. She was enjoying his company. She didn't want to ruin things by delving into all of that. 'Oh, no. You just, you know, you do so much maths.'

Jack laughed, but he still looked a little worried.

Clare chewed her lip for a bit, then said, 'You weren't entirely wrong. I did apply for this job because I wanted to travel again. It had been a while since I could afford to go anywhere.'

'Have you always loved travelling?' he asked.

'Once I'd started,' Clare said, smiling ruefully. 'I never went anywhere till I was twenty-one, but I used to talk about it all the time with my dad.'

'He liked to travel?'

'He never got to,' said Clare. 'He was always talking about places he wanted to go. He'd watch every travel show he could find and take all these notes about what he'd do if he ever could. The TranzAlpine in New Zealand. Alcatraz in San Francisco. Ice hotels in Norway. But my mum thought it was a waste of money. I hoped that when they split up, he'd finally go away somewhere, but he never did. I made him promise, though, that after I graduated from university, we'd go somewhere together.'

'What happened?' said Jack.

Clare shrugged and looked at her plate. 'He died.'

'Oh, God,' said Jack. 'I'm so sorry.' He reached out and took her hand.

'Yeah,' said Clare. 'That's why ...' She hesitated. Somehow, she didn't want to tell Jack about her failed academic career, him with his MBA. But maybe you have to be honest with someone who's read Meg Cabot for you. 'That's why I didn't finish my degree,' she said. She held her breath, worried he would be shocked, that he would think she wasn't qualified to be running the shop with him. But he didn't look shocked. He looked sad.

'Grief has a way of interfering with stuff, I guess,' he said.

'I'm not even sure it was grief, really,' she said. 'Or it was, but ... I don't know, I started to feel like I was wasting my time.'

'Getting a degree felt like a waste of time?' he asked.

'Kind of. Getting an education didn't, but a degree ...' She fell silent. She didn't know how to properly explain how completely her father's death had thrown her life off its rails.

'I don't, at all, understand what you're talking about.'

Clare laughed and then sighed. 'No, I suppose it doesn't make any sense. It's like ... It's like I still loved the learning part of it. Reading and going to lectures and tutorials – with some of the professors at least – but when it was time to prove what I'd learned, to write essays and sit exams and whatever, it just felt pointless. Partly because he wasn't there any more to be proud of me. Because I loved making him proud. But also because it all felt so arbitrary. And I understand that they need to know who's learned enough to qualify for a degree, but I just found it hard to care about that.'

She paused, frowning. She'd never really put all this into words before. She was still figuring it out for herself. 'My dad always did what you're supposed to do,' she said. 'He followed all the rules, did everything right. And he always thought he'd have a chance, one day, to get what he really wanted. Like it would be his reward. I didn't want that to happen to me.'

'So, what did you do?'

'I kept going for a while. My dad had left me some money, so I was able to pay off my loans with some of it.'

'But eventually you stopped?'

'I did everything except my final thesis,' she said.

'Why did you stop there?'

'By that point I think I was running on fumes. And one day I just . . . couldn't read.'

He looked at her. 'You couldn't read?' he asked.

'Well, I could read, you know, I could recognize words. But they wouldn't stay in my mind long enough to make sense. I'd get to the end of a sentence and not be able to remember how it had started.'

'That definitely sounds like grief to me,' he said.

'Maybe,' she said. 'But I think it was more than that. It was thinking about his life. All that time spent dreaming of something and never getting to do it.'

'So what did you do?'

'I asked for an extension and went to Italy.'

'And never went back?'

'And never went back. I used the rest of his money to take

the trips he'd never taken, or as many of them as I could. Until the money ran out, and I had to move back home to my mum's. I got a sensible office job. Got fired. Got another and got fired again. And since then, I've been wasting my time in café jobs and temp work, wondering why I wasn't trying to find something better.'

Jack didn't say anything.

'Oh, God,' said Clare, 'you're wondering the same thing.'

'No!' he said. 'Well, maybe. But it takes time to decide what you want. You can't just do it out of nowhere.'

'Well, my mum wanted me to,' said Clare, 'and she was probably right. She always seemed perfectly happy having a job that meant nothing to her. Putting in the hours so she could pay the bills.'

'Why did you get fired?' Jack asked. 'I mean, you don't have to talk about it, obviously. That was rude.'

Clare pulled a face. 'The first time was understandable,' she said. 'I really did give nothing. I was doing data entry in this grey little office block and it was like a week after I got back. I'd just been in Cuba and I was so resentful of being in a grey little office block. It was exactly what I'd been afraid of, you know? Putting in the hours and feeling at the end of every day like I'd wasted a little bit of my life.'

'So they let you go?'

'Yeah. I mean, I was miles away from the productivity targets. They were right to do it.'

She fell silent. Jack looked at her hesitantly for a bit. 'And the second time?'

Clare groaned and rubbed her eyes. 'I really tried,' she said. 'I tried to make a good fist of it. It was just a reception job, at this small accountancy firm. I'd thought to myself, *This time you need to bring something to the role.* And I thought that since the receptionist is the first person someone sees, I should be welcoming and cheerful. So I tried to be. I smiled and joked with the clients, I put bright flowers around, and I spent my own money on a candy bowl.'

'They didn't like that?'

'I'd barely been there two months when a woman from HR pulled me into a meeting,' Clare said. 'I really thought I'd been doing a good job. Clients seemed to like talking to me. Some of the staff commented on how much energy I had or complimented my clothes. And I was so pleased, because I put a lot of thought into them. I wanted to seem professional but also friendly, not intimidating.'

She sighed and took a sip of her drink.

'But this woman, she just talked for ages about how everything I'd done was wrong. My clothes were too bright. I talked too much. I'd cluttered the reception desk. She made me feel like I was twelve years old. She told me that staff were expected to behave like adults. She said I wasn't a good fit because I'm not a *serious person*. She said a lot more than that. She could have just told me I was fired and let me go home, but she took an hour out of her day to list all the ways I was insufficient.'

'Jesus.'

'So I just signed up for temp work where you're expected to give nothing, and I gave nothing. Because if I had to waste my time, I could at least not waste energy. But I still felt like a failure.'

Jack looked down at his hands. 'Well,' he said, 'everyone feels like a failure sometimes.'

'Please,' said Clare. 'Somehow I doubt that's true for you.'

Jack cleared his throat awkwardly. 'I wouldn't say that,' he said. Clare glanced up at him, startled. He was biting his lip, his brow furrowed. 'Yeah . . .' he said slowly. 'I lost a company a twenty-million-dollar deal last summer.'

Clare gaped at him.

He looked at her and laughed softly. 'It wasn't fun.'

'What . . .' Clare said '. . . how . . .'

'I was interning for them,' Jack said, 'and I had to put together the pitch deck for a meeting with the client. It was supposed to be a formality – they'd been working on it for months. Just going over the final details. And I made this interactive profit projection tool, so they could see the probable outcome of investing however much in each part of the business after the merger. But there was a mistake somewhere in the formula. It made it look like the profits would be much, much higher. The client noticed it and thought we'd done it on purpose. Decided we'd been trying to con them the whole time and backed out.'

'Oh, my God,' said Clare.

'Yeah.'

'But you were just an intern. Wasn't it someone else's responsibility to make sure everything was in order?'

'Yes. And she got fired. Because of me.'

'Oh, no.'

'I've been trying to figure out where the mistake was ever since.'

'Is that why you were always on your laptop?'

'Yeah. It wasn't exactly healthy, but I couldn't stop

hunting through my work, trying to figure out how I'd made that mistake. At least, I couldn't until . . .'

'Until?'

'Until you forced me to go out and do something better with my time. Have an adventure.'

Clare gave a small smile. 'Is that why you were so determined to sort out the finances at the shop?' she asked. 'I couldn't figure out why it seemed so important to you.'

'Basically. I wanted to do something right. Restore the karmic balance or something.'

Clare smiled in sympathy. 'I know the feeling,' she said. 'I'm out here trying to prove to myself I have something to contribute.'

Jack let out a long breath. 'God,' he said. 'I really didn't want to tell you that but it's kind of nice to have it out there, instead of just sitting inside my head.'

'You haven't told anyone else? You haven't talked to your family about it?'

'No one,' said Jack. 'Obviously the people I was working for know, but no one else.'

'Why?' Clare asked.

Jack frowned. 'I don't like talking about my mistakes until after I've corrected them,' he said. 'I don't like admitting I'm struggling until after I've overcome it.'

'But then no one can ever help you.'

He shrugged. 'I don't want people to help me. I don't want to need help.'

'That's ridiculous,' said Clare. 'Being able to help someone is a gift. It's a privilege when someone lets you see that they need you.'

Jack was staring at his hands again. 'I've never really thought about it like that.'

Clare breathed in slowly and out again. 'Well,' she said. 'I guess we're both fuck-ups. In our own special way.'

Jack laughed wryly. 'I guess we are.' He smiled at her with a warmth that went right to her centre.

'I think we're doing an okay job here, though,' Clare said.

'I think we are too. And you seem to be enjoying it,' he said. 'You seem extremely enthusiastic about it.'

'I am,' said Clare. 'I love it. More than I thought I would. I mean, there was a fantasy version of it in my head and I knew I'd love *that*. But I also knew that the real version probably wouldn't be anything like the one in my head. But now I think I'm enjoying the real one even more than the fantasy.'

'And you're good at it,' Jack said. He looked concerned, as if he was trying to will confidence into her. She laughed.

'I am, aren't I?' she said. 'I really want to save it, Jack. I really, really do.'

Jack didn't reply.

'But there's only two months left,' Clare said. 'And then I have to go home.'

Two months, she thought. *And then I have to decide what to do for the rest of my life.*

Chapter Fifteen

It was Jack's day off, and Clare was in the shop by herself. She was starting to wonder what he was doing with himself. He often came back with small cuts and blisters on his hands. Maybe rock climbing. If that was it, though, he'd have a much darker tan by now. But he wasn't asking her about her days off so she wasn't asking him about his. He'd nod at her when she came back, but the most he ever said was 'Seems like you're having fun,' and she wouldn't dignify that kind of thing with a response.

There had been a short burst of customers first thing, and Clare had wondered if it would be a busy day. But then there had been a lull, which had, by this point, stretched on for two hours.

Finally, the door opened and a woman came in, already speaking. 'Hi,' she said, 'I wanted— Oh.' She'd noticed Clare and stopped short, looking around the rest of the shop. 'Is the other person here?' she said. 'The man?'

'Sorry,' said Clare. 'It's his day off. Can I help with anything?'

'Well, maybe,' said the woman. 'It's just he recommended me a book – one for me and my son to read together – and it was perfect, just completely wonderful. We both adored it, and I wondered if he might have an idea for something else.'

Clare felt a warmth spread through her chest. It took her a moment to recognize that she was feeling . . . what? Proud? Proud of Jack?

The woman was walking towards the till, still talking. 'Something Adair, her name was. Sorry, I should have noted it down, but I assumed he'd be here.'

Clare smiled. 'Simone Adair, I think it would be,' she said, trying to act like she didn't know exactly what the woman was talking about.

'Yes!' the customer said. 'Yes, that sounds right. Do you know her?'

'I do,' said Clare. 'I think we have a couple of her other books in stock if you want to try one. Or . . .' She trailed off. The woman was gazing at the stand by the till.

'Yes,' she said slowly, and it wasn't clear whether she was talking to Clare or herself. 'After all, if I tried something for him, he could try it for me. And I think they're not dissimilar, are they? If you liked the one, you'd like the other, even if there are no spaceships,' she said, as if she was continuing a conversation Clare was actually part of.

'Um,' said Clare, not sure what to say to the woman, who was now looking at her again but not as if she was actually seeing her.

'Yes,' the woman said decisively, looking at Clare now, clearly coming to some sort of internal resolution. 'I will.'

'Great,' said Clare. 'But, sorry, you will what?'

'Oh!' The woman laughed. 'Sorry. This book club of yours. I think we should try that. That is, are there any other young people in it? Any teenagers?'

'I don't know yet,' said Clare. 'This will be our first one.'

The woman grinned, suddenly wolfish. 'So, you don't know there *won't* be other teenagers. That'll do. I'll take two, please.'

She pulled two copies of *House of the Spirits* from the stack and passed them to Clare, who beamed and rang them up.

*

Clare had got into the habit of video-calling her mum on her days off, showing off her adventures. She spent a day at the giant swings, holding her phone up so her mum could soar out over the rice paddies with her.

Maggie insisted that it felt just as exhilarating as if she was there.

'Are you sure you didn't just put the phone down until I was back on solid ground?' said Clare.

'Well, I put it on the table,' said Maggie, 'but I was still looking at it.'

Clare laughed. 'Well, I suppose that's fair enough.'

'How are things going over there?'

'I love it,' said Clare. 'I feel like I can make a difference to the shop. It was kind of a mess when we got here but we're turning it around.'

'I'm glad you're having a good time,' said Maggie.

'It's more than that,' Clare said. 'I feel, like, energized. I don't think I realized how much I was just going through the motions.'

'Well,' said Maggie, 'that's exactly what I hoped this would give you.'

'I was so worried that I'd end up never doing the things I wanted to. Because Dad didn't. But those years I was travelling I was just desperately trying to cram in as much as I could out of fear I'd miss out on something. There was no real purpose or decision. I just jumped from place to place. I hadn't really thought that hard about what I wanted at all.'

'But now you are?'

'I'm starting to, yeah,' said Clare. 'So, thank you, Mum. For being patient with me. And for running out of patience.'

Maggie laughed. 'Well that's my job.' She paused for a moment and then said, 'You know, your dad never got to travel. But he did plenty of other things he wanted to. It wasn't his only dream.'

'Just the one he talked about the most.'

'Did you ever think that maybe the reason he talked to you so much about travelling is because *you* were interested in it?'

Clare was silent.

'He had a full life that he loved. But no one gets everything. He knew that. And he knew he had the most important thing. You.'

*

Toby and Clare had been working their way through the restaurants between his hotel and her flat, but he and the boys had gone on a two-day trip to the other side of the island just as they'd got to the one she was most excited about, so she'd talked Jack into coming with her instead.

They sat comfortably at a table outside as she told him about his Simone Adair customer coming back to the shop.

Jack picked up a wedge of lemon and squeezed it over his fish. Clare noticed him wince as it splashed back up onto his hand. There were a couple of fresh scratches.

'What do you keep doing to yourself?' she asked.

Jack looked at her as he dropped the lemon on the side of his plate. 'What do you mean?' he said.

'You always have cuts on your hands,' she said. 'Unless you're extremely bad at turning the pages of a book, I can't figure out where they come from.'

'Oh,' said Jack. 'That. It's nothing. Not a big deal.'

'I didn't say it was a big deal,' said Clare, shrugging a shoulder as she lemoned her own fish. 'I'd just like to know what you're doing that scrapes you up so regularly.'

Jack sighed. He leaned forwards. 'Promise you won't laugh at me,' he said.

'No,' said Clare. 'What if it's really funny?'

Jack rolled his eyes and shook his head a bit in exasperation. 'You were the one who snapped at me about not experiencing Bali.'

'I didn't snap.'

'Whatever, you said I was too obsessed with the shop and that I needed to get a life.'

'I don't think those were my exact words,' Clare said. Jack raised an eyebrow. 'But, okay, they may have been in the subtext.'

'Well, you were right,' he said. 'I thought I didn't need to worry that much about seeing everything because we did a lot of the tourist stuff when I came here as a kid, and loads of the stuff that tourists have no idea about too. But, I don't know, you made me think about what else there was that I could learn about while I'm here, to make the most of it, because three months isn't a long time, whatever, blah, blah, blah. And the thing is, my great-grandfather – the grand-mother we used to visit, her dad – he was a leatherworker. His father was too. So, I thought, *Why not learn a little about how to do that?*'

Clare's brow furrowed as her mouth slowly curved into a smile. 'You've been learning leatherwork?' she said.

'Please don't la—'

'I'm not laughing.' She leaned forwards eagerly. 'Can you show me?'

'You want to see?' he said.

'Yes, please.'

Jack seemed unsure of himself. Then, all of a sudden, he stood up and moved around the side of the table until he was standing beside her. He pulled up his shirt a little and Clare instinctively drew back. 'I made this,' he said. 'The belt.'

'Oh,' said Clare. 'Oh.' She bent down to look at it properly. It was slim and tan, with a line of diagonal stitching down the centre and an embossed pattern repeating a bit unevenly around the edges. 'Wow,' she said. 'That's really great.'

'It's not,' said Jack. 'It's all very clumsy. But it's the first thing I made myself.'

'Yeah,' Clare said. 'It's really well done. I like this wavy bit by the buck—' She pointed at the part she was talking about and froze, suddenly very aware that she was peering very closely at what was essentially Jack's crotch. She cleared her throat and leaned away from him, looking steadily at his face. 'Well done,' she said. 'That is good. Good belt.'

Jack blushed and she didn't know if it was because he was embarrassed to have shown her what he'd made, or because he'd just had the same thought she had.

He made his way back to his seat and picked up his fork. They ate in silence for a minute or two. 'Good fish,' he said.

'Yes,' Clare said firmly. 'Very good fish.'

*

Suddenly the days when she was in the shop alone started to feel dull to Clare.

There was still a lot to do – roughly a third of the junk on the mezzanine remained, and there were still a few boxes from the cupboard to go through – but it wasn't so much fun when she couldn't interrupt Jack every few minutes with whatever thought had popped into her head.

It was strange that having someone to distract her all day made her more productive. It gave her a level of energy to tackle the mammoth task in front of her that she just didn't have when she was on her own.

It was a drizzly day, and she was in the shop alone and grumpy. She had wondered if, given the weather, Jack might elect to reschedule his day off, but he had disappeared quite happily.

She was picking through the bottom shelves of the cupboard, not really sorting the boxes so much as moving them from one side to the other, when she saw a document folder that had slipped down the back. It was much newer-looking than most of the stuff at the bottom – crisp and clean where everything else was battered and greying. It must have been shoved in recently and fallen through the cracks.

Clare pulled it out and opened it. There were a few pages in it that appeared to be out of order, including a floor plan of the shop, and a list of equipment. She leafed through them until she found a memo cover page.

It read:

From: Bellwether Holdings
To: Adam Hearn, owner Seashore Books
Re: Confirmation of Assets

Dear Mr Hearn,
Please see the attached list of assets associated with the business known as Seashore Books. Ahead of agreement of sale, we require confirmation of the accuracy of this list, along with the previously arranged survey of the property. Failure to provide this could render any agreement null and void.

Clare felt the world spin away from underneath her. This was why Adam had seemed so reluctant to help them arrange an event here. This was why he didn't seem to care about the bookshop at all. Celestina had been wrong: he didn't have any hope left.

He'd already decided to sell.

Clare looked around the shop. It glowed with a soft orange light against the grey of the weather outside. It was welcoming and homey. The shelves invited you to browse. The mezzanine was still a mess but she could see what it would become so clearly. It was more than just a project now. She wasn't only doing all this because she needed to prove herself anymore. She loved this place. She'd nurtured it and it was growing. She couldn't bear the thought of it being closed, or turned into some shiny, impersonal chain.

She let out a sob, grateful there was no one in the shop to see or hear her. But she didn't want to be alone.

She pulled out her phone and called Jack, pacing the floor and chewing a nail as she waited for him to answer. It went through to voicemail, and she swore. She felt more tears prickling at her eyes and flicked through to Toby's number. He answered on the second ring.

'Can you come to the shop?' she said, through her tears.

He was there within twenty minutes, his hair wet and salty.

'You were surfing?' she said, distracted. 'In the rain?'

'Course,' he said. 'The waves are great today.'

'Oh,' she said. 'You didn't have to stop just – just for me.' She dissolved into sobs.

Toby took her in his arms. 'Yeah, nah, you sounded like you needed me to,' he said. 'There'll be plenty of good waves.'

He deposited her gently on a chair and went into the shop kitchenette to make her a cup of tea.

Clare cupped her hands around the hot ceramic and tried to slow her breathing. Toby waited as she drank her tea, then asked what was going on.

'He's selling,' Clare said, her voice breaking again. 'Adam's selling the shop.'

'Oh,' said Toby. 'Well, I suppose he's around the right age to retire. And it doesn't seem like he has a lot to do with it any more anyway.'

'But we were saving it,' Clare said, her voice small and plaintive. 'We were fixing it for him.'

'Right. But, the thing is, are you sure he wanted you to fix it for him?'

'Of course he does! Or he will! When he sees that we can, that we have . . . We just need time to show him we can do it. That it can be the way it was before, better even. That it can be everything he wanted it to be.'

Toby didn't say anything.

'Don't you believe me?' said Clare.

'I don't know anything about this kind of thing, babe,' he said. 'I'm sorry, though. I know you really love this place.'

Clare didn't reply. She didn't want sympathy, she wanted him to understand. She wanted someone else to be as hurt by this as she was. As betrayed.

*

Toby hung around for the next hour or so, saying he didn't have anywhere better to be since the rest of the guys would still be surfing. Clare was glad to have him, if only because he was willing to take care of the few customers who came in through the rain.

She didn't feel particularly up to making small-talk over Kate Atkinson books right now.

It was mid-afternoon when Jack walked in, looking worried. 'You called me,' he said. 'I'm sorry I missed it. Is everything all right?' He took in Clare's face and Toby standing behind the till. 'God, Clare, what's happened? Are you okay?'

Clare's breath caught in her throat as she fought to stop more tears falling. 'It's over, Jack. Adam's sold the shop.'

Jack went white. 'What?' he said. 'Has he told you?'

Clare took the document folder from beside the till and handed it to him. He flipped through it wordlessly. 'We shouldn't be talking about this here,' he said. 'We shouldn't be talking about it in front of . . .' He glanced at Toby.

'I already told him,' Clare said. 'That's why he's here.'

'Clare, do you—' Jack said, but Toby interrupted.

'Yeah,' he said. 'I think this is probably something the two of you need to talk about without me. Clare, I'll call you later, take you out or something, get your mind off things.'

Clare let him go without demurring even though going out was the last thing she wanted to do. She didn't want to take her mind off it: she wanted to stop it.

'Clare,' said Jack, after Toby had left, 'you shouldn't have told him. It's none of his business. It's none of *our* business.'

'How can you say it's none of our business? After all the work we've been doing?'

'Because it isn't! We're only here for three months. We're a blip for this shop. You can't fix everything just because you want it to be fixed. You can't come in with a sunny attitude and assume that's enough to make everyone want the same things as you.'

'But I'm doing this for him,' Clare protested. 'We're fixing the shop for Adam—'

'Are we?' Jack had a hard look in his eyes. 'Is this really about Adam? You told me yourself that you want to prove yourself, that saving this shop would prove your worth. And I wanted to help you with that, Clare, I really did. But if it's not what Adam wants, it's not our place to change things.'

Clare stared at him. 'What are you talking about? I thought we both wanted this – to save Seashore for Adam.'

'Oh, come on, Clare. This has always been about you. You weren't happy with the way things were so you had to change everything to suit yourself. You steamroll over people without stopping to ask what they want. You wanted an idyllic life with a golden himbo and a little shop in paradise where nothing is ever wrong, where nothing is ever hard, or just boring and ordinary, and you're trampling over everything else to make it real. Adam doesn't want this shop any more. Clearly. He wants to be done with it.'

Clare wasn't crying any more. She was too shocked. Jack had taken the wind out of her lungs, accused her of being the worst possible version of herself.

'No,' she said. 'You just want to give up again. You always thought this was a waste of energy. If we give up then you don't have to be worried about failing again. It's always risky down here, isn't it? That's why you're going to work for a corporation, because there's safety in numbers. You're too scared to be out here alone trying to make something work against the odds.' She felt it again, frustration rising to rage, and she couldn't stop it. She knew she was being unreasonable, that she wasn't making any sense, but there was some fear in her that needed to get out and this was the route it was taking. 'For all I know it's your company that's doing it,' she said, 'this Bellwether Holdings. For all I know, that's the job waiting for you at the end of this.' She took a step towards him. 'For all I know, you wrote this memo.'

Jack looked baffled. 'Of course I didn't write the memo,' he said. 'What are you talking about?'

'Do you work for Bellwether Holdings?'

'Clare, no! I don't . . . I know them, but—'

'Ha!' said Clare. 'I knew it. I knew you were—'

'I was what?' said Jack. 'I know who they are, I know people who work there, but this is nothing to do with me.'

'Well,' said Clare, 'so what if it isn't? This is still what you do, isn't it? This is what you studied. You interned for companies like this.'

'It's not what I do!'

'It might as well be. That's the natural end here, for you. You see a failing business and you see something to be swallowed up by a company with "holdings" in its name, the logical thing to let happen, nothing worth saving. Might as well give up.'

'Oh, is that right?' said Jack, turning away from her and walking towards the window. 'That's why I've been slaving away here for weeks? Going along with all your schemes because you've decided this shop is your new identity so you can't admit that even with all our work it might still never be a viable business?'

'See? This is what I'm talking about,' said Clare. 'You have to talk about things in terms of "viable business" but this could be so much more than that. Celestina told me Adam wanted it to be a source of community, of connection, and we can build it back to that.'

'But it still has to make enough money to stay open.' Jack turned back to face her. 'The shop can't survive just because you want it to. And you can't want it hard enough to make it survive.'

'So – what?' Clare said, taking a few steps towards him. 'You just give up on something? Something that could be so great? You just give up because it's easier?'

Jack moved closer to her. He suddenly seemed small and sad. 'Sometimes you have to admit that something is impossible. That no matter how much you want it, it's never going to be yours.'

'But can't you feel it?' said Clare, taking another step, almost involuntarily. 'Doesn't it feel like we're supposed to be doing this? Like we're both here for a reason?'

Jack was gazing down at her. They were standing very close now. 'It's just a feeling,' he said. 'That doesn't mean it's real.'

'But . . .' Clare was almost whispering. 'You do feel it.'

Clare stood looking up at him. Her cheeks felt hot, and she was suddenly very aware of Jack's eyes on hers. 'Jack,' she said.

Jack brought his hand up to her cheek. 'Clare,' he said, 'I—'

And she rose to her toes, bringing her arms around his neck and pressing her lips to his. She stepped back and let go, flushed and breathless, but he pulled her back to him, wrapped his arms around her, and they were kissing desperately, achingly. Clare felt Jack's hand running over her back, pressing her closer into him.

He tasted of salt and sun, and Clare wanted to sink right into him.

Just then, the door opened, and a voice said, 'Oh! I'm so sorry.'

Clare and Jack sprang apart, wild-eyed. It was Joyo. 'I can come back,' he said. 'I just . . . I think you got a book in for me.'

'Of course,' said Clare, a manic edge to her voice. 'Sorry, I'll get that for you now.' She went to the till and bent down to pull out Joyo's book, and by the time she straightened up again Jack was gone.

Chapter Sixteen

Jack didn't come back to the shop. Clare put the 'Back in five minutes' sign by the till and dashed to the flat to see if he was there, but it was empty.

She walked slowly back to the shop, still feeling dazed. It had been a mistake. Obviously a mistake. The heat of the moment.

She would text him and apologize. She pulled out her phone. It buzzed in her hand and she almost dropped it. It was Toby calling. Like he'd said he would. He always did what he said he was going to do. He was so dependable. It was good to have a dependable person, she thought.

She answered the phone with a brightness she was sure he'd see through. 'Hi,' she said. 'Hello! How are you? How was your afternoon?'

'Are you okay?' he said.

'Yes!' she cried, panicking. 'Of course! Why wouldn't I be?'

'Well, you know,' he said, 'because of the shop. You were pretty upset about it.'

'Right, yes.' She felt a stone drop in her stomach. For a moment, she'd actually forgotten what had started the whole thing. 'No, I am, I'm upset, but I can't do anything about it right now. So I'm trying to be positive. It doesn't look like things are final yet. I'll talk to Adam tomorrow and see what the situation is.'

'Sure,' said Toby. Clare felt her phone buzz in her hand again. Someone had texted her. She swallowed but didn't pull it away to look.

Toby was still talking. 'Look,' he said, 'I was thinking I'd swing by for you when you close. Come out with me and the guys – come out for dinner and then let's go dancing.'

Suddenly spending the night in a club so loud she couldn't hear her own thoughts sounded perfect. 'Yes,' she said. 'God, yes. Thank you, Toby.'

She hung up and tapped through to her texts. The message was from Jack: *I'm sorry. I crossed a line. It won't happen again.*

She felt heavy for a moment, then shook her shoulders and lifted her head. She didn't have to think about that right now. She was going dancing.

*

Clare had thought nothing could be more awkward than her first couple of weeks in Bali, when she and Jack had barely known each other but were forced to live together in that shoebox flat. When they barely talked except to argue over the petty cash.

But she'd been wrong.

Now they moved around the tiny flat like satellites,

listening to check if the other was around before venturing out of their bedrooms. When they were both in the shop they kept as far apart as they could – Clare working on the mezzanine while Jack sifted through the rest of the documents in the cupboard. She found herself moving automatically, opening boxes and sorting the contents on autopilot while her mind whirred. Part of her longed to talk to Jack about the kiss, and part of her was desperate for it never to come up again. Suddenly the way he sometimes looked at her, the expression she had taken as judgement, was thrown into a new light. Had he been into her this whole time?

But he'd said horrible things to her as well, things that implied he thought as little of her as she'd assumed back in the early days. She was so confused. Why couldn't he just tell her how he really felt?

But what would be the point of him doing that when Clare didn't know how she felt herself?

Clearly, he was attractive: she'd known that right from the first day. He wasn't a massive ripped beach demigod, like Toby, but that wasn't always what you wanted. She hadn't admitted it to herself, but sometimes, laying her head on Toby's chest felt like lying on concrete.

Jack was leaner, a cleaner shape. He had those neat, well-rounded shoulders, and those forearms. Whenever she caught him chopping vegetables or shelving books with his sleeves rolled up, she had to force herself to look away. And his eyes, soft, warm and brown, with his hair – longer now, and a little scruffier – falling into them so he needed to sweep it back sometimes. With those hands. And forearms.

Clare realized she'd put a couple of perfectly good Sarah Waters books into the pile meant for the bins and swore softly at herself. She needed to get a grip.

Jack called up to her from downstairs to let her know he was heading out for lunch and could she mind the till. She peered over the balcony as he left. He also had a really good butt.

Shit.

She knew it was better to keep herself safe. Jack was still two different people in her mind. The one who always made fun of her ideas, but also the one who had helped her make every single one of them happen. The one who'd read *The Princess Diaries*. The one who'd felt so good in her arms, whose lips she could still feel on her own. The one who seemed to care so much about saving Seashore Books. But also the one who was here to learn about how small businesses worked so he could better dismantle them. The one who was becoming harder and harder to believe was real.

There was another layer to it as well, if she was willing to be honest with herself. Jack wasn't like Toby. Toby was a perfect Bali boyfriend. He was fun, he was good to her . . . and he was very temporary. She and Toby were both extremely content to enjoy each other for a few weeks, then go their separate ways.

Somehow she knew that, even as things were now, Jack was going to be very hard to leave when her time here was up. If he became more to her than he already was? It would be impossible. And what would happen then? He had a job lined up in Chicago. Was she expected to move there for him? Would he even want her to? What would she do there? Just the same kind of miserable jobs she was doing at home?

No. She had to figure out a place for herself that was hers, not just end up somewhere because of a guy.

Suddenly Clare was laughing at herself. She was rejecting a future no one had even offered her. It was just a kiss! Just one kiss. She had firmly decided it wouldn't turn into anything more.

She needed to keep herself safe, and that meant fun, frivolous, temporary Toby.

And that was fine. That was just fine.

*

Clare went for her own lunch after Jack got back, taking her disordered thoughts for a walk through the market. She popped into Buana's shop to see how the chairs and tables for the mezzanine were coming along and chatted to him about his son, who was just starting university – 'A great shame,' Buana said. 'He is better at carpentry even than me, and he insists on studying bioengineering' – and his daughter, who had just opened her own accounting business in Jakarta.

Clare had hoped that this would take her through her full lunch hour, but when she walked away from Buana it had only been forty minutes. She was furious with herself. She was more scrupulous now than she ever had been about not taking more than her allotted break for lunch, but that didn't mean she wanted to go back early. That would be even more embarrassing than being late, especially since Jack would absolutely not comment on either, and his silence would hang in the air between them for the rest of the day.

She begrudgingly bought herself an ice cream and sat on a bench by the sand, watching the minutes tick by until she could go back. Finally the hour was up and she walked towards the shop, planning to nod casually at Jack and return to her perch upstairs.

But when she opened the door, it was to find him pacing around, running his hands through his hair, a feverish look in his eyes. 'I was going to call you,' he croaked, as she came in. 'I found her.'

'What?' said Clare. 'Found who?'

'Simone,' he said. 'I found Simone Adair.' He waved his hand distractedly in the direction of the till. On the bench there was a thick brown notebook, with one word embossed in gold on the front. It read: 'Addresses'.

Chapter Seventeen

Clare screamed. 'Oh, my God,' she said.

'Oh, my God,' said Jack.

'You found her.'

'I found her.'

Before Clare knew what was happening, they were dancing around holding hands, yelling into each other's faces.

'Oh, my God,' said Clare, again, coming to a breathless stop. 'I can't believe it. I can't believe you did it.'

'I know,' said Jack. 'I know.' He was looking at her, his eyes glowing. The room suddenly grew very still around them.

Clare cleared her throat. 'Okay,' she said. 'We have to call her. We have to call her right now.'

'Yes,' said Jack.

'No,' said Clare.

'No?'

'We have to figure out exactly what we're going to say to her. We have to make her feel special, to make her realize how many people would love to see her.'

'Right,' said Jack. 'Right. Let's make some notes.'

'Yes!' cried Clare, running to find pens and paper. They huddled over the bench, staring at the paper and saying nothing.

'This is easy,' said Clare. 'We just have to tell her all the things we've said to each other. All the things the people on the internet have said.'

'Right, yes, we just have to say, "You're amazing and everyone loves you and here is why,"' said Jack.

'Yes, exactly,' said Clare. 'Yes.'

They were silent. For several minutes.

'I'm sorry,' said Jack. 'I can't think of anything. My head is all busy and empty.'

Clare put her pen down. 'Maybe we need to take a step back and calm down,' she said. 'I'll make a cup of tea.'

She went to the kitchenette and boiled the kettle. She put teabags in cups, poured hot water over them and let them brew for four minutes. She took out the teabags and added milk to hers and sugar to Jack's and carried them out into the shop. She and Jack sat sipping their tea, staring at the address book, looking up at each other, then staring at the address book again.

When a customer came in, Jack jumped up to help them with so much excess enthusiasm they almost fled the shop.

They finished their tea, and Jack carried their cups back to the kitchenette, came back to the till and sat down. They stared at the address book and at their blank pieces of paper.

'Maybe . . .' said Clare.

'Yes?' said Jack.

'Maybe we can't do this over the phone. Maybe we need to talk to her face to face.'

Jack was nodding way too much. 'Do you mean just drop in?' he said.

'Well, let's call her first,' said Clare. 'But just to say, like, "We're local booksellers. Might we come to see you with a proposition?"'

'Might we?'

'Shut up. But yes, basically.'

As soon as she'd said it, it seemed like the best plan. No awkward cold call, just a casual visit where they could talk naturally instead of coming up with some strange and awkward script. Clare insisted that Jack make the call since Simone was his favourite author, but when he went to dial, he froze. 'I can't do it,' he said, his voice small. 'Please do it for me.'

Clare nodded and picked up the phone. She dialled the number, obsessively double-checking each digit as she entered them. The phone started to ring. Clare's eyes were locked on Jack's. The phone kept ringing.

Clare found her head moving closer to Jack's, her eyes wide as she listened to the phone ring over and over and over.

She pulled it away from her ear and hit the speakerphone button.

It continued to ring.

She propped her chin in her hand.

'No answerphone,' said Jack.

'No answerphone,' said Clare.

'We should hang up,' said Jack. Clare nodded but didn't move. Jack walked away from the bench, shaking his hands, then turned back and thrust out his hand to hit the hang-up button.

Silence echoed through the shop.

'It wasn't disconnected,' said Clare.

'It wasn't disconnected,' said Jack.

'We can try again. Later. Or tomorrow.'

'Yes!' said Jack. 'We'll try again.'

'People go out,' said Clare.

'People go out all the time,' said Jack.

'We'll try again,' said Clare.

They stood there for a moment in silence.

'Jack,' said Clare.

'Yeah?'

'You found her.'

He beamed. 'I found her.'

*

They tried again.

They tried again the next day and the day after that. They kept each other's spirits up saying things like 'We just have to pick the right moment one time,' and 'I've got a good feeling about tomorrow.'

At least, after the excitement of that first afternoon, the lingering awkwardness between them was gone. Clare was embarrassed to admit it, but her relief at having their old friendship back was almost as great as her excitement over finding Simone's number.

And if they occasionally locked eyes for a moment too long, if the atmosphere in the room sometimes suddenly shifted, that was nothing she couldn't deal with. They didn't mention it and they didn't act on it. Clare found time to spend with Toby almost every day, and Jack did . . . whatever he did.

Clare didn't mention the hope that was again rising in her chest. If they could actually pull this off, maybe it would convince Adam to back out of the deal. Maybe he wouldn't sell the shop after all.

*

The night of the first book club came around and, all in all, it went off well. Clare and Jack had elected to make it a bring-your-own-wine night to save the shop money. They'd scrounged up a mismatched collection of chairs – the one benefit to business still being on the slow side was that they didn't have more people than they could find seating for.

The woman who'd bought two copies for her and her son came along, introducing herself as Lauren, and the lanky youth lurking behind her as Max. Joyo made it, too, but he kept his phone in his hand, and looked at it frequently over the course of the hour. Aside from them, there were only two other people, neither of whom had bought their copies of the book in the shop. Everyone seemed interested in making the book club a regular thing – with the exception of Lauren and Max, who were only in Bali for the next few weeks.

'I made him come,' Lauren joked. 'He spent the whole summer vacation with his dad, and I decided I needed some quality time with him too.' The boy blushed and didn't say anything.

And Toby was there, although he hadn't read the book. He slotted himself into the role of waiter, busying himself with making sure everyone's glasses were always full.

The small group made awkward chit-chat for the first few minutes. Aside from Toby, Lauren and Max were the only people who didn't live in Bali. Joyo and Siti had grown up on the island, while Valarie was a Canadian who'd moved there in her twenties.

Once they started talking about the book, everyone started to slowly come out of their shells – even Max, who said he'd been surprised by how much he'd liked the book, but still wished it had a bit more action.

Clare noticed Lauren looking at him in delight. It seemed like she was bursting to say, 'I told you so,' but was holding herself back.

'He doesn't like it when I push things too hard,' she confided in Clare, when everyone was gathering their things at the end of the session, 'but I'm so proud of him for reading it. And enjoying it! It's a relief, to be honest.'

She sighed, and looked over at her son, who was talking to Jack on the other side of the shop. 'He's always had so much more in common with his dad. They go camping together, they go see all the *Star Wars* films together, which I thought was wonderful when we were still married. My dad never gave me or my brothers the time of day. But since we divorced, it just feels like I have nothing to share with Max. I brought him here because I thought there'd be things we could both enjoy, and there are, but not together. He wants to go surfing, I want to visit temples. He wants to learn why the rice fields are in steps, like they are, I want to go to a spa. I thought it was all a mistake, coming here. And then I came into the shop, and I'm so glad I did.'

'Will you still be here for the next one?' Clare asked.

'I think so,' said Lauren. 'I think we might just be able to make it.'

Clare was a bit worried about what they'd do for the second book club. She wasn't sure Jack would be okay with ordering in more copies. But she was wrong: he was the one who suggested the next option.

'*Melmoth*,' he said, 'by Sarah Perry. It's a bit darker, a proper Gothic horror, but I think people would like it.' Clare agreed and, to her surprise, Jack looked relieved, and a bit shame-faced. 'I may have ordered it in already,' he said. 'If they'd arrived and you hadn't said yes, it would have been embarrassing.'

*

Business was continuing to improve slowly but surely. It was clear that it was partly thanks to word spreading online, but there were more walk-in customers, too. Clare was redoing the window every week, highlighting new releases with a selection of related recommendations, and painting the glass with designs pulled from the covers. Jack had found an old street sign that they'd freshened up and set out on the corner every day.

Clare was trying to persuade him to let her put an Instagram wall on the mezzanine now that it was almost clear of boxes, and she was sure she would eventually win. 'We could put up some floating shelves,' she said, in what she thought was a honeyed, persuasive tone, 'and let people put their own favourite books on them for their posts. As recommendations, you know? So it's not just about the visuals it's a way to start conversations.'

'Or we could just put up a normal shelf,' he said, 'and fill it with books.'

'It would be really great for events,' she countered. 'A way to highlight the books related to each one, but also to keep our name visible in people's posts. Because it would be painted on the wall.'

'What would be painted on the wall?' said a voice from the doorway. Clare turned to see Celestina walking in, followed by a couple of people carrying crates of wine. She waved them up the stairs to the mezzanine.

'I'm trying to persuade Jack to let me do an Instagram wall upstairs,' said Clare.

'Oh, marvellous,' said Celestina. 'It's crucial to keep a strong presence on social media. I myself have found great success on TikTok.'

'You're on TikTok?' said Jack, staring.

'Yes, dear. Film has always been a wonderful medium for me,' she said. 'Now, darlings, you know I think you've done a splendid job with this shop, but have you thought of putting some tables up on the mezzanine? You *are* intending it as an event space still, I gather?'

Clare looked at Jack. 'We have some on order,' she said. 'A local carpenter is making them for us. Buana. But they're not ready yet.'

'Oh, Buana. Yes, perfect. You know he did our sideboard – did you notice it? At the house?' She turned to one of her lackeys. 'Will you go and see if Buana has a table or two he can lend us until the ones we've ordered are done? Biggish ones, you know the kind of thing, just for serving from.'

'Thank you, Celestina,' said Jack, 'but we don't need—'

'It's nothing, my dear, and of course I do need somewhere to put the wine tonight.'

'Right,' said Jack. 'Tonight.' He flashed Clare a helpless look, but she was as mystified as he was.

'My reading, of course. I told you I would do a reading here.'

'You did,' said Clare, 'of course. Did you tell us when—'

'And you don't need to worry about a thing. It's all taken care of. And you are both, of course, invited. Now let me just review the space.'

Celestina walked up the spiral staircase, Clare trotting behind her.

'There's still a bit of tidying-up to do,' she said. 'We've not quite gone through the last couple of boxes, and the floor needs sweeping.'

'That's fine, of course. I assume you'll have time for that before this evening.' Celestina looked around and sighed. 'I suppose it's too late now to have that wall set up.'

'Well, properly, yes,' said Clare. 'We haven't got to decorating up here at all.'

Celestina looked at her with a mournful expression.

'But,' said Clare, 'I can try to rig up a makeshift one? And we can prove to Jack that it's a good idea!'

Celestina brightened immediately and breathtakingly. 'See?' she said. 'I knew Adam made the right choice with you.' She spun around, her silk robe flaring out around her, and started back down the stairs. 'I must go. The rest of the day is for strict vocal rest. The boys will set up the tables. See you anon!' And she was gone.

Clare and Jack stared after her.

'Did you ever find any digital copies of her books?' Jack said.

'No,' said Clare. 'No ebook versions and the only second-hand ones were like sixty quid each. Did you find someone who can rebind the ones from the mezzanine?'

'Turns out that would be significantly more than sixty quid each.'

'Now that is tragic,' said Clare. 'But it does mean our day just got a lot more exciting. I cannot wait to hear her read.'

*

Clare and Jack spent the rest of the day sweeping and mopping the mezzanine and replacing dead light bulbs. The remaining handful of boxes they stashed behind the till to look through later. The walls all needed painting, so they used the dimmest bulbs they could get away with – although Clare made sure there was something brighter and more flattering on the Instagram wall. This she decorated as best she could, pinning up a spare section of cloth from her window displays so it draped gracefully to the floor. She put an old, wrought-iron stool in front of it, with books piled on each side. She'd uncovered a small blackboard a few days earlier, so she wrote 'Seashore Books' on it and tacked it at roughly just above head height.

Jack had run out to get some fairy lights, which were now wrapped around the railing, and he'd surprised Clare by also grabbing a couple of potted ferns.

Buana himself brought the tables Celestina had demanded, saying, as he helped winch them up over the railing, 'Ah, you do these things for Celestina, my friends.'

Jack and Clare took turns to pop back to the flat and change from *daytime shop worker chic* to something more appropriate for a reading by the single most glamorous person either of them had ever met. Jack went first, coming back in charcoal dress trousers and a cool blue batik dyed shirt he must have bought recently from one of the local clothing boutiques.

Clare also chose something she'd bought in Bali, donning a light silk midi dress in a rich green that brought out her eyes. She swept her hair casually off her face, and added gold drop earrings.

By six, everything was ready, and Jack and Clare sat back to wait for the guests to arrive. By seven, they were each drinking a glass of wine and still waiting. At twenty past, Jack slipped out to get them some food, and at eight, they poured themselves another glass of wine.

At a quarter past eight Toby turned up, saying he'd thought the event would be starting to wrap up by now and that he and Clare could go out. Clare told him to pour himself a drink and settle in.

Finally, at around ten to nine, a group of six or seven lavishly decorated persons burst through the doors talking animatedly and all at once. They started roaming through the shelves, and from there, a consistent trickle came in, until around thirty people were milling around upstairs and down. They all seemed to know each other – and know exactly what they were there for.

Clare wondered vaguely if she and Jack should be offering to help them, but she was at a loss as to what they might need help with, so she stayed quiet, apart from asking someone what time they believed Celestina would be there.

'Whatever time it is, she'll make sure she's the last to

arrive,' they said. 'That's the only way to make a real entrance, darling.'

No one seemed impatient for her to arrive: the atmosphere had a contented excitement to it, as if something delightful but reliable was imminent.

The trickle of people slowed to a stop and an air of expectation started to hum through the room.

And then the door opened one last time, and Celestina was there, somehow looking as if she was bathed in light, although Clare couldn't tell where it was coming from.

She moved through the shop as if an aisle had been laid out before her, murmuring greetings to everyone she passed – she seemed to know them all – until she reached the stairs and glided up them with the grace of Veronica Lake. At the top she turned, positioning herself carefully to the side and by the railing. It was clear she had an unerring talent for finding the perfect spot. Everyone, upstairs and down, could see her. She was spectacular, of course, in a deep purplish blue, spangled all over with delicate stars. Her long silver hair was flowing down her back, giving her the appearance of an immortal being, of the head witch of some sprawling coven.

'Beloved ones,' she said, 'I have kept myself from you for far too long, but it is a joy to be among you again. Thank you for honouring me with your presence once more. Now, as you all know, I retired from my career as a romance novelist some time ago' – there were boos and theatrical sobs and even a feigned swoon or two – 'but I've always been one for returning to the classics.' Cheers and whoops erupted around the shop as, with a flourish, she pulled out a battered paperback with a cover Clare couldn't help thinking of as elegantly lurid.

Celestina opened the book reverently and began to read. The passage she'd chosen was not long, but she made a rich meal of it, drawing out every graphic detail of the torrid scene taking place in a shack on the beach beside a particularly stormy ocean. Clare, sitting against the wall downstairs with Jack and Toby, felt her eyes growing wider with every passing word. She glanced at Jack, whose face wore an expression of pure delight, and then at Toby, who was bobbing his head slightly from side to side, as if in time to music only he could hear.

He caught Clare looking at him and gave a small, distracted smile. 'Yeah, she's something else, isn't she?' he said.

The reading finished, and Toby went off cheerfully to get another drink while Clare and Jack stayed stock still where they were.

'I can't—' said Clare.

'I know,' said Jack.

'In your wildest dreams, did you—'

'Just beyond anything I could ever—'

They let out a sigh at the same time.

'I've never been this happy,' said Clare.

*

After Celestina had finished her reading, the party got going in earnest. Someone – Clare had no idea who – had found the sound system and put on some Fleetwood Mac, and people were, if not exactly dancing, swaying in each other's arms.

Toby was mingling with the crowd. Clare walked past him while he was talking to a tiny woman dressed from head to toe in black with a single anatomically correct heart on her cheek where you'd usually see a beauty mark. He was listening earnestly as she described a piece of performance art that had involved her dangling upside down from a tree for a full day. 'Well, it was supposed to be a full day,' she was saying, 'but I was forced to cut it short, due to a pressing medical need.'

Celestina was everywhere, talking warmly to everyone, and it felt like the night might last for ever.

And then, as suddenly as it had started, it was over. A group sailed out of the door calling for cocktails, the performance artist dragging Toby in her wake. Celestina kissed Clare and Jack on each cheek and wafted away, and the two were left alone, 'You Make Loving Fun' still flowing out from the sound system.

They wandered around the shop, collecting discarded glasses and carrying them up to the tables to deal with tomorrow. Clare hummed along with the song, and as she turned to go downstairs, she noticed Jack singing as he carefully lined up smeared wine glasses.

He looked up and caught Clare watching him. He reddened slightly, and then cocked an eyebrow at her, his mouth twisting up at the corner as he sang a little louder. He reached out a hand and when she took it, he spun her around and pulled her closer, still singing as they moved gently to the music.

Clare joined in on the second verse, bringing in a valiant attempt at harmony. The vocals faded away and she and Jack kept moving together as the instrumental played itself out.

Silence fell and Clare looked up at Jack. He was more serious now, gazing into her eyes, and Clare felt her hand compulsively tightening on his back, twisting into the cotton of his shirt. His hand holding hers gripped a little harder.

And then the next song started, blaring out of the speakers. Clare took a breath and stepped back. Jack dropped her hand and gave an exaggerated yawn. 'The Instagram wall looks good,' he said, a little too loudly. 'Maybe you're right. We should set up a proper one.'

'Yeah,' said Clare. 'We'll have to look at what Celestina's friends did with it tomorrow.'

'Yes,' said Jack. 'Yes, we will. Well. I guess we should lock up.'

'Yes,' said Clare. 'We should lock up. And go home. To our flat.'

'Yes, we should,' said Jack. 'It's late and we should be getting to bed. To beds. To sleep. We should be getting to sleep. In our beds.'

Clare nodded mutely and they walked normally downstairs, picked up their things, and locked the door, normally, like normal respectful adults, and walked together, but in a normal way, down the path that led to the flat.

And then Clare went straight to her bedroom, shut the door, and face-planted on her bed.

Chapter Eighteen

In the days after Celestina's reading Clare felt a buoyancy she didn't understand and chose not to examine.

She went hiking with Toby and the green of the jungle was brighter. She went swimming and the salt of the ocean was tangier. Food was spicier; drinks were smoother; the air itself seemed to have more oxygen in it. She could feel her mouth curving in a slight smile round the clock.

But nothing new was happening.

Adam and Celestina had brought down some paint left over from the last time they'd redecorated their house – a few buckets of a dusty blue, a bit of green and, because it was Celestina, a rich gold.

Jack and Clare spent a day painting the walls of the mezzanine, and if there was giddiness to both of them while they did it, they didn't acknowledge it. The Instagram wall they painted green, and Clare used stencils to add some palm leaves in gold, and painted the shop name in a flourishing curve across the top.

They'd asked Buana to put up three floating shelves on

that wall and were planning to have him install more shelving along the back.

Clare was inordinately proud of her wall. 'It looks good, right?' she said to Jack, as they stepped back to look at it after the shelves had been installed.

'It needs books on the shelves,' he said.

'Wait. We need to take turns,' Clare said, and dashed downstairs. She arranged her selection thematically: a comfort shelf with *A Song for Summer* by Eva Ibbotson, *Arabella* by Georgette Heyer, *I Kissed Shara Wheeler* by Casey McQuiston, and *Matilda* by Roald Dahl. A classics shelf with *The Tenant of Wildfell Hall* by Anne Brontë, *Nicholas Nickleby* by Charles Dickens and *The Count of Monte Cristo* by Alexandre Dumas. And a literary shelf with *White Teeth* by Zadie Smith, *The Crimson Petal and the White* by Michel Faber, and *Jonathan Strange and Mr Norrell* by Susanna Clarke.

She handed her phone to Jack and posed in the middle, smiling saucily at him as he snapped a few photos.

'Okay,' she said, taking her phone back. 'Your turn.'

'Oh, no,' he said. 'Instagram walls aren't really my thing.'

'You have to,' said Clare, planting her feet and glaring up at him. 'I've done all this work.'

Jack rolled his eyes and headed downstairs, coming back up a few minutes later. Unlike Clare, he did not arrange his by any theme or grouping, just stacking books randomly on each of the three shelves. He ended up with one holding *The Wind over Dofida*, *King Lear* and *The Princess Diaries,* one with *The Thursday Murder Club*, *Emma* and *Cloud Atlas*, and one with *The Three-Body Problem*, *Brother of the More*

Famous Jack and *The Secret Diary of Adrian Mole, aged 13¾*.

He stood in the middle, his arms hanging awkwardly by his sides as Clare raised her phone.

'Come on, Jack,' she said. 'You have to give me a little somethin' somethin'.'

He scowled at her, and she held her thumb down, letting it go into burst mode.

'Vogue it,' she yelled. 'You're an animal.'

Jack laughed, covered his face with his hands and dropped them again. 'Can we stop, please?' he said.

'Sure, babes,' said Clare, 'take five. Got to keep the models happy.' She was already flipping through the photos she'd taken to find something suitable. '*Yesss*,' she said. 'Burst mode triumphs again.' She pulled the shot through to an editing app and began adjusting the levels. Jack had been shifting his weight and fidgeting, in self-consciousness, but in that one half-second, he looked relaxed, assured, even a bit teasing. He was standing at a slight angle, his head a bit lowered, looking up and forward from under a slightly furrowed brow, his mouth twisting up at one corner.

Clare found herself smiling as she looked at the photo, tweaking the brightness, bringing the contrast up, the shadows down. Suddenly she felt heat behind her and realized Jack was looking at it over her shoulder. 'Oh, God,' he said, giving a shudder that somehow went through Clare's chest. 'Tell me you're not going to post that.'

Clare turned to face him, keeping her face entirely straight. 'I'm not going to post it,' she said.

Jack narrowed his eyes. 'Liar,' he growled, and Clare found herself feeling a bit light-headed.

She blinked, shook her head clear, and said, 'It's for the shop, Jack. It's for the shop.'

Jack groaned and walked back downstairs. 'Okay,' he said, 'but don't ask me to look.'

Clare gave a sinister cackle and leaned on the bannister as she pulled up Instagram. She posted the two images together with a caption that read, 'Testing out our lush new Instagram wall with a few of our favourite books. What do you think and when are you coming to try it?'

She spent a few moments looking through the posts and stories that had tagged the shop to see if there was anything worth sharing, and when she went back to check the comments, there was one from @LinaJWeddings that made her gasp.

It read: 'How's tomorrow?'

*

'You okay?' Jack called up from downstairs. 'You gasped.'

Clare shushed him and pressed her phone to her ear – she'd immediately gone to call her cousin and the phone was ringing. And ringing.

'Did you see my comment?' said Lina, when she finally picked up.

'Why did you take so long to answer when you know I know you had your phone in your hand?' said Clare. 'What do you mean tomorrow?'

'I'm at the airport,' said Lina. 'You've been out there

on your own for weeks now. I thought you'd like some company.'

'What are you talking about?' said Clare.

'I was going to arrive and surprise you,' said Lina, 'but then I saw your post and couldn't resist the spoiler. Also, I should probably ask if I can stay with you. I can find a hostel or something, but it'd be preferable.'

'It's okay with me, but it might not be okay with *you*,' said Clare. 'Our flat's the size of a postage stamp.'

'*Our* flat?' said Lina.

'Yeah, mine and Jack's, the other person who works here.'

'Oh, hooo, the Henry Golding type from the second photo? And you live with him too? Yes, delicious.'

Clare blushed and turned away from the railing, walking to the back wall. 'Don't be silly,' she said.

'Come on, coz, he looks like the perfect holiday fling.'

'Well, he isn't,' said Clare. 'That's Toby.'

'There's a Toby as well?' said Lina. 'This is the hottest trip you've ever taken.'

'Yeah, you'll meet him, I guess. Lina, are you sure you're not kidding? You're actually coming here?'

'I'm actually coming there. And I cannot wait. I haven't been to a nice tropical paradise where I didn't have to shoot someone's location wedding in literal years.'

Clare felt dazed as she walked downstairs. She was excited to see Lina – they'd always been close, even though Lina was fourteen years older than her. But it felt strange to have someone from home coming to see her here. It felt like a different world, and she felt like a different person. It felt odd that the two parts of her would meet.

She went down to tell Jack about the phone call and check he was okay with Lina staying. 'She'll have to sleep on the couch,' she said, 'but I can put her stuff in my room so there's no clutter.'

'It's fine,' he said. 'I actually think there's some spare bedding in my wardrobe – I'll help you make up the couch tonight.'

'Oh, that's okay—' Clare started to say.

'Don't worry about it,' said Jack. 'It's not a big deal.'

And it wasn't a big deal. It wasn't a big deal that when Jack swatted her with a pillow, she refrained from retaliation because she was afraid of where that might lead. And it wasn't a big deal that when they were tucking a sheet into the back of the couch his fingers brushed hers and sent a jolt through the centre of her. And it wasn't a big deal that when he bent to smooth the covers he looked up at her with that damned twist in his mouth and she felt like she might expire on the spot.

It was a good thing Lina was staying here, Clare thought, as she lay on her bed with her pillow over her face to hide her shame. A loud, overly chatty third wheel was exactly what this situation called for.

*

Lina arrived the next morning, much fresher of face than Clare remembered being on her first day there. She announced her intention of having a nap and demanded to be taken out for dinner that night.

'You'll bring Toby, of course,' she said imperiously. 'I have to know more about him. And bring that slice from the shop too.'

'God, Lina,' said Clare. 'Keep it together. It's just a normal man. An innocent man.'

Lina laughed and collapsed on the couch. 'Away with you,' she said, 'and let a woman snooze.'

Clare was left to wander to the shop with Jack, happy to have Lina there but still confused. 'I don't know how she could have afforded it,' she said to Jack, as they opened the shop. 'Especially last minute. She's usually so careful about money because she never knows how the year's going to go. And that's another thing . . .'

Jack's eyebrow rose as her voice got louder.

'How can she be taking time away now? It's not wedding season yet, but usually she's taking a million meetings with couples at this time of year, trying to convince them to hire her.'

She looked pointedly at Jack, who blinked bemusedly back. 'Hmm,' he said, when it became clear that she wanted an answer. 'Well.'

Clare laughed. 'Sorry,' she said. 'It's just not like her to do something like this, something spontaneous. She plans everything months in advance because she's terrified of missing out on a possible job.'

'That makes sense,' said Jack. 'But I think your time would be better spent interrogating Lina than me.'

Clare scowled at him, and he laughed.

She dashed back to the flat a few times during the day, but Lina was always sleeping soundly on the couch, her quiet snores echoing round the room.

*

By Clare's watch, it was seven p.m. before she got any answers out of Lina.

She'd swanned into the shop just as they were closing, and before Clare could ask her anything, Lina had demanded a tour, wandering up and down every shelf, examining the signs, commenting on what Clare and Jack had on the staff-recommendations table, asking what kinds of books sold best.

Just as she was running out of bookshop-related material to probe Clare about, Toby arrived, responding to Lina's summons as passed on by Clare. That took up more than half an hour, Lina plying him with questions about his life, his friends, his time in Bali, while staring at Clare behind his back whenever she got the opportunity and mouthing, 'Oh, my God.'

Then there was a long debate over where to eat to make the most of both the food and the location, and all in all it wasn't until the waiter had taken their orders that Clare had a chance to plant her hands on the table, glare at her cousin and say, 'What is going on with you?'

Lina grinned, looking a little sheepish but mostly delighted. She flicked her eyes from Toby to Jack, then back to Clare. 'I'm booked up for the next two years,' she said. 'Every weekend from April to October and quite a few others besides.'

'What?' said Clare. 'What the hell happened?' She knew how much Lina had to hustle to keep her schedule full enough to survive. The weddings industry was brutal, the competition was fierce, and Lina spent almost as much time finding work as she did doing it.

Lina was still grinning at her. 'I forgot to bring you a copy,' she said. 'Completely slipped my mind.'

'A copy of what?' Clare almost yelled. She could tell Lina was driving her crazy on purpose.

'*Harper's Bazaar*,' said Lina. 'They did a profile of me.'

Clare's mouth fell open. 'Wha . . .' she said. 'How . . .'

Jack laughed. 'I think,' he said, 'that Clare would like a little more information.'

Clare glared at him. 'Shut up,' she said. 'But, yes, I would.'

'It was just this random thing,' Lina said. 'I shot the wedding of this nice couple. Posh, but I thought they were just normal posh, like private school, skiing holidays posh. But it turned out that they were properly, embarrassingly posh. They don't have titles themselves, but they have relatives and friends who do posh.'

'Holy shit,' said Clare. 'And they hired you?'

'They hired me, and then they sent the photos to *Harper's* for an article about their wedding, and *Harper's* liked them so they wanted to do a full profile, which came out just after you left. And since then I've been inundated with bookings. Everyone wants a piece of me and they're all paying non-refundable deposits. I put up my rates! I hired an assistant! Which is why I can come on holiday for a week or so because she'll set up meetings for when I'm back and I don't have to worry about missing anything.'

Clare was speechless. For as long as she remembered Lina had been worrying about work. When she did take time off, she was always glued to her phone in case an enquiry came through – she didn't want to take too long to reply in case the couple went with another photographer who got back to them faster. She'd been slogging away at her dream job for more than a decade and it was refreshing to see her able to relax a little.

'Lina,' she said, a little choked up, 'I'm so happy for you.'

'*I*'m so happy for me,' said Lina. 'It's bloody taken long enough.'

'It's just so nice to see you get what you deserve,' said Clare. She gave her cousin a hug, and straightened up, wiping a tear from her eye. When she looked up it was to find Jack watching her. He gave a small smile, and looked away again, taking a sip of his water.

Clare heard Lina make a weird noise, a low 'hmmm' sound in her throat. She turned back to her, and Lina raised an eyebrow, angling her head towards Jack. Clare kicked her under the table. That wasn't going to help anything.

During the rest of their dinner, Clare made a point of showering attention on Toby. She flirted with him, and leaned on him, and told Lina about all the beautiful places he'd taken her. 'He comes here every year,' she said, keeping a hand on his shoulder, 'so he's been my Bali guidebook. He's made it a really special trip.'

'I'm sure he has,' said Lina, raising an eyebrow. Jack was leaning back in his chair and saying nothing.

'Yeah,' said Clare, a little too loudly. 'I'm really lucky to have him.'

'Surely not for much longer,' said Jack. 'You must have to go back to Australia soon, right?'

Clare stared at him. Toby took a moment to reply. His eyes flicked from Lina to Jack to Clare. She swallowed guiltily.

'Yeah,' Toby said. 'I guess I'll have to get back to reality next week.'

'Next week?' said Clare. She'd known he would be leaving eventually but not so soon.

'Well, that's a shame,' said Lina, but she was smirking.

'Yes,' said Clare, glaring at her briefly, before turning back to Toby. 'That's a real shame.'

Chapter Nineteen

'I have a proposition,' said Jack, after he and Clare had listened to the fruitless ringing of Simone Adair's phone for the thousandth time.

They had started planning a contingency event, and had teased the date online, describing it as a night to celebrate 'the groundbreaking work of Simone Adair' without giving any details in the hope that they'd still get through to her.

Clare had been keeping an eye on the Reddit thread, and some people definitely seemed interested. She was confident that she and Jack could put on a good event on their own – they could ask Celestina to read and host a discussion on one of the books. It would be a good time.

But she also knew that both she and Jack had let themselves hope for too long that they could actually convince Simone to come, and now anything less would feel like failure.

'Propose away,' she said. 'I mean, proposition away. Which somehow sounds worse.'

'Can I actually tell you my idea, or are you going to spend

the next five minutes on the difference between "propose" and "proposition"?'

Clare made a show of pressing her lips closed between her teeth, widening her eyes in an expression of innocence.

Jack sighed. 'I think,' he said, 'that we should just try to pay her a visit.'

Clare had also been wondering if this was the next step, but something about it felt like crossing a line. 'Isn't it a bit like, I don't know, escalation?' she said. 'Doesn't it make you feel like a stalker? If she won't answer the phone she probably doesn't want us turning up on her doorstep.'

'Trying to,' Jack corrected. 'We don't even know if the address Adam had for her is still right.'

'So, we could just be stalking some random who's moved into her old house.'

'Look,' said Jack, 'we're not getting an answer on the phone. Which means we're not getting a no. So, we can't stop calling because we're both desperate to get a yes.'

'But isn't it a no?' said Clare. 'If she doesn't answer the phone doesn't that mean she wants to be left alone?'

'You don't answer the phone,' said Jack.

'No one rings me,' said Clare. 'If someone's ringing me it's spam because no one actually rings me.'

'Maybe it's the same for Simone.'

Clare was sure she shouldn't be indulging this idea, sure that they should just call it and give up, but it was like Jack had injected a little more air into the balloon of hope still floating around in her chest, and she couldn't resist letting it rise.

'Okay,' she said. 'But you'll have to go alone. We can't

show up unannounced in the evening – and someone needs to look after the shop.'

'I'll look after the shop,' came a voice from upstairs. Lina's head popped over the railing.

'How long have you been up there?' said Clare.

'I came in with you,' said Lina. 'I said I was going to spend the morning reading. I can't believe you forgot I was here. Anyway,' she went on, 'this definitely seems like something the two of you should do. Together.' She winked at Clare, who glared at her. 'I can look after the shop while you do it.'

Jack was grinning at Clare. 'Come on,' he said. 'Or are you giving up?'

*

The address in Adam's book was on the other side of the island so they hired a car for the trip. Clare's heart was racing as they drove past the rice fields. She couldn't stop herself speculating about Simone Adair's house and what it would be like.

Where does a reclusive author live? She pictured a large and intimidating gate with a watchful camera and an intercom that only existed to tell people to go away. She played out the whole short scene: a red eye blinking like HAL, a scratchy voice telling them they were trespassing. And then a long, sad drive home with the beauty of nature grating on them in their despair.

Despair doesn't belong in a place like this, she thought. *That's what Surrey in January is for.*

She didn't say any of this to Jack, who was happily humming along with the radio, a slightly manic sparkle in his eyes. He seemed sure they were doing the right thing, but also a bit like he was talking himself into it so hard there was no room for doubt. His excitement seemed to grow as they got closer, while Clare only felt more and more afraid.

This was a bad idea, she was sure. She wanted to turn and run. She wanted never to arrive. They'd planned their trip carefully – they wanted to arrive no earlier than ten thirty, and no later than eleven. Late enough to be after breakfast, early enough that there was no danger of running into lunch.

They didn't quite make their target – it was ten past eleven when they found the right place and stepped out of the car. And it was nothing like Clare had pictured it. Instead of a great tall fence with an intimidating gate, there was a low fence with mandevilla growing over it, and no gate at all. A stone path led through a garden to a small, unassuming bungalow with a stained-glass front door.

Clare's heart was in her throat as she looked at Jack. He was quieter now that they were here, and paler. But he gave Clare a small nod, stepped up to the door, and gave a quick, decisive knock.

*

Clare expected to wait and wait only for no one to answer, like they had done time and time again when they'd called. Or she expected someone to come to the door furious at the interruption, at the impertinence. What she didn't expect was for a head to pop round the side of the house and say, 'Yes? Can I help you?'

Jack opened his mouth, but no sound came out. He swallowed and tried again but there was only air.

Clare stepped towards the head and said, 'Hi. I'm Clare.

I'm sorry to interrupt you, but we're looking for Ms Adair. Simone.'

The head smiled and a body came around the corner to join it. 'I'm Simone,' she said, walking forward with her hand outstretched. 'What can I do for you?'

She was a tiny woman, even shorter than Clare, dressed in grass-stained trousers, holding gardening gloves in one hand. Her hair was in a neat bob, mostly grey but with a few sudden streaks of orange.

'Oh, my God,' said Clare. 'It's such an honour to meet you. This is Jack, by the way. He'll probably regain his voice soon. We're both such fans of your work. Especially him. You're his absolute favourite author.'

'You've read my books?' said Simone. 'How delightful. Thank you very much.'

'Love . . .' gasped Jack '. . . love them.' He tried for something else but then contented himself with nodding fervently.

'The thing is,' said Clare, 'we work at a bookshop. At Seashore Books.'

'Oh, I used to love that place,' said Simone. 'For some reason I thought it had closed down.'

'Not yet,' said Clare, 'although we're afraid it might. We're hoping you can help with that.'

Simone gave a small frown. 'Well, I'm not sure what use I'd be, but why don't you come through? We'll have a cup of tea and you can explain it to me.'

The little house was very full but neatly organized. There were bursting bookshelves all over the place, art wherever it would fit, colour crammed into every spare inch. Simone led them through to the kitchen, then out onto a small deck that looked over an exquisite garden, which sloped away, down towards the distant ocean.

They settled down with their mugs, and Simone said, 'Now, what did you want to ask me?'

Clare glanced at Jack, who still seemed overwhelmed, and turned back to Simone. 'I'm sorry again for turning up unannounced,' she said. 'We've actually been trying to call you, but we couldn't get an answer, so coming here was sort of a last-ditch effort.'

'Oh, yes. I should plug my phone back in. I knew I'd forgotten something.'

Clare stared at her.

'Sorry, yes, sometimes when my phone rings and I don't want to answer it, I just unplug it from the wall. I always mean to plug it back in again, but . . .' She gave a shrug. 'But I am sorry if you've been trying so hard to get in touch with me. It is the one downside.'

'Oh, that's okay,' said Clare. 'It's really very impertinent of us to be doing this at all. But, well, we wanted to ask if you'd be willing to do an event with us. At Seashore. A reading or a signing . . . anything really. I know you were asked to do an appearance there some time ago and you weren't interested, but we were hoping that maybe you feel differently now.'

'Yes, I remember that,' said Simone. 'My husband had died a couple of years beforehand, and I'd stopped doing events. Stopped writing. Didn't think I'd ever want to start again. When that nice man – Andrew was it? – approached me it just felt, I don't know, like a completely alien request.

Something that had belonged to my previous life – it didn't make sense in my new one.'

'We understand,' said Clare. 'If that's not something you want to return to, we get it.'

'It does feel strange,' said Simone, 'but not as strange as it did back then. And, after all, I did start writing again.'

Jack let out a strangled sound.

Simone's eyes twinkled. 'Well, I won't say any more about that,' she said. 'I don't want to kill him.'

Clare laughed. 'If you were willing to consider it,' she said, 'you'd really be making our day. We think we could get quite a lot of people to come, and we could sell your books. Also, it would give us a boost online, help spread the word about the shop.'

'That seems wildly optimistic,' said Simone. She looked out over the lush green of her garden. 'Do you know?' she said eventually. 'I always hated gardening.'

Clare stared. 'But all this . . .' she said.

'My mother-in-law's,' said Simone. 'We moved here to take care of her when she got sick. I felt so helpless and small. Looking after her garden felt like the one real tangible thing I could do. And then she died, and then my husband died, and I kept going just to be busy. It became a routine and then it became a solace. Gardening doesn't flick you on the raw the way that writing does.'

She gave a laugh. 'You'd think, wouldn't you, that if you got a rave review in the *New York Times*, a little spiteful hatchet job in some small-town gazette wouldn't hurt you? But it does. It always does. To this day I remember almost every word of it, but the positive reviews are just' – she waved a hand in the air – 'gone.'

'But so many people love your work,' said Jack suddenly, fervently.

'Hmm,' she said. 'Maybe. But maybe that's not enough. When I started writing again it was like a compulsion. I didn't want to, I just couldn't stop myself. But even then it was only because I knew I would never try to publish it.'

Jack's hand shot out and gripped Clare's arm. 'Ow,' she said, turning to glare at him. He let go and grabbed the arm of his chair instead.

Clare took a sip of her tea. 'I have to confess something,' she said. 'I'd never heard of you before a couple of months ago.'

Simone chuckled. 'That doesn't surprise me. It's been years since anyone's cared about my books.'

Clare leaned forward. 'That's the thing. I overheard Jack recommending one to a customer. I'd never heard him talk about something with that much passion. Or with any emotion at all, to be honest. So I read it and I loved it, of course. And it seemed so strange to me that these books could exist and I wouldn't have heard of them. It seemed like they should be everywhere, that people everywhere should have read and loved them. And then I found out that they do.' She pulled out her phone and opened Reddit. 'This is a forum for fans of your books,' she said, passing it to Simone. 'It has more than two hundred thousand members.'

Simone didn't reply. She scrolled silently through the page.

'Did you know that every year for the past fifteen years,' Clare went on, 'a group of fans come to Bali just to celebrate your work? They throw parties and read passages aloud to each other on the beach. They'll be here in a couple of weeks, more of them than ever, to celebrate the thirtieth anniversary of *Dofida*. That's why we want you. It's not a question of whether people still care about your books,' she said. 'This is a way to thank the ones who do. For turning up for you, year after year.'

There was a long silence. Simone took a deep breath. 'I don't know,' she said. 'I'm afraid I . . . I don't know . . .'

'That's okay,' said Clare, quickly. 'I know it's a lot to ask. But will you think about it? Take your time. Just . . . it would mean a lot to people. To a lot of people.'

She looked at Jack, and he nodded. They stood up to leave. Simone was silent as she walked them back through the house to the front door.

Clare started walking down the path to the car, but noticed Jack wasn't with her. She turned back to see him holding out a hand to Simone. 'In case you decide to say no,' he said, 'in case I don't get another chance, your book kind of changed my life.'

He looked down, as if gathering himself. 'I was having a rough time. My brother was away at college, my dad was working a lot. I was starting to grow apart from my friends. I didn't know it at the time, but I was really lonely and I didn't know how to fix it. Teenage boys don't, you know. I didn't like going home when there was no one else in the house, so I started staying in the school library to do my homework. And one day someone had left a copy of *A Wind over Dofida* on one of the tables.'

Clare was practically holding her breath as she listened to

him. They'd talked so much about that book, and she'd never thought to ask him why he loved it so much. How he'd discovered it.

'I picked it up and started reading it and . . . I didn't stop,' Jack said. 'I loved it so much I bought a copy and sent it to my brother. He read it and called me that weekend to talk about it. We started doing that a lot. It hadn't even occurred to me that he'd want to. I went away to college the next year and added a literature class just to make sure I kept reading fiction while I studied, so we could still have those phone calls.'

He swallowed and took an unsteady breath. 'I'm so grateful to you,' he said. 'It means a lot to be able to tell you that. To have an opportunity to tell you that part of who I am is because of you.'

'I—' said Simone. There were tears in her eyes. 'Thank you,' she said. 'Thank you.' She waved to Clare and walked back inside her house.

*

Clare drove on the way back, letting Jack gaze silently out of the window. When they got back to the shop, he walked wordlessly to the till and sat down beside it.

Lina stared from him to Clare, mouthing at her, 'Is he okay?'

Clare shrugged.

Lina dragged her to the other side of the shop, pretending she needed help restocking some books. 'What the hell happened?' she whispered.

Clare gave her a rough outline of their visit.

'Aw,' she said, 'poor boy. It is kind of adorable, though. You know,' she went on, dropping her head to the side and peering at Clare, 'I can't imagine Toby being that overcome by meeting his favourite author.'

'Will you stop?' said Clare.

'I can't imagine Toby having a favourite author, actually,' said Lina.

'You are a snob.'

'I'm not! There's nothing wrong with not having a favourite author, I just think that, for example, someone like you might be happier with someone who does.'

'Lina!' Clare said, and walked back across the shop. She heard her cousin chuckling behind her as she went.

Jack was still sitting at the till, but he had his phone in his hand and was staring at it as if he'd never seen it before.

'Everything okay?' said Clare.

He shook his head as if to clear it. 'Yeah,' he said. 'I just got a text.'

Clare stepped forward eagerly. 'From Simone?' she said.

'No,' said Jack. 'From my brother. He's coming here. He's coming to visit.'

Chapter Twenty

Fortunately Ben had no intention of staying with Jack in their tiny flat. He had booked a room at the Four Seasons.

'The Four Seasons?' said Clare, when Jack told her. 'I didn't think anyone actually stayed in places like that.'

'Clare,' said Jack, an amused glint in his eyes. 'How did you imagine they kept operating if no one stayed there?'

'Oh, you know what I mean,' said Clare. 'I mean, like, real people. Ordinary people. People other than, I don't know, Paris Hilton.'

'I would imagine Paris Hilton stays at the Hilton.'

'Shut up,' she said. 'Is it weird that he's coming here? You seemed surprised about it.'

'No,' said Jack, slowly. 'He does this. He's spontaneous. Like Lina, I guess. Or unlike her, but like her this one time. And he did say he'd come over at some point while I was here. He said he wanted to see me working in a shop.'

'What's so weird about that?' said Clare. 'Hasn't he ever worked retail?'

'No,' said Jack. 'Neither had I.'

'What, not ever? Not even when you were at uni?'

'No, our parents always said it was important to be able to focus on our studies.'

'But how did you pay for things?' She stared at him, and then understanding slipped into her brain. He was rich. His parents were rich.

'Oooh,' she said slowly. 'Wow.'

'What?' he said. 'Don't be weird.'

'I'm not weird,' she said. 'I'm normal.'

'You,' he said, 'inherited enough money to travel the globe for two years on a whim.'

'Only because I was very unwise with that money,' she said. 'I used it all up doing that. And I was travelling on a shoestring, staying in hostels and working in bars to help it go further. Just like I worked in retail while I was studying so I could buy clothes and food and beer because that's what you do.' She put a hand on his shoulder and looked at him in mock-sympathy. 'That's what normal people do.'

'I'm working retail now,' he said, laughing ruefully. 'Does that count?'

She shook her head mutely at him. 'I bet you didn't even have to take out student loans,' she said.

'What's the point of taking out a massive loan when—'

'When your parents can just pay for it?' Clare finished for him. 'And presumably also give you an allowance while you're there?'

She picked up a stack of books and carried them away to shelve, still shaking her head in astonishment. And then she thought of another thing.

'Wait,' she said, poking her head out from behind the shelf, 'you did a master's. Did your parents . . .?'

Jack's face was scarlet.

Clare slid back behind the shelf. 'Unbelievable,' she said. 'You think you know a guy.'

*

It wasn't until a couple of days after Ben arrived that Clare got to meet him. Jack had told her he was keen to see some of the island first – it was his first time visiting since he and Jack had been there as kids and he wanted to see the places he remembered.

Clare covered the shop for a few days to let Jack make the most of it, like Jack had done for her during Lina's first few days in town.

Jack's order of *Melmoth* came in and, to her surprise, Clare found he'd ordered a few extra books as well. He was slowly beginning to reconcile himself to spending money on the shop – she suspected only partly because business was picking up a bit. *He knows I'm right*, she thought. *He doesn't like to admit it, but he listens to me.*

Clare let the previous book-club members know what the next book was going to be and that copies were ready to be picked up in the shop. Siti preferred reading on her ereader, but Valarie came in for one the next day, and a couple of days after that Lauren and Joyo came in together.

Clare was surprised but she tried not to show it. They were chatting to each other with much more familiarity than you would expect after just an hour spent talking about a book, and when they came to the till with their copies, Joyo insisted on paying for all three. Clare smiled to herself but said nothing.

Towards the end of the week, Jack showed up again, his brother in tow. The two of them came into the shop, looking windswept and salty.

Ben was a bit of a surprise. He was several inches taller than Jack, and looser, somehow. The kind of person who gives the impression that they chew gum a lot, even if they don't. 'So, this is your little shop,' he said to Jack, as he walked through the shelves.

'What were you expecting? Macy's?' said Jack.

'It's not bad, though, is it? Good light, nice spacing. Quaint little signs, very cute.'

'The signs were all Clare's work,' said Jack.

Ben spun around to see Clare sitting by the till. 'Yes,' he said. 'Clare, right, Clare. Yes.' He glanced at Jack, raising an eyebrow, before walking over to her, a hand stretched out, his mouth curving up at one side the same way Jack's always did.

It made Clare smile, to see the family resemblance.

*

After closing the shop, Clare came home to find Jack sitting on the floor, already in pyjama trousers and a T-shirt, bending over a large piece of leather. He looked up at her as she came in.

'I brought some home to practise,' he said. 'I'm still not very good at the stitching.'

'Oh,' she said. 'Is it okay if I . . .' She waved a hand at the couch. 'I was going to read.'

'Sure,' he said. 'But don't watch. It'll put me off.'

'Of course,' said Clare, sitting on the couch and thinking, *He'd better hope this is a bloody good book.*

Jack returned to his leather, bending over it with what looked like a screwdriver.

'What is that?' said Clare. 'I promise I'm not watching. But what is that?'

Jack looked at the tool in his hand. 'I, ah,' he said, 'I bought my own awl.'

'I see,' said Clare. 'Very good.' She opened the book, flicking slowly through the pages, her eyes drawn back to Jack again and again.

The muscles in his forearms twisted as he worked the awl through the leather. He kept brushing a hand against the hair that was falling gently into his eyes. Clare couldn't tell if he was eyeballing the holes very precisely or if he'd marked them out in a way she couldn't see from where she was sitting, but he was extremely focused as he lined up each hole and punched it through.

Eventually he laid down the awl and moved back to lean against the wall, looking up at Clare as he moved. She snapped her eyes to her book and casually turned a page. When she glanced back at him, he had a large needle in his hand, threaded with a thin leather thong. He was passing it through the holes in a pattern – two diagonal stitches one way, another passing over them.

She peered at him, fascinated. He was taking this very seriously. Like he did with everything. He always wanted to be sure he was doing the best possible thing in every circumstance, choosing the best possible option. He made every stitch slowly, passing the leather through his fingers to be sure that when it was pulled tight it would be laid flat and perfect against the surface.

She found herself entirely captivated by him: his eyes, down and clear, focusing all his attention on his work. His hands, strong and capable, turning the leather, moving with careful precision, guiding the needle home, then with swift vigour, pulling the leather tight.

Out of nowhere Clare saw those hands pressed on her skin. Curling in her hair, grazing her waist, pressing into—

He glanced up at her and caught her watching. 'What?' he said. Then, 'You said you wouldn't look.'

'Sorry,' Clare said, smiling and red-cheeked. She cleared her throat. 'You're really good at that,' she said.

'No,' he said. 'I'm not. Stop watching.'

She wanted to tell him that she wouldn't stop, that she couldn't. That there was something about watching him absorbed in his work that tugged at her. That turning away when she could be seeing him felt like a tragic waste of time.

And they didn't have any time to spare.

'I—' she began.

The door crashed open. Lina walked in, a beatific smile on her face. 'Lads, I just had the best spa day. I've never been so relaxed.' She plopped down on the couch beside Clare. 'What are you guys up to? Jack, what's that?'

'It's nothing,' he said. 'Just a hobby.'

'Jack's been learning leatherwork,' said Clare, a bit too enthusiastically. 'He's really good at it.'

Lina arched an eyebrow at Clare. 'I bet he is,' she said.

Clare stared at her pointedly and stood. 'I'm going to bed,' she said.

'Yeah,' said Jack, 'me too.'

'Kids, I'm already asleep,' said Lina, stretching out into the space Clare had just left and beginning to snore lightly and fakely.

On the other side of her door, Clare gave herself a shake. *Get it together*, she said to herself.

This was starting to get ridiculous.

*

Toby took Clare sailing the day before he left. She had been surprised when he'd announced he was leaving at dinner a few days earlier, but now she thought about it, he'd been around for much longer than he'd initially said he would be.

'Weren't you meant to leave a while ago?' she asked.

'Yeah,' he said. 'Seemed like a good idea to extend the trip. The place has had a couple more attractions than normal.' He held her gaze.

'Oh,' said Clare. 'Okay.' She felt guilty. She'd enjoyed Toby's company, but she hadn't really thought about him that much. She knew neither of them had expected their relationship to be more than a holiday fling, but she hadn't known she was important enough to Toby that he'd extended his trip for her. And she knew she wouldn't have done the same.

She looked back at the island, the wind whipping her hair into her face. 'You won't be here for Simone's event,' she said sadly. 'I'd always pictured you there.'

'In the background, right?' he said. He was smiling, a little sadly.

She twisted her mouth at the truth of his words. 'Sorry,' she said.

'Don't be,' said Toby. 'Look, the way I see it, there are always going to be opportunities to make things a little more fun in life. Maybe those things will last for ages. Or maybe they'll just be around for a bit. You've got to take them, right? And enjoy them for however long they are around. Even if they're hard to let go of.'

Clare blushed. 'I don't think I'll be that hard for you to let go of,' she said.

'Yeah, well,' said Toby. 'I wasn't entirely talking about me.' Clare stared at him. He gave a rueful smile. 'I think your cousin would know what I mean.'

'Oh,' said Clare. 'Don't worry about Lina. She just says what she wants to say even if it's not at all based in reality.'

'Hmm,' said Toby, then fell silent for a while. 'Did you know you have a really expressive face?' he said eventually. 'You should maybe be aware that you have a really expressive face.'

'Oh,' said Clare. Had the connection between her and Jack been that obvious? 'Oh, God. I – I'm sorry.'

Toby laughed. 'Want a beer?' he said.

'Only if you don't have anything stronger,' said Clare.

'Sorry,' he said, and tossed her a can. They sat together on the deck for a while. The sea around them sparkled under the hot sun, but Clare felt somehow cold.

'It's been fun hanging around with you, Clare,' said Toby.

'You too,' said Clare. She held out her can and they gently cheersed each other.

'What are you going to do now?' he asked.

'I don't know,' said Clare. 'I'm going home in a month.'

'Hmm,' said Toby. 'Seems like it could be a pretty great month.'

Chapter Twenty-one

Clare was alone in the shop when Simone Adair came in. Jack and Ben had gone off hiking together, and Lina was out shopping.

It had been a busy morning, with a lot of customers trying to find very specific books they didn't know how to describe. Clare had just finished dealing with someone desperate to find a book that 'I think has a house on the cover?' and was enjoying a brief moment of respite. She smiled as she realized how much rarer those moments had become. When she heard the door open, she was almost a bit annoyed, but when she saw who it was, she leaped out of her chair.

'Simone!' she said. 'Hello! It's so nice to see you! Hi!'

'Hi,' said Simone, laughing a little. 'It does look lovely in here,' she said.

'Thank you,' said Clare. 'It was a bit, um, under the weather when we started, but we've tried to bring it back to health.'

'I suppose that up there is where you do events,' she said.

'Yes,' said Clare, eagerly. 'Well, there are books up there too, but we wanted to keep some space for people to sit and read and stuff, and, yes, also things like our book club and, you know,' she cleared her throat, 'any other, um, things we might want to, um, do.'

Simone twinkled at her. 'Yes,' she said, 'about that—'

'No!' Clare yelled. 'Sorry,' she said, 'but Jack's not here. You can't tell me when Jack's not here.' She looked around hopelessly for a moment.

'Oh,' said Simone. 'Is he due back soon?'

'Noooo,' Clare wailed. 'He's off hiking. For the whole day! Would you . . . that is, can we . . . would it be okay if we called him?'

Simone smiled. 'Yes, I think so,' she said.

Clare nodded distractedly, nervously. 'Okay, okay,' she said. 'Thank you. Thank you so much.' She felt a frantic sob rising in her throat as she pulled out her phone. She set it on the counter while it rang and put it on speakerphone.

Eventually Jack's voice came crackling out. 'Clare,' he said. 'Is everything okay?'

'Jack!' she said. 'Everything's fine. Simone's here.'

'What was that?' he said. 'The reception here is terrible. I can't hear you.'

'Simone's here,' Clare yelled. 'In the shop. Simone.'

There was no reply, just crackling on the line. Then, 'Is that . . . Simone's there? Did I hear that right?'

'Hello, Jack,' said Simone.

Garbled yelling came through the phone. 'Jack,' said Clare, 'Jack, can you hear us?'

'Yes,' he said. 'Sorry, I . . . had to tell Ben, carry on.'

'Jack,' said Simone, 'I just wanted to come into the shop and tell you and Clare that I've decided I will do this event you're planning.'

There was crackly silence again and then Jack's voice came through again: 'Are you sure?' he said. 'Are you sure you want to?'

'I'm sure,' said Simone. 'But I can't promise to stay out all night. I like my sleep.'

'No,' said Jack. 'Yes, of course. Yes. No. Oh, my God. Yes. Thank you. Thank you so much.'

Clare heard a sound in the background that she was sure was Ben whooping. Jack was still talking but the static was getting in the way.

'Jack, you're dropping out,' said Clare. There were more garbled crackles. 'I'll talk to you later,' she said, and hung up. She gazed at Simone, grinning all over her face. 'I promise,' she said, 'we'll make it as easy and lovely for you as we can. Anything you need, just let us know.'

'Well, thank you, but I'm sure I'll be fine. I did so many readings back in the day, I'm sure it'll come back to me. Like riding a bike. Is there anything you need from me to promote it?'

'Oh, no,' said Clare. 'We'll take care of all— Wait. There is one thing, if you don't mind. It'll be super-quick.'

'What – now?' said Simone.

'Is that okay? I just want to take a photo for Instagram.'

'Oh, God,' said Simone. 'I always hated having my photo taken. But if you must.'

'Thank you,' said Clare. 'We'll do it upstairs. Luckily, we

just got a bunch of your books in. If you'd come last week we would've had none – they keep selling out.'

She stacked Simone's books on the floating shelves and took a bunch of quick photos. She let Simone pick her favourite before she left, then gave it a few tweaks before uploading it to Instagram. She hit post and leaned back against the wall, a blissful smile on her face.

*

Jack and Ben didn't make it back for more than two hours. Clare was finishing up a sale when they burst through the door.

'Drinks!' Ben yelled. 'Celebrate!'

'Has she gone?' said Jack. 'Is she still here?'

Clare looked at them, bemused. After Simone had left, the shop had picked up again: she'd been dealing with non-stop customers all afternoon and hadn't had a chance to think any more about Simone, although the beatific smile had stayed put on her face. 'Yes, Jack, she's gone. She's been gone for ages.'

'We came straight here!' he said.

'Bro, we were at the top of a mountain,' said Ben. 'Took us a minute, didn't it?'

Jack let out a sigh. 'Yeah,' he said. 'I just thought . . .'

Clare giggled. 'But she'll be back,' she said. 'She's coming back. Because she said yes!'

'She said yes!' said Jack, perking up.

'She said yes!' said Ben. 'So we get drinks! Drinks! Drinks!'

He was striding around pumping both his fists in the air when Lina walked through the door.

'Good Lord,' she said. 'I thought you were supposed to be quiet in bookshops.'

'That's libraries,' said Ben. 'Besides we're celebrating. Drinks!'

'Lina, she said yes,' said Clare, running forward to meet her cousin. 'Simone Adair said yes to our event.'

Jack was standing beside her, nodding his head endlessly in silence.

'Well, look at that,' said Lina. 'And look at the two of you. A pair of absolute buffoons.'

'Hey!' said Clare. 'We're excited!'

'And so you should be,' said Lina. 'Well done, kids. Well done. And this idiot's right. We need to go out and celebrate.'

Ben insisted on taking them to the fanciest bar he could find, insisting that the night was on him when Lina and Clare balked at the prices. And when Clare, embarrassed to be letting him treat them, meekly asked for a house wine, he cut her off with 'Silence!' before turning to the bartender and saying, 'The lady will have your fanciest cocktail, please, and thank you.'

He looked to Lina, an eyebrow cocked.

'Oh,' Lina said. 'I will absolutely have the fanciest cocktail too.'

Ben turned to Jack, who shrugged and said, 'I don't want to be left out.'

'Right,' said Ben, turning back to the bartender, 'that's three of your fanciest cocktails and one very manly whisky, neat—'

Clare involuntarily cried out, 'Oh, come on!' and Ben gave her a steely glance.

'Fine,' he said. 'Four fancy cocktails, thank you so much.'
He spun his finger imperiously in the air and ushered them
all out to a table overlooking the ocean.

The night sparkled around them. Every joke was hilari-
ous, every drink more delicious than the one that came
before. Clare couldn't stop smiling, and she found herself,
every so often, having to glance at Jack to check that it was
real, that they'd done it.

'We'll have to talk about arrangements,' said Clare. 'We
should ask Celestina who we should go to for food—'

'Yes, and we have to make a formal announcement, con-
firm the date and time. I wonder if we should ask people to
sign up so we know how many to—'

'Oh!' said Clare. 'I haven't checked Instagram! I posted
but the shop got so busy . . .'

She pulled out her phone and brought up the post. It had
gone wild. There were hundreds of comments, many of them
just strings of exclamation points or scream emojis. One
read, *That's it, I'm booking flights, screw my sister's wedding.* Another said, *Find me camped out at Seashore Books
for the next three weeks.*

Clare's grin spread wider and wider as she scrolled. She
looked up at Jack, who was beaming back at her.

'No phones!' Lina yelled suddenly. 'We are at too fancy a
place to waste it on our phones.'

'What are you two mooning over anyway?' said Ben, pulling Clare's phone out of her hand. 'Holy shit,' he said. 'There
are twenty-three thousand likes on this post. This lady must
be a big deal.'

'Yeah,' said Clare. 'That's why we're celebrating.'

'No, yeah,' said Ben. 'But, like, I thought we were celebrating because you guys wanted it so much. I didn't know she was actually, I mean, properly famous.'

'Ben, I've been telling you about her for at least ten years,' said Jack.

'Yeah, but, bro, you also spent ten years telling me about why grass-type Pokémon make the best starters.'

'Wow,' said Jack. 'You really just said that. In front of everyone.'

'I sure did,' said Ben, smirking at Jack. 'But actually, for real, well done. Proud of you, man.'

He clinked his glass against Jack's and took a swig. 'You too, Clare,' he said. 'But there's less of a long-term emotional connection. You get it, you understand.'

Clare laughed and slid her phone back into her pocket. 'That's fair,' she said. 'I'm happy with that.'

'It was all Clare, though,' said Jack. 'When we asked Simone, it was all Clare. I could barely talk I was so nervous, and she was all . . .' he waved a hand drunkenly through the air '. . . eloquent. And shit.'

Ben stood up, holding his third or fourth fanciest cocktail aloft. 'To Clare!' he cried. 'All eloquent and shit!'

Everyone cheered and raised their glasses, a little more sloppy than they had been a couple of hours earlier.

'But if it weren't for Jack, we would never have got to talk to her at all,' said Clare. 'I would never have just' – she waved her glass, the liquid inside sloshing around – 'gone to her house like that.'

Lina stuck her glass into the air. 'To Jack!' she said. 'Just going to her house like that!'

Everyone cheered and raised their glasses again, and Clare flopped back in her seat, feeling giddy and content.

She looked over at Jack, and he was looking back at her, a glow in his eyes. Suddenly, she was extremely grateful that they were out with Lina and Ben. She wasn't sure what would have happened if she was celebrating this moment with Jack alone.

No, actually. She was sure. She just wasn't sure she could handle it.

Flustered, she put down her empty glass and stood up. She grabbed Ben's shoulder and looked intently into his eyes.

'Dancing,' she said.

He turned to face her and gripped her shoulder in return, his jaw clenched in fervour. 'Dancing,' he said.

*

The four of them took to the dance floor together, and Clare felt the fun of it fizzing inside her chest.

Ben danced with such determined abandon that the rest of them – and a few other random club-goers – couldn't help but follow along. For a while it was all noise and chaos, bass pumping through Clare's veins, people passing around her.

Then, without being sure how it happened, she found herself in Jack's arms, sweaty and exhilarated, battered on all sides by other bodies.

Clare's heart rate slowed as she looked up at him. He smiled softly, and unexpectedly twirled her away from him, and back in. She laughed as she spun under his arm, and back again, her feet moving against his.

He said something but she couldn't hear him over the noise.

'What?' she shouted back. He shook his head and looked around, then pointed at the door. She nodded, but as they went to move, a body crashed into hers. It was Lina.

Lina laughed, and then Ben was there too, grabbing his brother's shoulder and it was the four of them again and the moment was gone.

*

No one wanted to look at the time as they happily stumbled towards home.

Lina dashed into an all-hours corner shop to buy them each a one litre bottle of water, and stood in front of them like a drill sergeant forcing them to down them – if drill sergeants yelled, 'Skull! Skull!' when they were trying to hydrate the troops.

Clare still had a blissful glow coursing through her, even as she could feel the impending hangover. She walked slowly along, happy, and happily conscious of Jack walking a couple of metres behind her, with Lina and Ben in between.

'I can't believe we all just let you pay for that,' Lina was saying to Ben.

''S no big deal,' he said. 'I have to get used to covering that one's nights out. If we're to keep having them in the manner to which I have become accustomed.' He turned to yell over his shoulder, 'Isn't that right, bro?'

Clare, from the front of the group, heard Jack yell, 'What?' in response.

Ben yelled back, 'You're going to be on that non-profit salary when you get back. You'll only be able to afford the twelfth fanciest cocktails.'

Lina laughed and changed the subject. But Clare's mind was racing. Non-profit salary? That was not what Jack had told her. She wanted to ask him about it, but Lina and Ben had started arguing about the lyrics to 'Alien Superstar' and she didn't know how to manoeuvre the conversation back around. And by the time Ben had peeled off to go to his hotel and the rest were back in the tiny flat, she was too exhausted and drunk to think straight.

Lina headed straight to the bathroom, and Clare looked at Jack. His eyes were almost closed, and he was moving a little, dancing to some song playing in his head. Clare laughed, and he looked over at her and beckoned.

She shook her head, and he moved towards her, shuffling his feet rhythmically on the floor. He took her hand and pulled her into his chest, bringing a hand to the small of her back as he moved.

Clare moved with him, feeling the heat of him spread into her, pooling in her belly. Jack was nuzzling the side of her neck, making happy, sleepy noises. At first Clare thought they were just that, but then she caught a couple of words.

'Mmm,' he said. 'Now gone . . . maybe want me . . .'

'What?' she said.

'. . . glad he's gone, though . . .' he said. 'I'm . . . me . . . my turn . . .'

'Jack,' Clare said. 'What are you saying?'

He stepped back from her, bumping into the couch. 'Oh!' he said, and sat down suddenly. 'Yes,' he said. 'Need to.'

He keeled over sideways, then turned onto his back, stretching out on the couch. Clare leaned over him.

'Jack,' she said. 'What were you talking about?'

Jack's eyes were closed, and he mumbled something she couldn't make out. Then he said, 'Clare!' and raised his head a little.

'What?' said Clare. 'I'm here.'

His eyes opened, unfocused. 'Oh, good,' he said. 'Yes, you're supposed to be here.' His head fell back again, and his breathing deepened.

Lina came out of the bathroom. 'Fussake,' she said. ''S my bed.'

She wandered into Clare's room and tumbled onto her bed instead.

'There'd better be room for me too,' said Clare, following her. She grabbed a pillow and squeezed in beside her cousin, her mind still very much on the couch with Jack.

Chapter Twenty-two

Jack and Clare trudged to the shop the next morning to find a parcel on the doorstep, with three takeaway cups of coffee on top. They opened the package to find three bottles of Lucozade, a packet of ibuprofen, and three greasy and delicious-looking breakfast sandwiches.

'Did Ben send us a care package?' said Clare. 'That's so sweet.'

'This means he's not leaving his hotel room all day,' said Jack. 'Lucky bastard.' He groaned and ran a hand over his eyes.

Clare couldn't face carrying Lina's to the flat, so she just texted her saying, *Breakfast*, and a few minutes later Lina stumbled in.

She grabbed the waxed-paper-wrapped sandwich and pressed it to her face, breathing in the smell. 'Mmm-mmm,' she said. 'Yes.'

The three of them hunkered in the bookshop, moving in slow motion, playing gentle, comforting music and, despite the hangovers, passed a pleasant morning.

It wasn't until lunchtime that Clare was reminded of Ben's

comment from the night before. He'd sent another care package at around one o'clock – this one containing three cartons of *mie goreng*, three brownies, with more coffee and Lucozade.

There was a lull in customers, so they sat outside to eat together, backs against the window. They'd been eating in companionable silence for a while when Lina said, 'So, what's the job you're going back to? Ben said something about non-profit.'

Clare froze, her eyes growing wide. She was desperate to hear Jack's answer, but she didn't want to show it. She realized she was holding her breath and tried to start breathing again in a way that seemed natural.

'Yeah,' said Jack. 'A place I did an internship with last year offered me a business consultancy role – I'll be giving struggling businesses advice on how to turn things around. Places that are facing forced acquisitions or bankruptcy. Trying to establish whether there's a way for them to remain independent, and if not, finding a good franchise fit that won't force them to become something new entirely. Often it's personality matching as much as financial support.'

Clare could hear Lina responding but her voice seemed to be coming from very far away. Her heart was thumping, and she could feel a smile crawling onto her face. He wasn't a corporate stooge! He was working for a charity! He was going to be helping people like Adam, not ripping their businesses from them.

All of a sudden she felt she'd been unfair ever to have expected otherwise. Of course Jack was going to work for a non-profit. Of course he was going to be helping people.

Even if he'd interned with companies like Bellwether Holdings, he'd never work for one. Not Jack, not *her* Jack.

Her Jack.

Hers.

She turned to look at him as he sat chatting with Lina. She took in every detail. That hair, now so much longer and softer, all sexily rumpled. The way he waved his hand around when he was looking for the right word to say. The way he thought so hard about how to phrase something, like he was worried he wouldn't express himself clearly. The way his mouth curved up at the side, the way Clare had hated at the beginning, thinking it meant he was judging her. But now she knew it meant . . . something else.

She thought about that moment in the flat last night. He'd talked about someone wanting him. Did he mean her? Was he hoping something would happen between them now that Toby had gone? There had been so many moments between them, so many almost moments. And that kiss, that one kiss that she'd never been able to scrub from her mind, although she'd tried so hard to.

She'd been holding all this at arm's length for so long. It was a relief to sit there in the sun letting it all in, letting it slip down her consciousness like honey.

Her Jack.

Jack noticed she was watching him and turned, a question in his eyes. She smiled slightly, tipped her Lucozade to him, and stood up, taking the remnants of her lunch inside to throw away.

*

Clare didn't say anything to Jack about his job. She didn't want to remind him of how stupid she'd been when they'd found the memo from Bellwether Holdings. She'd known at the time she was being unreasonable, but in retrospect, it all seemed so much worse. She'd been so afraid of him seeing her as just some shallow, useless idiot that she'd gone on the attack without thinking and she didn't know how to explain herself now.

Well. There were other things to think about. There was only a week left until Simone's event and they were both in full planning mode. They'd set up an event page for people to register, and more than a hundred guests already had.

Already people were coming in to ask if it was true that Simone Adair would actually be there in person, some of whom insisted on taking selfies with Clare and Jack, which they then posted to Reddit, saying things like, *I talked to the staff, it's really happening.*

There was a special Simone Adair book club scheduled for a couple of days before the main event, with one of her lesser-known books, *And the Rest Was Dust*. They hadn't asked people to register but they were banking on there being more than their usual six or seven attendees, so there was a bit of organizing to do for that as well.

Clare and Jack were operating at a constant low level of excitement that was playing havoc with their emotions. Clare found herself in tears when a customer complimented the shop. Jack welled up when Clare made him a cup of tea. They were both laughing manically at anything even remotely resembling a joke.

Their conversation often devolved into debates about

what kind of food to get and how much they could afford to spend on drinks. Whether there should be an interview segment at the event and who should host it if there was. How many books they needed to order and whether they could safely assume that people would bring their own copies.

Clare and Jack were so focused on it that they barely noticed when Ben and Lina went home. Clare was sad that they wouldn't be there on the night, but part of her preferred it that way. This felt special. Personal. It belonged to her and Jack. As much fun as it would have been to have Lina and Ben there, neither of them would really have understood.

It suited Clare as well to have so much work to do, so many little decisions to make. It all took up the space in her mind that would otherwise have been left for the one big decision that really mattered. She'd let herself acknowledge that she was falling for Jack. But she didn't know if she was ready to act on that feeling. If she was ready to tell him about it.

It was, of course, always anxiety-inducing to have feelings for someone and not know if they felt the same way. She knew Jack felt *something* for her: she wasn't the only one who was suddenly overcome with blushes if they were caught looking at one another for too long, and she wasn't the only one who grew still for a moment whenever they touched.

And there was that kiss . . .

But that could just be physical. It could all just be desire. It could just be the curiosity of living and working so closely with someone for so long and knowing that things . . . that things could happen. And, God, she wanted those things to happen. She was shocking herself with how often she thought about them.

But she knew now that it wasn't just physical for her. It wasn't just desire or curiosity. Jack made her feel lighter and happier than she'd felt in a long time. He made her feel at once excited and comfortable.

As much as she wanted to tear his clothes off, she knew that if she did and found out that, for him, things didn't go deeper than a base physical connection, she'd be devastated.

And if she was going to be devastated, it couldn't happen until after Simone Adair.

*

Clare had been optimistic about their next book club, but at first it looked like it would be even smaller than the first. By five past, only Joyo, Siti and Valarie were there.

'I'm sure Lauren and Max will be here soon,' said Joyo. 'Max and I were talking just yesterday about the book, and he definitely said they were coming.'

Everyone looked at him enquiringly.

'Ah,' he said, 'yes, he and Lauren were kind enough to babysit for me yesterday. I recently became my granddaughter's guardian, and I'm afraid I haven't got the most robust system in place yet.'

Clare's heart swelled. So that was who Bethany was. She was curious about how Joyo had ended up taking charge of her, but didn't feel she could ask.

He was right about Lauren and Max: they arrived two minutes later, shortly followed by another three people Clare didn't recognize.

The discussion was more energetic than last time. People were getting comfortable, Clare realized with pride. Towards the end of the hour, she proposed a toast. 'To Lauren and Max,' she said, 'who made space for us during their holiday, and whom we will miss.'

'Well,' said Lauren, looking down, her cheeks slightly flushed, 'we might be back sometime. We like it here, Max and I.' But she was looking at Joyo. 'We might make this our regular vacation spot.'

Max rolled his eyes. 'Gross,' he said, but there was warmth in his tone, and his mother just laughed.

She was clearly in another confiding mood when she helped Clare clear away the chairs at the end of the session. 'Honestly,' she said, 'I didn't expect to meet someone like him at all. He's still, I think, processing a lot. His daughter died, you see, and he hadn't seen her for years. She ran off the moment she turned eighteen, went to college in the States and never came home. Married young, and then she and her husband were in a car crash. Both died. Joyo didn't even know she'd had a daughter.'

'Wow,' said Clare, not sure she should be receiving all these confidences, especially second hand. 'That's a lot,' she said.

'I think he feels guilty,' Lauren went on. 'He was always working when his daughter was growing up. He's convinced he was a bad father. But she named him as Bethany's guardian in her will. Well, he's making up now for whatever he didn't do back then. Hiring managers so he can step away from work. I think he might even retire early.'

Clare was misty-eyed as she and Jack locked the door to

the shop after they'd left. 'See, this is what I wanted,' she said.

'A book club that doubles as a matchmaking service?' he said.

'No – well, yes! Somewhere people can meet and get to know each other. A place that can be something beautiful in people's lives.' She was suddenly embarrassed about how earnest she was being. 'Or whatever,' she said.

Jack laughed. 'Yeah,' he said. 'You should be proud. You've really made this place special.'

Clare felt a warm glow spread in her chest. She looked up at Jack and beamed. He smiled back down at her and the warmth spread.

Chapter Twenty-three

And then, all of a sudden, it was time for Simone. Clare unlocked the shop on the morning of the event with shaking hands, Jack shifting from one foot to the other behind her.

They went through their usual morning routine in silence, then stood in the still-empty shop, arms hanging at their sides, looking at each other blankly.

'What do we do now?' said Clare.

'We work all day like normal,' said Jack, 'I think? How are we meant to wait till six?'

They had already made sure the shop looked its best. There were no books in the window display, just a large sign advertising the event. Both tables at the front were laden with Simone Adair books.

And the mezzanine looked incredible. In what she was counting as one of her greatest triumphs, Clare had persuaded Jack to have Buana put large strips of trellis across the ceiling, which she'd then woven with ferns and fairy lights.

The bookshelves they'd had installed upstairs were full of Simone's books, as well as others they thought her fans might enjoy, like Octavia Butler, N. K. Jemisin, and Terry Pratchett.

A big table to the side was already set with glasses, with a second waiting for the finger food that was due to arrive just before six. They'd placed candles on each of the new café tables, ready to be lit later, and the perfect spot that Celestina had so naturally stepped into at her own reading was marked out clearly with a small dais, on which stood two microphones ready for the night.

They'd asked Celestina to interview Simone and moderate audience questions if there were any.

'Yes, angels, but I think it would be wise if we kept audience questions to a maximum of five, don't you?' she said, when they asked her, casually confirming just why she was the perfect person for the task.

At around two thirty, Jack turned to Clare.

'Does it seem like there's a weirdly high number of people browsing?' he said.

Clare peered into the shop. He was right. The shop had become a lot busier over the last few weeks, the initial trickle of customers growing into a steady stream. But it had never been crowded like this.

'Some of them aren't browsing,' said Clare, in a low voice. 'They're just milling around.'

They watched them for a while. Some were making a show of looking at the shelves, but others were standing around chatting to each other, and there were even a couple sitting on the floor leaning against the 'Mysteries (Thrilling)' shelf.

'Do we just let them hang out here?' said Jack. 'All afternoon?'

Clare was about to answer when the door opened and another three people came in, one of them wearing a *Persephone's Arrow* T-shirt. They spotted the people on the floor, waved, and walked over to them.

'I don't think we can turn this tide,' said Clare. 'Is it too late to build a holding cell?'

Jack gave a low laugh. 'This is all you, you know,' he said. 'You did this.'

'Oh, no,' said Clare. 'I would have ruined this place in the first month if it was just me. Gone over budget in every conceivable way, throwing around money that didn't exist.'

'It's not the same,' said Jack. 'The stuff you do is special. It would never occur to me to do half of it. Anyone can keep a budget.'

'Anyone but me,' said Clare, with a wry smile.

'Stop that,' said Jack. 'Take a moment to be proud of yourself. You're a force, Clare. And you should know that about yourself. Everyone around you does.'

Clare was silent. 'Thank you,' she said, after a while. 'I've never really thought of myself as, I don't know, a capable person. I thought I was flighty and unreliable and that was why my mum was so worried about me. But maybe she saw me better than I did. Maybe she just knew I could accomplish something. If I really wanted to.'

Jack was looking down at her, his mouth curved at the side, his eyes warm and brown and so deep Clare felt as if she could swim in them.

'Clare,' he said, his brow furrowing, his voice softening. Clare felt herself leaning towards him, her skin growing hot. 'I wanted—'

'Darling ones.' Celestina's voice broke in on them. 'We're on our way for an early dinner, or maybe a late lunch, with Simone. One requires sustenance, you understand, and why events like this must always take place just when one most wants to eat I have never understood,' she said. 'You'll have noticed, of course, that my own reading started at a much more reasonable time.'

Jack and Clare glanced at each other and grinned, remembering their long wait for Celestina's appearance.

'I just thought we'd drop by to check if there's anything we can help with for tonight,' she continued. 'And if you need me to make a few calls to bolster numbers you have only to say the word.'

'Thanks, Celestina, but I think we're all right. A lot of these people are already waiting,' said Clare.

Celestina looked around and gave a start, as if noticing for the first time how many people were in the shop. 'Waiting already?' she said. 'But it doesn't begin for three hours.' She arched an eyebrow at Clare and Jack. 'My, my,' she said. 'A coup indeed.'

As she'd been talking, Adam had been slowly walking around the shop. Clare watched his progress with her heart in her mouth. She and Jack hadn't mentioned the memo to him or to Celestina. Even though she'd found it accidentally, Clare didn't want them to think she'd been snooping.

Plus, she'd known she couldn't promise that her efforts would work, that they'd be enough to get the shop properly back on its feet, and she hadn't wanted to disappoint them. Or perhaps she was afraid to hear directly that Adam was determined to sell.

'You both really have done a wonderful job,' he said. 'But I do worry about how much work it must have been. You can't have been having a very restful time.'

'It's been a pleasure,' said Jack. 'Truly, we've loved it.'

'We have,' said Clare. Suddenly she had a thought. 'Can I take a photo of you? In front of our Instagram wall? We ought to have a shot of you up. You are the owner, after all.'

'Oh, I don't know about that,' said Adam. 'No one wants to see me.'

'Nonsense, dear,' said Celestina. 'We'll take one together. I understand we're to select our favourite books?'

She herded Adam upstairs and Clare took a photo of the two of them, Celestina with an arm raised and her head thrown back, like an icon of the silver screen, Adam standing with his hands in his pockets, twinkling up at her.

Clare posted the photo, captioning it, 'Our wonderful founders, our glorious hosts, our Adam, our Celestina.'

*

The early fans continued to trickle through the door and Clare started to get a little worried there wouldn't be room for everyone.

By the time the food was delivered, the shop was so full that they had to weave through the crowds holding trays high above their heads to get them to the table upstairs. The sight of it caused a ripple of excitement to run through the crowd, and people started looking towards the door more and more.

'God,' Clare said to Jack. 'I hope she's prepared.'

All at once a hush fell over the shop. Celestina had

appeared in the doorway. She smiled regally at the assembled crowd and stepped to the side with a flourish as Simone walked in behind her. She was dressed in a simple black shift dress, shot through with silver, her silver and red bob artfully tousled and windswept.

There was a collective gasp and then, from somewhere in the back, a sob, and the crowd burst into applause.

Simone looked completely taken aback, her eyes flitting around the room, and Clare moved forward to meet her.

'Are you okay?' she asked.

Simone stood there blinking at the crowd. 'They can't all be here for me.'

'They're all here for you,' said Clare.

'Wow,' Simone said softly.

'Come on,' said Clare, and led Simone up the stairs, Celestina and Adam following them. She got to the dais and picked up one of the microphones, unexpectedly nervous.

The mezzanine was full of people, a tide that spilled down the curving stairs and into the shop below, all of them craning their necks to see her better and waiting in a crackling silence. She took a moment to gaze out over the assembled crowd. She wished her dad could see her up here. She wondered what he'd think of everything she'd done.

She felt a rush of emotion and swallowed hard before opening her mouth to address the audience.

'Hi, everyone,' she said. 'Thank you so much for being here tonight. I'm Clare and I work here at Seashore Books. Along with Jack, who's down at the till if anyone wants to buy a book, I arranged this event with Simone Adair.' Someone somewhere whooped and Clare took a shaking breath.

'We know that, for a lot of you, this is a long-established tradition, and we hope it doesn't feel like we're elbowing in on something you've all cared so much about for ages. But we love Simone and we wanted to celebrate her with you.

'I want to thank, in advance, the shop's owner Adam, and his wife Celestina, who'll be moderating the event tonight. But without any more nonsense from me, it gives me no end of pleasure to introduce the genius that is Simone Adair.'

She swept her arm to the side, and Simone stepped onto the dais to a roar of applause. Clare saw at least three people with tears streaming down their faces and felt herself welling up in response.

'Oh, my,' said Simone, after she'd taken the mic. 'This is somewhat overwhelming. I wonder, Clare, if I might trouble you for a glass of wine?'

'I'm on it,' came a voice from the back by the tables, and a glass full almost to the brim came floating through the crowd, passed from person to person till it got to Clare, who handed it up to Simone. She took a long sip and continued speaking.

'I haven't done one of these in such a long time,' she said. 'I hope I remember how.' There was a burble of laughter. 'I thought I'd read you something you might know,' she said. 'And then my wonderful friend Celestina is going to ask me a few questions. If you're well behaved, she might let you ask some too. And then, if it's all right, I'd like to read something you won't know.'

Clare looked over the railing to Jack at the till. His eyes found hers, and he gripped his chest dramatically. She laughed and turned back to Simone, who had pulled out an extremely battered copy of *A Wind over Dofida*. She read from the end of part one, a beautiful scene that saw a young couple stepping onto the ship that would take them away from everyone they knew for ever. It was full of sadness but also hope and anticipation. It was a scene of possibility but also of the grief that comes with having to choose which path to follow, knowing that you're turning your back on all the others.

There was not a dry eye in the house when Simone reached the end of the passage. Celestina waited a moment before she stepped up to join her on the dais, picking up the second microphone.

'Well, my first question,' she said, wiping her eyes, 'is how dare you?'

As she and Simone talked into the mics, Clare felt someone take her hand. She turned to see Jack, his eyes blazing. She smiled up at him and gripped his hand tighter.

Celestina and Simone kept the crowd captivated. It was less an interview and more a series of incredible anecdotes from the literary world of the nineties. Simone seemed to have met everyone and was not afraid to share stories that showed them all in the most embarrassing light possible, herself included.

Clare could have listened to the two of them talk for hours, but eventually Celestina stepped down and Simone turned back to the crowd.

'I had some news today,' she said. 'It was not the sort of news I ever expected to have again. Not the sort of news I ever expected to want again. But, well, I've never been particularly self-aware. Now, I know at least one person in this room' – she glanced round at Jack, who gave a gasp and gripped Clare's hand in both of his – 'will be quite pleased to hear that in the autumn of next year, my new book, *What We Were When We Lived,* will be published worldwide.'

There was silence, and then there was noise. It wasn't applause, although people were clapping. It was disbelief. It was a hundred sentences started and left hanging. It was joy inexpressible. Clare turned to Jack, whose mouth was opening and closing, and who was gripping her arm as if he'd never let her go.

Simone cleared her throat quietly and the room fell silent again. She looked at Clare and grinned. 'Is he okay?' she asked. Clare shrugged and there was a ripple of laughter.

'Now, if it's all right,' said Simone, 'I'd like to read you the first chapter of that book.'

*

Clare had never heard stillness like it as the crowd listened to Simone read for the second time. They leaned towards her, their entire bodies tense, as if they were trying to absorb the words from the air around them. She could swear she saw some people's ears move on their own, craning towards Simone.

When she finished, Clare realized she hadn't taken in a word of what Simone had been reading: she'd been too busy watching other people listen. She looked back at Jack. His head was bowed, and he was wiping his eyes with the back of his hand.

'Okay,' Simone was saying, 'I believe there's a table for me up here. If you promise not to ask me any more questions, I'd love to sign some books for you.'

Chapter Twenty-four

After Simone was safely installed at a table, the queue of fans snaking away and devolving into a muddle, Clare found Adam leaning against a wall in the corner, a glass of wine in his hand and a small smile on his face.

'Ah,' he said, as she came towards him, 'you should be proud. It's all gone off extremely well. Events like this can be dull sometimes. Authors are not always the most vibrant people.'

'Oh, it's all Simone,' said Clare, 'and Celestina. She makes a great moderator.'

'Oh, yes, she's always wonderful at drawing people out.' He gave a sad smile. 'It used to feel like this a lot more often. It's nice to see it back for a bit. One last time.'

Clare felt a sob rising in her throat. 'But why does it have to be the last time? You don't have to go through with it.'

Adam stared at her.

'Jack and I found a memo,' she admitted. 'About you selling this place.'

'Ah,' said Adam. 'I didn't realize I'd left a copy in the shop. That was careless of me.'

'It's why we've been working so hard,' she said. 'Well, it's not the only reason. We were already trying to turn things around. But it spurred us on. We wanted to get it making money again. Enough so you can keep it.'

Adam gave a little laugh. 'Ah,' he said. 'I might have been just as optimistic at your age.'

Clare frowned. Did he think they couldn't do it? That all the work they'd done wouldn't be enough?

Adam was watching her quietly. 'It'd take more than a couple of months of good business to turn this place around,' he said gently.

'But we could give it more time,' she said. 'This shop is special. We can't let it just die.' She felt a lump growing in her throat.

'Well, everything's temporary,' said Adam. 'People come through places like this, and they make it feel magical for a while, but they don't stay. They can't. They have lives elsewhere.'

'But this is still important to them. Still magical.'

'I don't know,' said Adam. 'I used to think it could be.'

'But it is,' said Clare. 'Don't you know how much it is?' She pulled out her phone and brought up Instagram, tapping on the photo of Adam and Celestina from that afternoon. 'Look at these comments,' she said.

This was one of my favourite places when I lived in Bali, one comment read. *I need to go back soon and visit it again. So glad it's still going.*

Another said, *OMG, I worked here for a bit like ten years*

ago. *It was wonderful and the owner was the best – it felt like a proper home.*

Another: *I took myself off to Bali after a bad break-up when I was 23 and that shop was such a solace to me. An unforgettable place.*

Clare looked up at Adam. He had a tear in his eye. 'There are loads of them,' she said. 'People who haven't been here in years still remember this shop, remember what it was and what it meant to them. Remember *you*. It's not transitory. It's become part of them. Part of all of them.' She paused for a moment, trying to put everything she was feeling into words. 'It's such a gift. It's so generous to give people a place like this, a place that stays with them for ever, even if they move on. To give them this even though you know they can't hold on to it as tightly as you do. And every so often,' she went on, 'there'll be someone who will hold it tightly. Like me.'

'Oh, Clare,' Adam said.

'Working here has saved me, I think,' Clare said. 'I was lost. After my dad died, I started to forget how to relate to the world. I started to forget what I wanted from life – and what I could give to it. This shop has reminded me of who I am. It's built me back up. I can't tell you how grateful I am to you. What you've given me, what you've given so many people, it's so precious.'

Adam took a moment. 'Well, my dear,' he said, 'what a lovely thing to say. But I'm afraid I don't have the energy I used to. I'm afraid I . . .' He trailed off, staring across the shop.

After a moment, he looked back at Clare. 'Thank you for showing me that, Clare. And for saying, well . . . Thank you.

247

I think I'm going to have to call it a night. Find that wife of mine and retire for the evening. Well done. Please pass on my congratulations to Jack. You've both done a marvellous job.'

Clare was desperate to stop him leaving, to grab him and beg him, to refuse to let go until he promised not to sell the shop. But she watched him walk away to Celestina, who was holding court in a circle of new but ardent admirers, her arms soaring through the air as she told some dramatic story.

As Adam approached her, she turned, as if some sixth sense was pulling her attention to him. She took one look at his face and stopped talking, her head falling softly to the side. She gave him a small smile and caressed the side of his cheek, then waved a casual goodbye to her new acolytes and tenderly took his arm, moving with him serenely downstairs and out of the shop.

Clare's chest felt heavy and full. She held back a sob and turned to look for Jack. He was standing by Simone where she sat chatting to fans and signing their books. He was watching and listening and beaming all over his face, and Clare felt the lump in her throat abate.

She gave her head a shake to clear it and walked downstairs, where a few people who didn't have their own copies of the books were waiting to buy them.

*

Clare felt a little breathless as she watched the last of the guests leave the shop. She could never have imagined it would go so well.

The shop looked beautiful, Simone had seemed to have a

great time, and several fans had come up to Clare in tears to thank her for throwing an event that had let them actually meet their hero.

She stood surveying the wreckage – dirty glasses on every surface, crumbs on the floor – with a smile plastered across her face. Jack came up to her, sharing her smile, and silently handed her a broom.

They worked in a contented, satisfied silence for a while, taking sips from half-empty bottles of wine, packing up glasses to be taken away for cleaning, wiping down surfaces, replacing books on shelves. Every so often they looked up at each other, smiles widening.

Finally it was all cleared away, and they stood at the railing, surveying their shop.

'We did a pretty good job, didn't we?' said Jack.

'I think so,' said Clare. 'I think we did a great job.' She sighed happily and hiccuped. 'I'm so glad I was wrong about you.'

Jack let out a bark of laughter. 'Oh. You were, were you?'

'I was,' Clare said. 'And I'm sorry.' She glanced up at him, gave a rueful laugh, and, leaned on the railing looking down at the books below. 'I thought you were a soulless corporate drone,' she said. 'That you were just using this place to learn how to dismantle people's businesses, how to maximize corporate profits. When I heard about the company you're working for, I was so relieved. I was so happy to be wrong.' Jack didn't reply and Clare didn't look up at him. 'But I was right about you too. I could tell you cared about this place, and I could tell you were trying your hardest to help it. To help me. And it was so confusing for so long. I didn't know how both versions of you could be real. But they're not. Just the good one is.'

She suddenly realized that Jack had gone very still. She straightened and turned to look at him. There was a hard look on his face.

'Wow,' he said. 'You've certainly made some judgements.'

'N-no,' Clare said. 'Not about y—'

'Yes, about me,' he said. 'Do you know why I took that job with the non-profit? Because they offered it to me. It wasn't the only job I applied for, Clare. And if I hadn't got it, I'd have taken a different one, yes, with a corporation. Just like my brother. Do you think he's a corporate drone?'

'But you're not—'

'Do you know what Ben does? Do you know what his actual job entails?'

'I—'

'You don't because you didn't ask him because you assumed you already knew.'

Clare didn't say anything. She could feel tears prickling at her eyes and shame pulling at her stomach.

'He vets the contracts businesses sign to make sure no one is being exploited. He checks for hidden clauses, he verifies that the buyout amounts are fair, he makes sure the people selling actually want to sell and he makes sure they get the best deal possible.'

'Jack, I—'

'And did you know that he chose that job over one at a non-profit? One that claimed to be focused on real-estate support for disadvantaged communities but was lobbying behind the scenes for fewer building regulations?'

'I . . . I didn't know.'

'No, you didn't,' said Jack. 'You just assumed.' He shook his head and walked downstairs.

A sob caught in Clare's throat, but there was something else as well. Frustration, no – indignation.

'Wait,' she said, following Jack. 'I didn't just assume. You said it. You said you'd studied this, that you'd interned in places that took over businesses like this one. You told me that yourself.'

'And that made me the villain, didn't it?' said Jack, moving towards the door. 'Because to you everything is so cut and dried, so simple. You want things to be special more than you want them to be practical. Making a profit is for suckers. How dare someone take a job just because it'll pay them a decent wage? Corporation bad therefore Jack bad. Things are more complicated than that Clare. You're so naïve.'

At that, Clare sped up, reaching the door before Jack and slamming her hand against it, barring his way. 'No, you're naïve,' she said. 'You might do good work, your brother might do good work. You might pick a company that cares about people, that is aiming to do good, but it's still always going to be about making money. And always more, always growing. Year after year, you have to make more than you did before. It's built in. At the end of the day caring for people is optional. Caring about money never is. Ben might get paid to help the little guy, but he flew here first class. He stayed in a luxury suite. Which do you really think is more important to him? To his company?'

Clare flung open the door and stormed down the path to

the flat. She heard Jack fumbling with his keys, swearing as he dropped them and, even in her anger, she felt a bubble of affection for him rising in her chest. So determined to lock up properly, even in the middle of a fight.

She let herself into the flat and stood in the middle of the living room. Suddenly she felt drained and desperately sad.

She heard the door open behind her.

'I know he makes a lot of money,' Jack said. 'And he spends a lot of it on himself. I do too, to be honest – this shirt was, like, three hundred dollars. We could give more away, fly economy—'

Clare turned. 'I wouldn't wish economy class on anyone,' she said. 'Bump everyone up to business. That's what we should be doing.'

Jack gave a small smile. 'I get that the system isn't perfect. Tear it down all you want. But is it so much to ask that you realize everyone is also just trying to survive it? That they're doing the best they can? Even if that best is sometimes pretty shit?'

Clare shook her head hopelessly. 'Why does it matter so much to you?' she said. 'We're just two people who were thrown together for a few months. And it's nearly over. In two weeks we'll be back home. We may never see each other again. Why does what I think of you matter so much?'

Jack stared at her. 'Clare,' he said. 'Don't you know?'

Chapter Twenty-five

They stood for a moment, gazing at each other, and to Clare it felt like the earth had spun away from under their feet, like they were standing in space with nothing else around them. She was frozen and breathless.

Without being fully aware of it, she took a step forward and the stillness shattered around her. Jack closed the space between them, and then his lips were on hers, his hand in her hair. Clare pressed herself against him, crumpling his expensive shirt in her hands as she fought to be even closer to him, to be touching him even more.

Jack's hands were on the buttons on the front of her dress. She shrugged it off and pulled his shirt over his head, pressing her skin against his, running her hands over the muscles of his back.

'Jack,' she said, between kisses. 'I'm sorry, Jack. I don't think you're a villain.'

''S okay,' he said. 'I don't care.'

Clare pulled away from him a bit. 'But you should care! I care! I care that you thought I thought you were a villain.'

'Okay,' he said, cupping his hands around the sides of her face, 'I did care. I have cared. I will care.' He kissed her again, pulling on her bottom lip gently with his teeth. 'But is it okay if I don't care that much right this second?'

He twisted his hand into her hair, his other snaking around her waist and pulling her into him until she felt entirely wrapped up in him. She nodded against him and he growled, 'Good,' against her neck, and she moaned.

How had she gone so long without his hands on her? She felt like all these weeks she'd been waiting for this to happen and somehow it still wasn't happening fast enough.

Jack tumbled back on the couch, pulling Clare with him. She stretched out on top of him, letting one leg fall to the floor. They lay still for a moment, looking into each other's eyes. Then Jack lifted a hand and brushed a finger down the side of her face.

Slowly Clare lowered her head, slowly she let her lips meet his, slowly moved against him, no longer trying to take his kisses but give him hers. Jack's hand moved to the back of her neck, pulling her into him, then travelled down her back. Clare moaned again as he undid the clasp of her bra and slipped it off her shoulders. She sat up to let it fall away.

She brought her hands to his waist, unbuckling his belt, and shifting her weight onto her leg. Jack groaned as she stood and grabbed her hand to pull her back down.

'I'll be back,' she whispered, pressing a kiss into his hand. She ducked into her room for a condom. When she came back into the living room, Jack had his hands behind his head, propping it up to look for her.

'What?' she said.

'Nothing,' said Jack. 'Just admiring the view.'

'Oh,' said Clare, as she came to the side of the couch. 'Well, likewise,' she said, as she looked down at him. Jack grinned as he grabbed her hand, sitting up and pulling her onto his lap. She hooked her leg around his waist, and gripped his hair, kissing him hungrily.

Jack ran a hand down her side, sending shivers rocketing through her. His fingers met her centre and unbearable tension coiled under them. She pushed him down and rose up on her knees to give him room, and as she closed the gap between them, drawing him into her, she shook her head slightly, wondering why it had taken them so long to get there.

She was still scared. She still knew that this had the power to break her, but she also knew she couldn't keep it at bay any longer. She pulled Jack as close as she could, and as he rose to meet her again and again, she knew that, whatever happened, it would be worth it.

*

They fell asleep on the couch, pressed into each other, clinging to each other. But couches were not made for two people to sleep on, and sometime in the middle of the night Clare was awoken by the crash of Jack falling to the floor.

She leaned over the side and blinked down at him.

'Are you okay?' she asked.

'Ow,' he said, pouting up at her.

'Oh, no,' said Clare.

She leaned down and kissed him on the tip of his nose, and as she pulled away, he moved up with her, catching her mouth with his. He put up an arm and pulled her off the couch with him, and she laughed as she rolled onto her back on the floor.

'This sleeping situation,' he said, kissing her mouth, kissing her neck, kissing her ear, 'is insufficient.'

'I agree,' she replied, running a hand up his arm and gripping the back of his head. 'It needs some serious adjustments.'

Jack pulled his head back and looked at her. 'What?' he said. 'Right now?'

She grinned up at him wickedly, sliding a foot along his calf. 'Not right now, no,' she said, pulling his mouth back down to hers. He kissed her deeply, running a hand along the side of her thigh, and over her hip. His fingers played across her waist, moving up over her ribs and grazing her breast.

Clare shuddered as Jack ran his hand down the length of her arm, raising it above her head. He pulled back a bit and gazed at her, before bending down and kissing her mouth, her cheek, her neck. He nibbled her earlobe, and she let out a moan.

Jack nuzzled into her neck, breathing her in, and began moving down her, kissing her collarbone, before running his tongue around her nipple. Clare arched backwards, gasping, and Jack's hand came to her side, as he moved further down.

And then his teeth were grazing her inner thigh and she felt like she could explode right there. This time, as Jack brought her to her peak, she couldn't hold on to any thoughts at all.

*

Some time later, Jack silently deposited her on the couch, before going first to his room, then to hers, dragging out the mattresses from each of their single beds. He covered them with blankets and pillows, then sleepily grabbed Clare's hand and pulled her over to him.

He laid her down and curled up behind her, his arm wrapped tightly around her waist, holding her against him. He nuzzled the side of her neck, and murmured, 'This is better. This is much better.'

*

Jack was still asleep beside her when Clare woke up the next morning. He'd moved away from her and was lying on his back, one arm thrown up above his head.

She sat for a moment looking down at him, smiling, blissful, but with a sadness tugging at her. She sighed and bit her lip. Jack's eyes blinked slowly open, and he looked up at her. 'Hi,' he said, closing his eyes again as a smile spread over his face.

'Hi,' said Clare, shuffling over towards him and lying back down, her head on his chest. His arm came down around her shoulders and he stroked the side of her arm with his thumb.

'We should get up,' she said, after a few moments. She felt him nod underneath her.

'We need to open the shop,' he said, and she nodded too. They lay still for a minute, then both sat up. They stayed there looking at each other. Clare put out a hand and ran her fingers over his chest. He shuddered and closed his eyes, then took her hand in his, raising it to his lips. He kissed her fingers, then put his other hand to the side of her face, pulling her towards him, and kissed her lips.

He pulled back and smiled at her contentedly, then pulled her to her feet and pushed her towards the shower.

*

The shop was busy all day with the now-standard steady hum of customers, some regulars, along with a few tourists who'd seen the shop on some BuzzFeed list or other.

Just after lunch Joyo came in, holding the hand of a tiny girl with enormous eyes. Clare walked forward to say hello, crouching down in front of her. 'Well, hello,' she said. 'You must be the Bethany of legend.'

Bethany giggled shyly.

'She takes a while to get used to new people,' said Joyo. 'Usually, that is – she loved Max in an instant.'

He turned to his granddaughter. 'Now remember, I said you could choose two books.'

'Come on,' said Clare to Bethany. 'I'll show you where the good ones are.'

It was clear that Bethany and Joyo adored each other. They spent half an hour reviewing the selection of picture books and wound up selecting three. 'I'm such a soft touch,' said Joyo. 'Can't seem to keep to my own rules.'

'Well, there's no such thing as too many books,' said Clare. 'Did you want one for yourself?'

'Actually I did wonder if you've decided on the next book-club book.'

'We have,' said Clare, 'and the order came in this morning.' She pulled out a copy for him.

'Can I have three, please?'

'Sure,' said Clare, confused.

'I'm going to send them to Lauren and Max,' he said. 'They can't participate in the club, of course, but I thought the three of us could have our own supplementary club.'

'That's lovely,' said Clare. 'But won't they be expensive to post? They could probably buy them at home.'

Joyo looked a little crestfallen, but then he said, 'No, I'd like to send them a copy. It's nice to have something through the mail because someone has sent it to you, and not just because you ordered it online.'

Clare smiled. 'You're right,' she said. 'That's one of the nicest things.'

Clare was sure that everyone would be able to tell that something was going on between her and Jack. She'd look up in the middle of helping someone to find Jack staring at her and flush red to her roots. Every time the door closed, they would start towards each other, and every time, another customer would come in at just that moment. It became a wordless running joke. Every time the shop was empty, they'd lock eyes and start counting. The longest Clare counted before the door opened again was thirty-seven.

'It's good, really,' she said, around three thirty, one of the first chances they'd had to talk to each other. 'It's good for the shop.'

'It's our fault,' said Jack, his voice low. 'Think of all those days we sat around in an empty store.'

'Doing maths,' said Clare. Jack laughed and moved his hand towards her hair, just as the door was pushed open again. His head fell to his chest, and Clare giggled and went to help the customer, a smile on her face and butterflies in her stomach.

*

But that night she lay awake a while after Jack fell asleep. She lay on her side gazing at him as he breathed softly, deeply.

It felt so perfect. It felt so necessary. The future she'd had, the normal one waiting for her at home – it just didn't feel real any more. She'd always known it would be hard to go back. This was paradise. And it was deferral. When she went home, she knew she'd have to make a decision about what was next. She couldn't go back to temp work. She had to find a future that meant something to her. That let her feel like she was contributing. Building something.

But now she knew she'd have to do all that with a broken heart.

Next week, she thought. *I'll think about that next week*.

Jack turned onto his side, facing away from her. She curled up behind him, placing a hand on him. He moaned quietly and grabbed her arm, pulling it around him. She buried her face in his back and breathed him in.

And she slept.

Chapter Twenty-six

A week after the event, Adam and Celestina had Jack and Clare to dinner in their home again.

Clare thought Adam had seemed a bit lighter recently, a bit more energetic, but she wasn't sure if that was just her. If her happiness was making everyone around her seem happy too.

She and Jack still hadn't talked about what they were going to do when their three months were up, or acknowledged how soon that would be. They hadn't even talked about whether they would tell anyone what was happening between them. Maybe because of that, because it seemed so separate from the rest of their lives, it had started to feel precious. Sacred.

Their nest on the floor in their microscopic flat felt like a bower. There was something bohemian about the way they were living. Clare loved to lie sprawling in the blankets on the floor, watching Jack potter around the kitchen, half-naked, making her toast and coffee. He'd bring it over to her, and sit beside her, their backs against the wall as they ate, reading or doing a crossword together. Clare had never liked having breakfast in bed – she hated getting crumbs in the sheets – but somehow this was different. They were in their bower and the normal rules didn't apply.

Clare clung to it with all she had. It was safe there. Outside the bower there was only uncertainty.

The bookshop felt like it was doing well, humming with activity, but was it enough? They might have made it special but had they saved it? Adam had seemed happy with it at Simone's event, but he didn't look as if he was going to change his mind about selling, and the thought of it disappearing broke Clare's heart. So she tried not to think about it.

What she did think about was what she'd be doing next. She felt energized about her life in a way she hadn't for years. She felt like she had something to give, and all she had to do was find some way to give it. Her mind ticked through options constantly.

She'd loved bookselling: she could try to find a job in a bookshop back home. But it was more than that: she'd loved building the shop into a hub, into somewhere that felt like home. She didn't know that they'd let her do that in a high-street chain. But she couldn't just start her own shop: that would take money she didn't have. Were there companies that helped businesses refresh themselves?

Her mum had given her a deadline. She had to figure out what was next. But she wanted to for herself as well. She couldn't go back to temping, and she didn't want another job where she just didn't fit.

She held Jack's hand in the taxi, gazing out of the window. It had been a perfect three months. Magical.

The magic was going to die soon, Clare knew. There was no escaping it. This dinner was the beginning of their farewell. They were leaving next week, and they would need to have a difficult conversation soon. Clare shivered and gripped Jack's hand a little tighter.

They got out of the car and walked up the front path. Clare went to ring the doorbell, but Jack pulled on her arm. He stepped in to meet her, and cupped her head in his hand, breathed her in slowly, and kissed her. He leaned his forehead against hers for a moment, his eyes closed.

Finally, he stepped back. His mouth twisted at the corner, and he nodded. Clare stepped forward and pressed the button, and as they heard the bell pealing through the house, she let go of Jack's hand.

*

Celestina flung open the door and ushered them in, kissing each of them in turn on the cheek.

'Angels,' she cried, 'how can it have been three months already? It seems criminal.'

She led them through to the magnificent dining room, where Adam was waiting.

It was just like the first dinner and nothing like it. No dinner with Celestina or Adam could be boring, and the conversation sparkled just as much as ever. Instead of three months, Clare felt like she'd lived a lifetime there. She cared about these people and this place more than she could bear, and as she laughed and joked with them, pain throbbed through her at the thought of walking away from it all.

After dinner was over, Celestina led them out onto the

balcony for one last drink, then quietly slipped back into the house. Clare wondered why she wasn't joining them and instinctively looked at Jack to see what he was thinking. But he wasn't looking at her. His head was down, his eyes on his drink.

Adam cleared his throat. 'Well,' he said, 'I know I've said it before, but it really does bear repeating. The two of you have done a marvellous job in the shop. I haven't seen it so full of life in years, and I can't tell you how much it's meant to me. So much, in fact—'

He broke off.

'I have to confess something to you. You might have guessed . . . you might have noticed that I've been a bit . . .' He took a breath. 'For some time, the shop has been a source of pain to me. It had become so . . . so broken. I didn't want to let go of it, but I couldn't somehow bring myself to repair it. And its upkeep was costing more than it was bringing in. Earlier this year I received an offer from Grantham Books for the property and any remaining merchandise. They're part of a large conglomerate that owns bookshop chains all over the world. It wasn't an enormous offer – not really reflective of something I've devoted years of my life to – but it was enough to let me walk away and retire. And walking away and retiring felt good to me. So, I decided to accept. I had made that decision just before the two of you arrived. You were to be my last booksellers.'

Clare looked over at Jack, but he was still motionless, staring at his drink.

'A few weeks ago,' said Adam, 'I had another offer. An offer of a partnership. This partnership would put me, and some key deputies, in charge of a franchise of bookshops around the world that would offer working holidays.'

Clare's head snapped up, and she stared at Adam, then back at Jack. She couldn't understand why Jack wasn't reacting. He was holding his glass in both hands, staring into it as if it could tell him the future.

Adam continued: 'The plan would be to slowly, one by one, find other locations that might suit. Sometimes it will mean opening a new shop entirely, setting it up, hiring a permanent manager to oversee the travelling booksellers. I realize, of course, that leaving people alone to do their own thing in the shop only works in exceptional circumstances.' His eyes twinkled. 'Sometimes it will mean finding existing shops that would mesh well with the idea and injecting a little cash to help them revitalize in exchange for a small share going forwards, to help contribute to running the programme.'

He looked at Clare and at Jack. 'Now, I wasn't considering this offer. I was ready to rest. But then you two . . .' He fell silent. Clare's eyes were full as she gazed at him. He put a hand on his heart. 'I hadn't grasped how much this place meant to people,' he said. 'It was something you said, Clare, about it being a gift that I can give. And I want to, I want—'

He took a moment, and Clare felt a tear slide down her face.

'Now,' he said, in a more businesslike tone, 'I don't have the energy I used to, and I don't like to be away from Celestina for extended periods of time. So, I would only be able to accept this partnership if I could run things from here. And to do that I need my deputies – the ones going to each shop

265

and helping them get started, then visiting from time to time to monitor them. I would need them to be people I can trust. Completely.'

Clare stared at him. Was this really happening?

'I think I can only accept this partnership,' said Adam, 'if it involves the two of you.'

Clare swallowed, breathless and tearful.

'So?' said Adam. 'Do you want the job?'

*

Clare lay awake for hours after she and Jack got home. She was struggling to take everything in. She couldn't have imagined for herself an opportunity so perfect. It couldn't possibly be real.

Part of her was sure that the next day would dawn and no one else would remember the conversation. That Adam would still be selling the shop, that Jack would still be going back to Chicago and his new job, and that she would still be facing a return to temp work with absolutely no idea how to find something she cared about as much as she cared about Seashore Books.

Adam hadn't let her and Jack answer his question. After dropping his bombshell, he'd immediately thrown up a hand. 'Don't answer,' he'd said quickly. 'Don't answer yet. This is a big thing I'm asking of you. This job would involve being on the ground for weeks, months even, setting up each shop, then visiting them regularly. It's a nomadic existence I'm asking you to accept, after telling you that it's one I wouldn't want for myself. And, of course, after you've put in all that effort, spent all that time away from your friends and family, it could all fall apart. It could be a catastrophic failure. Although I think that's less likely with the two of you on board.'

He beamed at them genially, very much with the air of the fairy godfather Clare had started to see him as.

'Take some time. Take a few days,' he said, 'and think about it. There's a contract being drawn up, of course, and a formal job offer. Don't make any decisions until you've seen those, naturally. But do think about whether this kind of job, this kind of lifestyle, might be something you'd like. Indefinitely. And, of course, whether you could stand to spend any more time in each other's company!' He laughed. 'Now where has Lissie got to?' he said, and she magically appeared in the doorway as if summoned, a tray of drinks in her hands.

As she passed a glass of red wine to Clare, Celestina murmured, 'I thought we'd save the champagne until everything's decided.'

That was the only reference she made to Adam's offer. She turned the conversation easily to much less life-altering subjects, and the rest of the evening passed almost as normal. On the way home, though, Clare couldn't remember anything that had been said by anyone, even herself.

She was desperate to talk to Jack about the job offer, but somehow she couldn't get the words out. Time after time, she'd open her mouth, only to close it again. Jack didn't bring it up either, but whenever she looked over at him, he was looking at her, warmth in his eyes, a small smile on his face.

As she'd got into bed, her nerves had been jangling, her mind racing, but she couldn't latch on to any of it for long enough to comprehend it. She felt unbelievably happy and excited, but strangely sick, too. It was a bit too much, a bit too fast.

No, it was a lot too much a lot too fast. It was three or four in the morning when she eventually drifted off, curled on her side with Jack's arm slung over her hip. As she finally felt her mind relaxing into sleep, he murmured something into the back of her neck.

'I'm so happy for you,' he said.

And she fell asleep with a smile on her face.

Chapter Twenty-seven

Clare woke up late the next morning, and for a couple of minutes she couldn't remember why she felt so overwhelmed. Jack wasn't beside her, and the flat felt empty.

She stood up and went to the kitchenette. There was a note lying there from Jack.

'Morning,' it said. 'I think you should have the day to yourself. I'll take care of the shop. Don't come in. Go for a walk, go swimming, think about things. Decide for yourself what you want to do.'

For a moment, Clare rebelled. How dare he tell her how to make this decision? And how could he suggest that it was something for her to decide alone? How was she supposed to face this, to take it in at all, without talking it through with him?

But by the time she'd dressed she knew it was a good idea.

She loved him. She loved him so much. She knew that now. Nothing was more thrilling than the opportunity to be with him, to travel all over the world with him, to work with him, to experience everything with him beside her.

But she knew that wasn't enough. Obviously this decision involved Jack, but she had to be sure she was choosing for herself too.

And she really tried.

She walked along a black sand beach and she imagined meeting with a bookseller in Iceland, and Jack was there. She swam out past the surfers and imagined planning a window display for a shop on the Riviera, and he was there, peering at the shop's accounts and occasionally looking up to check what she was doing. She imagined throwing a book launch on Zanzibar, renovating a shelving system in Cuba, and Jack was there. Laughing at her jokes, rolling his eyes at her schemes.

It was impossible to imagine any of this without him.

And, she decided, as she sat on the sand watching the sunset that evening, it was pointless. If you were offered the perfect life – the perfect job with the perfect person – you didn't spend hours trying to picture it differently. You just took it.

So, she let herself go. She stopped holding back all the images that were crowding her brain, filling her head.

She saw the future spilling out in front of her.

Long-haul flights with her head dropping onto Jack's shoulder as she nodded off. Hotels with midnight room service sundaes just because she'd mentioned that they could and he'd decided that meant they should. Visiting museums and cathedrals and ruins, running on ahead of him while he listened carefully to the audio guide. One Christmas spent in Surrey with her family, the next in Chicago with his, the one after that in some exotic location on their own.

And long hours spent brainstorming ideas, getting to know local authors, figuring out what was special in each different location, setting up hubs that would draw people to them, draw people together for years to come.

It wasn't until she was walking home in the moonlight, past clubs that were beginning to pump out music, past restaurants where people were lingering over the remnants of their dinner, that she remembered what he'd whispered to her as she dropped off to sleep.

I'm so happy for you, he'd said.

Did that mean he was saying no? Had he already decided? How could he make that decision so quickly?

Surely she was just overthinking it. Surely he couldn't turn Adam down.

No. This was real. This was happening. This life she never could have dreamed of was going to be hers. Hers and Jack's. It had to be.

She walked past the bookshop, which was already closed, and down the path to the flat. When she let herself in, she thought it was empty. But then she saw Jack walk past the open door in his bedroom.

That was strange. Since they'd moved their mattresses to the living-room floor, neither of them had spent much time in their own rooms. They'd become glorified closets.

But now, Jack was pacing his room slowly, his head down. Clare moved through to the doorway, and he looked up at her. One look at his face and Clare's stomach fell away. Tears sprang to her eyes and her mouth went dry.

'You're saying no,' she said. It wasn't a question.

'I'm saying no,' said Jack.

*

Dazed, Clare turned and walked back into the living room. She crossed the floor until she reached the wall, then turned and walked back again.

Jack was standing in his doorway, watching her.

'Why?' she said.

He sighed and passed a hand over his face. 'Different reasons,' he said. 'A few. Too many for me to filter and sort through in time to make a decision.'

'I don't understand,' said Clare.

'It's a big commitment,' said Jack. 'And I don't think I'm ready to make it. I don't think I can be ready to make it. I have a job waiting for me back home—'

'They can find someone else,' said Clare.

Jack smiled. 'I know,' he said. 'I'm very replaceable. But that's why I know you'll be okay doing this without me. Anyone can balance a budget.'

Clare couldn't talk around the lump in her throat. He might be replaceable for his job in Chicago. He wasn't for her.

'Look,' said Jack. 'I'm not like you. I'm not very . . .' He took a moment to search for the words. 'I'm not very agile of mind. I spent a week deciding to even apply for Seashore Books, let alone say yes when I got the job. That's how I do things. I weigh up pros and cons. I balance things out. I make sure I'm taking the best possible decision for myself. I don't trust my instincts, like you do. I don't know that my instincts are trustworthy.'

Then trust mine, Clare's brain was screaming.

'I didn't know,' Jack went on. 'I wasn't sure how my being

part of things would impact this decision. This – you and me – we haven't really talked about it. But we both knew we were going home soon so I didn't want . . . I didn't want you not to take the job because you thought I'd be there too. That maybe to you this was just a fling, and it would be too awkward to have to keep working together.'

He gave a quiet laugh. 'The relationship equivalent of saying goodbye to someone and then realizing they're getting the same train as you.'

Clare's eyes were swimming.

'And then,' Jack said, 'I thought that if this was more than that to you, if I was more than that . . . Well, that would be even worse, somehow. Like you might just take it so that we wouldn't have to say goodbye. And that's no reason to take a job. Especially one as life-changing as this.'

He reached out and took her hand. 'I knew immediately that I couldn't say yes,' he said. 'And I knew immediately that I couldn't tell you what I'd decided until you'd made your own choice. I didn't want that moment to come. I wanted to keep this . . . I wanted to keep us like this for as long as possible. But last night I knew. I knew my time was up. And I hoped you'd say yes, because you deserve this, Clare, and you'll be so good at it. But I was dreading it too, because I knew I wouldn't get to be part of it.'

'Wait,' Clare said, realization trickling through the centre of her. 'You'd already decided. But how did you . . .?' It dawned on her. 'Ben,' she said. 'He's the partner.'

Jack looked at the floor. 'No,' he said. 'Not exactly. He had a client who was wanting to invest in small businesses all over the world. Something that involved local communities as well as tourism.'

'Is that why he came here?' said Clare.

'No,' said Jack. 'He came to visit me. But when he saw the shop, when he thought about how Adam had used it to bring people here, he thought it might be a good fit and he set up a meeting.'

'Oh,' said Clare.

'The original deal, the one with Grantham – Bellweather, really – was terrible for Adam. Really underselling the value of this place, even given the bad shape it was in. This partnership lets him keep ownership but share the responsibility. And although he's putting up a lot of his own money, it's a formal investment to establish a business, with a solid projected return. He won't be dipping into his own pocket to fill the petty cash.'

'So, it wasn't us who saved the shop,' said Clare, feeling deflated. 'It was Ben.'

'It was you, Clare. Ben would never have suggested it if he'd seen the shop as it was when we arrived. And Adam said it himself, he was going to turn it down. It was you. You showed him how valuable the shop is to people. That's why this is happening at all. You're the reason for everything.'

Clare was silent for a while. 'How could you know and not tell me?' she said eventually. 'I feel so stupid.' Clare swallowed hard. She didn't want this anger – she didn't have time for it. She only had a few days left with Jack, and she didn't want them to be full of bitterness. But she couldn't stop the hurt spilling out of her. 'You let me spend all day thinking about this. Thinking about what it would be like to have these three months for the rest of my life. Assuming you were coming with me when all the time you knew. You could have told me the truth, let me make my decision with all the information.'

She saw tears forming in the corners of his eyes. 'Please,' he said. 'Please don't be mad at me. It's hard enough having to say goodbye to you without you being mad at me.'

Tears were spilling down Clare's face. Jack pulled her close and she let herself bury her face in his chest.

She didn't know how long they stood like that.

'I tried to do what you told me,' she said, at last. 'The note you left, I tried to follow your advice. But I couldn't. I can't picture this, any of it, without you. I spent all day trying. But you're there. In all my visions of what this job would be like, you're there.'

She was still angry with him, but she knew it wouldn't last. How could she stay angry when she loved him so much? She didn't want to fight. She didn't want to yell. She wanted to beg him to change his mind. To plead with him all night if she had to. To hell with anything else, she wanted to ask him to pick her.

But she knew she couldn't.

She closed her eyes and took a breath to steady herself. 'I can't imagine what it will be like,' she said, 'doing this without you. But I'll do it. I'm saying yes. With or without you I'm saying yes. So I suppose before long I'll know whether I can really do this. Whether I can do it alone.'

Jack smiled sadly and nodded. 'You can,' he said. 'I know you can.' He gave her hand a tug and pulled her into him.

He brushed a tear from her cheek and bent his head to hers, closing his eyes and breathing her in.

Clare put her hands to his chest, balling them in the fabric of his shirt. There was grief in their kiss, and farewell.

They clung to each other all night, pushing away the knowledge of a future spent apart.

Chapter Twenty-eight

'And you really don't know when you'll be back?' Clare's mum was saying. 'What kind of job doesn't let you know when you'll be able to go home?'

'My kind of job,' said Clare. 'But that's why I want you to come out here for a few days. A week or two, maybe. It's lovely here. Did Lina tell you?'

She'd signed her new contract that morning, and the moment it was official, she'd called her mum to tell her.

'I don't know.' Clare could picture Maggie's worried frown. 'I'd have to take time off work.'

'Mum, you must have weeks and weeks of annual leave owing,' she said. 'I don't even remember the last time you took a holiday.'

There was silence on the line.

'Please?' said Clare. 'I want you to see what I've been doing. I know you've been worried about me. Worried that I was, I don't know, becoming sort of shiftless.'

'I've been worried you were making yourself miserable, Clare. You were always so much happier when you had a goal or a project. I've been worried you didn't know how to find one to suit you.'

'Well, I found one,' said Clare. 'And it's wonderful. Please will you come and see it?'

'I would like to.' But she still sounded hesitant. 'You do know how proud I am, don't you? How proud your dad would have been?'

A lump rose in Clare's throat. 'Thanks, Mum. Please. Please come. I miss you.'

She heard a sigh on the line. 'Well,' came her mother's voice, 'I suppose I'll ask. And if they can give me the time, I'll come.'

Clare beamed through the tears that had sprung up in her eyes. 'They will,' she said. 'I know they will. I can't wait, Mum – I can't wait to see you. I'll teach you to surf.'

At that, her mum shrieked and laughed, before saying she had to go.

Wasn't a no, Clare thought.

She called Lina next, who yelled, 'Shit, yes!' in response. 'This is perfect, Clare, so perfect for you,' she said. 'I cannot think of a better person for this. Is your slice from the shop coming too?'

'No,' said Clare. 'He's going back to his job in Chicago.'

'Argh, *nooo*,' said Lina. 'I was really banking on something happening between the two of you. Had a bet with Ben, actually.'

Clare didn't say anything.

'Oh, hon,' said Lina. 'I'm sorry.'

'It's okay,' said Clare, but she couldn't keep a sob from her voice. 'It's not like I could have expected it to last. He was always going back to Chicago.'

'Yeah,' said Lina, slowly. 'Well, he's a fool, if you ask me. This is a much cooler job than that lame one he's going back for. Whatever it is. And also, well, you!'

'Thanks, Lina,' said Clare.

'I hope you're still excited,' Lina said. 'You should be. You're going to look so glamorous to everyone back home, jetting about everywhere like some kind of mogul.'

'It's not going to be glamorous,' Clare said, laughing. 'It's going to be long days of shifting books around. I'll be dealing with so much muscle strain and boob sweat.'

'Look, coz,' said Lina, 'last week I shot a wedding for a minor royal, and if there's one thing I've learned from that, it's that there's no such thing as glamour. Just the perception of it. Behind the scenes, things are always hard or boring or being held together by thumb tacks and hope. Or all three. Sometimes you have to take a moment to appreciate how your life looks from the outside. And yours is going to look incredible. And it will be loads of fun on the inside as well, of course,' she added. 'Just sometimes hard or boring or falling apart. Like everyone else's.'

Clare laughed. 'How's being the most in-demand wedding photographer in London?' she asked.

'I sprained my ankle at the wedding I shot on the weekend, and someone knocked my 35mm lens out of my hand as I was changing it and it smashed. And my second shooter for tomorrow has just cancelled and I'm already pulling my hair out trying to find a replacement.'

'It's the best?' said Clare.

'It's the best,' said Lina.

*

The next few days passed in a wild blur of excitement and heartbreak. Adam tried to persuade Jack to reconsider, but he was firm, and eventually Adam resigned himself, asking Clare if she could handle things alone for a few weeks while they looked for someone else.

Clare did her best to accept this cheerfully. She and Jack had decided not to tell Adam and Celestina about their relationship, although sometimes Clare caught Celestina looking at them as if she knew.

She tried to be even more cheerful when she was just with Jack. The more she went on as if she was fine, the easier it was to stop herself begging him to change his mind.

The easier it was to stop herself telling him she loved him, that she'd never loved anyone like she loved him. It was better that way, she decided. If they never put it into words, they could pretend it wasn't true.

She made herself hold him lightly; she made herself bring him her joy and not her sadness.

And there was a lot to think about. A lot to arrange.

The plan was for Clare to stay in Bali for another couple of months, recruiting the next team of travelling booksellers with Adam and training them properly. They'd be using that time to search for possible new locations and, once the new booksellers were installed, Clare would start visiting them to help decide where to start.

Ben was already working on this, using his network to

scout businesses that could use the support, and destinations that could use a bookshop.

He called her a day or two before her original three months were up to tell her about a possibility on the Amalfi coast. 'The building it's in now needs full renovation,' he said. 'You'd need to take care of serious structural stuff. Or find a new location.'

Clare nodded, swiping through the photos he'd sent her. 'It's such a nice spot,' she said. 'I think it'd be worth the work to keep it. But maybe there'll be somewhere just as good when I visit.'

She could feel herself beginning to settle into things already. The idea in abstract had seemed an impossible dream, something she'd never be able to achieve. But each little bit of reality crystallized it a little more. Looking at this shop, she already had ideas about how it could be renewed. She added a few notes to her growing folder of locations.

'I suppose you'll be sending Jack back to me in a day or two,' Ben was saying.

'Yeah,' Clare said, keeping her voice light.

'What an idiot,' said Ben.

'He has his reasons,' said Clare.

'His reasons are dumb,' said Ben.

'He has a job lined up. He can't just walk away from it. He doesn't want to let anyone down. And not everyone wants to spend all their time hopping around the globe. People like to be settled.'

'Dumb,' Ben said again. 'Jack likes adventures, but he's not good at seeking them out. He has to be pushed. It was always me who did that for him when we were kids. I dragged him out surfing, and then he loved it more than I did. I talked him into going on rollercoasters he was scared of, and then he'd want to ride them dozens more times. I can't do that for him any more. Man's an adult. He has to learn to jump for himself.'

'Maybe he just thinks he'll like the job in Chicago more than this one.'

'I think he'll like it fine,' said Ben. 'Don't know that he'll love it.'

'Not everyone has to love their job,' said Clare. 'Some jobs are just jobs. There's nothing wrong with that.'

'Sure,' said Ben. 'There are plenty of people for whom there's nothing wrong with that.'

*

Jack insisted on working his last day. Clare had told him he should take it off, that his last day in Bali should be a holiday.

'I want to spend it with you,' he'd said.

They could have asked Adam to cover the shop – he came in most days now anyway for at least a couple of hours to talk to Clare about something or other to do with the travelling-bookseller ad, or the growing list of possible locations.

But that might involve explaining why they wanted the day together. And somehow Clare couldn't imagine herself saying to him, 'Well, you see, we fell in love, but Jack's going home, so this is the last time we'll be together, you know how it is.'

Besides, though she and Jack had played tourist a few times over the weeks, it was here that they'd spent most of their time together. It was here that they'd aggravated each other and supported each other.

They were saying goodbye to the shop and to the people they'd been while they worked in it.

Clare did her best to keep things light. She knew that, even if he felt sure of his decision, he was going to find it hard to leave and she didn't want to make it any harder.

And it would make it harder, she knew, if she told him she loved him.

If she begged him to change his mind.

The words threatened to spill out of her mouth all day.

Stay, she'd say. *Do it for me. Put me first. Choose me over the job in Chicago. Choose me over staying close to your family, over having a settled, stable life. Choose me over everything else.*

She knew that was what she really wanted. To come first with him. And she knew it was selfish. Just like he hadn't wanted her decision to be impacted by her feelings about him, she should let him make his own choice, without reference to her.

She should want him to choose based on nothing more than which job would make him happier. Independent of who else was involved.

And she *wanted* to want that for him. But she couldn't get herself out of the way.

The minutes passed, customers came and went, and she thought, *Pick me*, and didn't say it. She went and got lunch from their favourite stall and brought it back and ate it with him, and she thought, *Pick me*, and didn't say it.

Part of her knew she didn't want to have to ask. That she

wanted him to choose her on his own. And part of her knew she couldn't bear to put it properly out there, to say the words, and have him still say no.

But, still, they hovered between her teeth, the words she wouldn't say. *Pick me, pick me, pick me.*

When they closed the shop for the last time, it was a relief. They were meeting Adam and Celestina for one last dinner, and it would be easier to keep the words back with them there.

You don't make desperate pleas for love over lobster with your boss.

Dinner was peaceful and comforting. Celestina and Adam talked about Jack coming back to visit regularly with such casual certainty that Clare could almost pretend that everything wasn't ending.

After dinner, Jack grabbed a bag from under his seat. He pulled out three small objects, each identical in shape and size, but wrapped in a different brightly coloured cloth, and passed one each to Adam, Clare and Celestina.

'I hope you won't mind, Celestina,' he said. 'I wanted to make you each something as a goodbye present. As a thank-you. Clare and I found these old paperback copies of some of your books, but they were falling apart.'

Clare was pulling the cloth away from the book he'd handed her. 'Oh, my God,' she said, looking up at him. 'You fixed them?'

The book was bound in a rich tan leather. A spiral pattern flowed from the centre of the front cover, spilling over the spine and onto the back, weaving together to read '*The Countess and the Hounds* by Celestina Lai.'

'Jack,' said Clare. 'This is beautiful.' She opened the book and flipped through the pages, securely bound within their new cover. She noticed writing on the dedication page.

'For Clare,' it read, 'I'm sorry for reading this behind your back. Jack.'

She laughed and looked over at him, but he was gazing nervously at Celestina. She was holding her book and turning it over in her hands, completely silent. After a moment she gave a start and looked up. 'Oh, my,' she said. 'I find myself speechless. I can't recall the last time that's happened.' She swallowed and patted Jack's hand. 'This is, well . . .' She cleared her throat. 'Thank you, my dear,' she said. 'Thank you so very much.'

Adam took her hand, and they shared a look that made Clare's heart throb. She looked to Jack, who swallowed and nodded.

'It's . . . It was a pleasure.'

By the time Clare and Jack made their way back to their nest on the floor, all words had evaporated.

She didn't know how she was going to make it through the next few days, but right now, in this moment, she grabbed the time she had with both hands.

She kissed him more deeply, she loved him more fiercely. She tried to show him what she hadn't told him. Not as a plea, but as a gift.

As a farewell.

Chapter Twenty-nine

Adam turned up at seven the next morning to take Jack to the airport.

There was time for one last, crushing kiss, and then he was gone.

Clare stood in the middle of the flat taking deep breaths, trying to hold on to that kiss. To keep feeling Jack's hands warm on her back, pulling her into him. To keep the smell of him in her nostrils. The sound of his voice as he whispered her name in her ears.

She closed her eyes and tried to stop the sobs that were threatening in her chest.

They could wait. They would have to wait. They would be here waiting tonight.

She had a brutally efficient shower, got dressed and walked down the path to the shop. She opened the door, set out the sign and tried to pretend that it was just Jack's day off, and that he wasn't at this moment lining up to go through airport security.

She sat at the till with the book he'd given her. Made for her.

The book she had said she'd give her left boob to read. She opened it and read the dedication again with a small, sad laugh. Then she turned the page and stopped. There was more.

'Just to prepare you,' Jack had written in pencil, 'this book contains some truly imaginative positions and part of me is relieved you'll be reading this after I've left so you can't make me try them. I think you'll particularly enjoy the scene at the bacchanal, and also the tryst with the nun.'

Clare laughed, then sighed, then laughed a little more. She turned the page to the start of the book. There were five sentences devoted to describing our heroine's boobs. Jack had underlined them and written, 'Wowzer!' On the next page the heroine defied her conservative father by stealing his horse and riding away through a storm. Jack had written, 'Bad idea. Someone riding through a storm can cause succession crises. See Alexander III of Scotland.'

Clare flicked through a few more pages. There were notes in the margins of every page. Tears sprang to her eyes as her mouth stretched into a smile. It was like having a little part of him back again, and she couldn't decide whether to read through all his comments at once, or hoard them, only reaching for one when she really needed it.

She idly flicked through, not reading, just taking in the existence of the book, until she got to a comment that jumped out. It was all in capitals and underlined.

'STOP,' it said. 'NO SPOILERS.'

She chuckled and nodded. *Fine*, she said to herself. *Have it your way*. And she flipped back to the beginning of the book.

*

A couple of chapters in and Clare was engrossed. Celestina's writing was sexy, obviously, but it was also funny and engaging. The heroine, with her magnificent, five-line-worthy cleavage, was captivating and somehow, even though the plot was implausible in the extreme, Clare wholly bought into it.

The door opened and she looked up, expecting to welcome the day's first customer. It was Celestina.

'Good morning, my darling,' she said breezily, as she walked in. 'How are we doing?'

'Oh,' said Clare. 'Hello. Good. We're doing good. Well, the day hasn't really started yet. I haven't had any customers. I should be making the most of it, really. I need to set out the display for the next book club. But I was actually reading.' She held up the book.

'My dear,' said Celestina, pressing her hands to her face. 'I'm not sure you should be reading that in public.'

'You shouldn't have written a book I can't put down,' Clare countered.

Celestina blushed and simpered. 'You are a dear,' she said. She took the book from Clare and examined it. 'Ah,' she said, 'the *Countess*. Yes, a particular favourite of mine. He'd done *Deadly Delicious* for me, and *An Abundance of Thunder* for Adam. More appropriate than he can have realized. I can't believe these books were up there all this time.'

'Neither could we,' said Clare. 'We were so excited to find them, and devastated when we saw what condition they were in. Jack said he'd look into how much it would cost to have them rebound. I had no idea he was doing it himself.'

Celestina was flicking through the pages. 'Yes, he's a very impressive young man,' she said. 'And, look, he's annotated it for you.' She peered at Clare over the top of the book. 'Now that is not something he did for me or Adam.'

Clare didn't reply. She didn't feel she could. Her heart felt too big in her chest; her lungs like they weren't getting enough oxygen.

'I see,' said Celestina. She closed the book and placed it gently back on the counter. 'You know,' she said, 'one of the last things that I did BCE was leave Adam.'

Clare stared at her.

'Yes,' said Celestina. 'I've told you about this before, of course. A little. Well, perhaps I skated over it. He'd always thought of himself as a gay man, you see. Simple. Clear. Straightforward – well, maybe not *straight*forward.' She laughed. 'Anyway, I didn't want to ask him to change himself just so I could keep him with me. I thought I was being wise. Kind. So, I broke both our hearts for a while.'

'What happened?' said Clare.

'Well, he was always a very sensible and perceptive man,' said Celestina. 'He came to see me. I'd just had the duchesses done' – she gestured to her chest – 'and, to be honest, I was a little groggy, but he came to see me and he said, "Thank you." Not for my leaving him, but for helping him see more of himself. He said he was grateful to know he wasn't so simple a creature, or so clear. That he contained even greater multitudes than he'd known. He said he didn't care to label himself any more. "What I am," he said, "is deeply monogamous and very much in love." And then he kissed me and we both cried, and we've never been apart since.'

'That's a beautiful story,' said Clare, with a wan smile.

'Yes, I think so,' said Celestina. 'Not all men are as

perceptive as Adam,' she said, giving Clare a beady-eyed look. 'Not all men know when we're trying to give them what we think they need against our own better judgement or desires. Some men have to be told.'

She was leaning forward now, staring intently into Clare's eyes.

Clare swallowed. 'Celestina,' she said faintly, 'would you be able to mind the shop for a while?'

'Darling, I'd be delighted,' said Celestina, gliding around behind the till and shooing Clare away. 'I came by taxi,' she said, as Clare ran for the door. 'I told him to wait.' Clare looked back at her, speechless, her eyes brimming. 'Oh, my darling one,' said Celestina. 'I know.'

*

Half an hour later, Clare sprinted across the car park towards the gleaming doors of the terminal, her breath catching in her throat more from emotion than exertion. She was half looking ahead of her, and half glancing at her phone, scrolling through the departures page of the airport website, trying to figure out which gate Jack would be heading for.

She stumbled, almost dropping her phone, and as she steadied herself, she heard a voice to her left say, 'Clare?'

When she looked around, she thought for a moment she was dreaming. But she wasn't. It was him. He was solid. He was right there in front of her.

'Jack!' she cried. 'Jack, wait, I have to talk to you. I lied. Or I didn't, but I did also. I didn't tell you—'

She broke off, not sure how to go on.

'Clare, you don't need—' Jack said, but she cut him off.

'No, please, you have to let me explain. I said I understood. I said I was okay that you chose Chicago, but I'm not. I hate that you're going back. I don't want to do this without you. And I know it's selfish. And I'm not going to ask you to stay just for me. It wouldn't be enough – it wouldn't be good enough. I don't want to be the only reason you stay. And I know it's a big decision to make quickly and I know you like to be careful, but can't you just take the leap this time? Can't you take a chance for me? Come on this adventure with me. If you're sure you'd rather go back to that job in Chicago, if you tell me that's what you really want, I'll believe you and I'll let you go. But I can't let you leave without telling you how much I want you to stay. Without telling you how much I want you.

'I want to keep working with you. I think we're good at it together. I think we're both better with each other. And I think we can really make this work. If I have to do it on my own, then I will, but I know I'd do it better with you. And . . .'

She paused for a bit, shaking her head and looking up at Jack. He was watching her with steady eyes, a slightly furrowed brow.

'Jack. I love you. I'm in love with you. I'm not going to ask you to do anything you don't want to do, but I couldn't let you leave without telling you. I don't want to let you leave at all, but I will. I just . . . I just wanted you to know everything before you did.'

The corner of Jack's mouth was turning up in that way she just couldn't get enough of. His eyes crinkled a little and then he laughed. 'Clare,' he said. 'You idiot. Didn't you notice what I'm doing?'

'Wha . . . what?' she said, confused.

'I'm *leaving* the airport.'

Clare blinked, taking stock of him. It was true: his suitcase was sitting beside him. This was not a man who had checked in for a flight that was due to leave in twenty minutes.

She blinked again. 'Oh.'

Jack smiled broadly and grabbed her hand, pulling her to him, his other hand cupping the back of her head. Clare looked up at him, her eyes sparkling.

'Clare,' he said, 'I'd go on any adventure with you.'

'Are you sure?' she said.

'I'm sure.'

'It's not *just* for me?'

'It's not just for you.'

'Is it partly for me?'

He laughed. 'A not insignificant part of it is for you. Any more questions?'

Clare beamed and shook her head.

What other questions could there be? she thought, as Jack bent to kiss her. Everything was perfect.

Chapter Thirty

Six months later

Clare waited at the arrivals gate of Naples airport, holding a sign in front of her with two names on it. She was buzzing with excitement. She glanced up at Jack, standing beside her holding welcome packs in his hands, and he smiled down at her, his eyes sparkling.

The welcome packs had been Clare's idea. They were full of chocolate and biscotti, hand lotions and candles, all of which were from local vendors. And there was a comprehensive list of the best places to eat, get *gelato*, learn about the area – all places she and Jack had spent a fair amount of time checking out.

The last six months had been an exhausting whirlwind of renovations and planning, but they were finally ready to begin. She and Jack had arrived to find the Libreria Amalfi had extensive damp in the basement, a crumbling façade, and wiring so frayed that turning on the lights felt like an extreme sport.

The owner, a small, round-faced woman in her forties

called Giuliana, had inherited the shop a couple of years earlier from her aunt and had been on the point of selling it when Ben had come across her and suggested the shop as a possible next location for the travelling-booksellers scheme.

Clare had fallen in love with Giuliana on the spot, and Giuliana had all but adopted her and Jack, making them vast piles of pasta and pushing them physically out of the shop whenever she decided they were too stressed and needed a break.

The efforts to get the shop back into shape had been exhausting: there had been a plumbing disaster, an extremely stubborn pigeon nesting in the roof, and several fervent arguments about paint swatches . . . and Clare had never been happier.

Every exhausting day ended in her falling asleep in Jack's arms. Every morning she felt as if she was waking into a dream, instead of the other way around. And it was only the beginning. Now she'd get to share this beautiful shop, this wonderful life, with two new travelling booksellers.

She stood watching people coming through the doors in a stream, thinking about the fantasy job that had sprung up in her mind almost a year earlier. She'd known she wouldn't get that fantasy life.

She'd never imagined she'd find something better.

Acknowledgements

Thank you to Alice Rodgers and the team at Transworld, and to our sensitivity reader, Josephine Chick. Thanks to my agent, Claudia Young, and everyone at Greene & Heaton.

A special thank you to Amy Jones for unknowingly providing my Clare mood board.

Thank you to Jamie. Thanks to my mum and dad, to my siblings Christy, Joyia, Eli, and Tineke and my niece and nephews, Theo, Libby, and Will. To Sean, James, and Sam.

Thanks also to Dolly (and Chidi), Norma, Emma, Conor, Caroline, Gavin, Ella, Anna, Alice, Sarah, Cornelius, Eley, Hux. To Katie, Lizzie, and Colin. To my quarantine film club, Duncan, Celly, Will, Sophia, Rachael, JP, Mike, Fiona. To Wheatles, Sam, Cal, Charlotte, Jude, and Ben. To Erin, Amy, Mel, Luke, and Cam.

Georgie Tilney trained as an actress and also studied English, history and linguistics. She lives in London but was born in Auckland, which is more beach than city. *Beach Rivals* is her first romcom.